SHE LOOKED UP INTO HIS EYES. "Zachary Taylor Cobb, I think you know I'd love you with no legs. I just don't want it to come to that. You and I both have got to make up our minds about what's important. You've got to decide if a family is more important than the manly pride you take in what you do, and I guess I've got to decide to let you be what God made you to be."

They walked down toward the waiting wagon. He stopped and straightened up to hear her better, to listen to her with his eyes.

"You're a man of courage who can't abide injustice, and I want you to know that I'm proud of you. If you never change, I'm proud to know you and I'm proud to love you."

Jenny's words were followed by a silence. He looked steadily into her eyes and took her chin in his left hand. With the fingers of his right hand he brushed her hair aside and stroked her cheek with his thumb. He leaned down and gently kissed her.

BOOKS BY JAMES WALKER

Husbands Who Won't Lead and Wives Who Won't Follow

THE WELLS FARGO TRAIL
    The Dreamgivers
    The Nightriders

THE
NIGHTRIDERS

✦ ✦ ✦ ✦ ✦ ✦ ✦ ✦ ✦ ✦ ✦

JIM WALKER

BETHANY HOUSE

MINNEAP

Cover by Dan Thornberg,
Bethany House Publishers staff artist.

Published by Bethany House Publishers
A Ministry of Bethany Fellowship, Inc.
11300 Hampshire Avenue South
Minneapolis, Minnesota 55438

Printed in the United States of America

Library of Congress Cataloging-in-Publication Data

Walker, James, 1948–
   The nightriders / Jim Walker.
     p. cm. — (The Wells Fargo trail ; bk. 2)
   Sequel to: The dreamgivers.

    1. California—History—1850–1950—Fiction. I. Title.
II. Series: Walker, James, 1948–   Wells Fargo trail ; 2.
PS3573.A425334N54   1994
813'.54—dc20   94–38346
ISBN 1–55661–429–2   CIP

This book is dedicated to the one who shows me the resurrected Jesus on a daily basis—

my wife, Joyce.

JIM WALKER is a staff member with the Navigators and has written *Husbands Who Won't Lead and Wives Who Won't Follow*. He received an M.Div. from Talbot Theological Seminary and has been a pastor with an Evangelical Free church. He was a survival training instructor in the United States Air Force and is a member of the Western Writers of America and the Western Outlaw-Lawman History Association. Jim, his wife Joyce, and their three children, Joel, Jennifer, and Julie, live in Colorado Springs, Colorado.

CHAPTER 1

+ + + + + + +

THE SADDLE LEATHER SQUEAKED in the rain as the men rode down the narrow path and toward the cabin that rested beside the fast-moving creek. The rain beat a steady staccato rhythm on the bright yellow rain slickers before pouring off the riders' backs in sheets. To keep the chill off, several of the men sucked on their tightly wound cigarettes while others blew on their fingers. Two of the riders who were lagging at the rear of the slow-moving column pulled up on their reins and passed a bottle back and forth while the others snaked on down the canyon ahead.

"I never would have know'd Tom Whipple to be in on something like this," said one. "He just don't strike me as no road agent. Him being all sweet on the marshal's sister and all. That Emily girl's pretty enough to straighten any man out."

"Naw, it don't figure to me neither. Now that old man Joe's a mean cuss. And that other little one—Mouse, is it?—he's as shifty a sort as I ever did see; but I wouldn't 'zackly make 'em out to be no highwaymen." The second rider held the bottle still and looked perplexed.

"Here, give me another pull on that."

"Go easy, we got to catch up with the rest of them, pronto. If Old Rube and Toby thinks them boys is guilty, then I guess it ought to be good enough. Still, hanging some men you done know'd without no trial or nothing gives a body pause."

"Shoot fire, I don't care 'tall about that. It's that shiny double eagle in my jeans that persuades me."

"Well, maybe so. Still, I hear tell them boys is showing good color. 'Fore you know it, this here whole wash will be filled with cabins, saloons and such. Can't figure out why they'd want to go and take it off the stage, when they're getting it out of the ground. Just gives a body pause, that's all."

The men slapped their spurs to the flanks of their horses and quickly took their place in the meandering line on its way down the muddy slope. There was a terminal and sobering silence to the night, invaded only by the driving rain and rushing water— no birds, no frogs, no crickets, only the sound of water on oil-skin and swirling torrents rushing past boulders, long toms, and sluice boxes.

Pulling up outside the darkened cabin, the men swung down from their horses and squashed the mud under their boots. Two of the unofficial posse held the reins of the animals while the men slipped their revolvers from their wet holsters and cautiously opened the cabin door.

A groggy voice sounded out from the far corner. "Who is it? That you, Mouse? Have you quit for the night?"

The men stood inside the open door and allowed the part of the rainstorm they still carried on their backs to drip onto the dirt floor. The wick of a lantern had been turned down to burn dimly and one of the nightriders reached over and turned up the wick to brighten the room. The fresh glare revealed a man huddled in the bed at the far corner of the cabin, rubbing his eyes. Another miner was fast asleep in the bed closest to the door, while a third cot was off to the side, empty.

A large man stepped to the front of the pack. He took off his dark hat and swatted it on his silver-studded chaps to knock off the rain. Even in the dim light, the badge pinned to his red vest blinked out from under his dark oilskin coat. "No, Tom, we represent a group of citizens known as the Vindicators. You better wake up Joe. We're here to try and hang you men as road agents."

Tom sat bolt upright. "Road agents! Us? Why would we want to do such a thing?"

The dark-eyed, long-haired peace officer replaced his hat and drew his revolver from across his body, pointing it first at the cowering figure in the corner and then at the sleeping man on the bed. "Like I said, Tom, you wake up Joe and don't go trying anything foolish. We plan to make this thing as easy and painless as possible."

Tom cautiously laid back his covers. Maintaining eye contact with the massed group, he inched toward his snoring cabin mate. He shook the man. "Joe! Joe! Wake up, Joe! These men say they are here to hang us!"

Joe snorted awake with a loud series of coughs. He scratched his long white hair and gawked at the mass of wet intruders. "What? What the blazes!" He blinked back the drowsiness from his eyes and rubbed his eye sockets before staring at the men through the glaring globe of the lantern. "Who in the sense of corruption is this?"

"They call themselves the Vindicators, Joe. But it's Toby Summers and some of the boys from Volcano and they're here to hang us. They say we're road agents!"

The gray-bearded miner sat straight up in the bed and kicked at his blankets. "Road agents. You boys is plain crazy. You all know us. Toby, we don't even spit on the floor at the Cosmo. What's this all about?"

"Where's Mouse? We know he's in on this with you."

The two miners looked at each other and blinked in disbelief. "In on what?" Joe asked. "I done told you we ain't done nothing."

Tom broke in, "Did Breaker send you boys up here? Is this all about Emily? 'Cause I can tell you, we ain't done nothing wrong. In fact, I plan on marrying her."

The big deputy marshal grabbed Tom by the neck of his long johns and pulled him up from beside Joe on the bed. "I done told you, this don't concern you and Emily Morgan. It's about your gang of hold-up men." He pulled Tom closer. "Now, what we want to know from you is who else is in on this with you, and where is the gold you done took? You answer that and you stand a good chance for a clean high drop. You don't, it might be long and slow." Tom leaned backward to try to wrench free from the frozen grip.

"You boys all know us." Joe Johnston pulled the deputy's hand away from his frightened partner and stood between the two men. He looked around the room at the others who were passively watching. "We been showing some color, but the only thing we been spending is placer gold and some bench placer stuff. We ain't seen an eagle in months. Where did anybody get the idea we'd hold up a stagecoach?"

The deputy snarled, "We got our sources and they say you're guilty as sin, so you might as well own up to it. It'll go a lot better on your consciences."

Tom stammered, "Bbb . . . boys, it's your consciences you'd better worry about. I tell you we're innocent men. We've had nothing to do with no stagecoach robberies."

One of the nightriders muttered from the rear of the room, "Come on, Toby. If we're gonna do this, let's get on with it. I wanna get on to bed."

"All right, Jake, tie 'em up. Let's take 'em out and get it done."

Joe dropped his head to his chest and slumped down on his cot. Tom, though, backed away from the men who filled the cabin and pressed against the far corner of the room. He spit out his protest with a jerky motion of his head. "You can't do this! We're innocent. We ain't held nothing up. Everything we got, we done dug outta the ground or brought it up in a pan."

He sank to the floor in the face of the approaching group. "Don't do this, don't do this!"

Several men were tying Joe Johnston's hands behind his back. "It'll go a mite easier on you boys if you tell us where the loot is hid." The deputy pulled the mattresses up from the cots and tossed them onto the floor. He seemed to be halfheartedly conducting a search.

"I tell you, Toby, there ain't no loot." Tom dropped his chin and stared at the floor. "Why? Why? Why is this happening to us? Toby, there ain't no loot."

Several of the nightriders lifted Tom from the floor, spun

him around, and tied his hands. Tom craned his neck, directing his words to the deputy. "Toby, tell the marshal he's hurt his sister enough. Breaker can't keep controlling her life forever."

The deputy turned from his search. "Now, I done told you, Tom, this don't have nothing to do with Emily Morgan. Jes' get that out of your head. It's about you two fellas, that scrawny little Mouse character, wherever he is, and the gang of gold thieves you're all riding with. Tie him up tight, men, and bring them both outside."

The deputy patted his shirt pocket. "Oh, one thing more." Reaching into it, he extracted a pencil and a printed document. "Before you fellas hang, you better sign this here quick claim deed over to the court, so's Judge Harkness can get it to your next of kin."

+ + + + +

The women ran hard through the rain. When Maggie had seen the nightriders ride out of town and head for the diggings on the creek to the west of town, she knew she had to tell Emily. Emily would know what to do. Emily was not a woman who would just sit back and let things happen. Maggie knew her well enough to know that.

Each clap of thunder sent Maggie into a panic. She lifted her head to the sky, anticipating some sort of judgment, some type of punishment for what she knew she deserved. Even while she ran along beside the raging water, she thought about how poorly she had turned out. She knew she was a far cry from the little girl who sat on her mother's lap and listened to stories.

Her life now seemed only to revolve around men—what they wanted and when they wanted it—with no thought for herself and no room left over for anything else. Being a crib woman was the only thing Maggie had left. It was lower down than a hurdy-gurdy girl, but pride had long since stopped being an issue in her life. Daily survival was the substance of Maggie's life these days.

The only friend she had, the only one she really wanted to give anything to, was Emily, and now she knew that she had given Emily her greatest heartbreak. She knew the pain they were both going through was because of her. As they ran together, she wondered if secretly she had wanted Emily to be as unhappy as she was. Maybe she was just too afraid of losing her.

Emily never looked up. She ran steadily down the mud-slicked road she had traveled so often at night. Each time she slipped, she paid no attention, and with every boom of thunder and each dart of lightning, she raced straight ahead, into the driving rain. Emily was a woman who knew her own mind, and when she knew it, nothing else mattered.

The lightning darted overhead, but Emily tried to focus Tom's face in her mind. She was going to do whatever it took to get to him, to Tom, to the only man who had ever treated her with kindness. She had never known any tenderness from the other men in her life, only her father's whip and the back of her brother's hand.

From the first time Tom had seen her at the hotel, he had treated her like a lady, even if she did just work in the kitchen. She had walked this road with him many times, hand in hand, listened to his dreams, and felt her heart melt into his. When he had asked her to become his wife only a week before, it had been the happiest day of her life. It was a feeling she was not going to give up, not without a fight.

CHAPTER 2

+ + + + + + +

MOUSE DREW UP SHARPLY at the sight of the horses outside the cabin. He had quit the tunnel for the night. The vein was rich and he hadn't wanted to set the pick and shovel down to go to bed, but he had finally left the mine and started back to the cabin. Scooting partway down the slope, he dug his heels into the slippery mud and grabbed onto branches to slow his descent as he strained to catch solid footing. Mouse held his balance on the slope and squatted down behind some scrub brush to watch.

The rain was falling harder now, but he could make out the struggling Tom and his older partner, Joe, being hauled out of the cabin. The nightriders gathered around the two men and the group moved toward the rushing stream. Mouse could see torches being lit and the light from the hand-held flames showed that the men were carrying ropes. He clung more tightly to the branches and tried to keep his feet from slipping. Craning his neck, he leaned forward to overhear the men who were now just below him on the makeshift bridge.

"All right. This'll do. Tie the end of them ropes on to them bridge timbers. We'll swing 'em right here over the creek."

The deputy pushed his way through to the front on the pack. The others secured the ropes around the two men's necks. "All right, boys, here we go. If you got any last words to say before the drop or some praying to do, you better get on with it."

"Tell Emily I love her." Tom dropped his head and stared down at the fast-moving creek.

15

Joe yelled into the rainstorm so that everyone could hear. "For Pete's sake, boys, tie that knot tight. I can't swim a lick!"

The sound of the taut rope as Joe hit the end of the knot shook Mouse to the bone. Several of the men then picked up the praying Tom Whipple and tossed him over the side. As Mouse strained to lean forward, the mud suddenly gave way beneath his feet.

He grabbed for the branches on the hillside but both his feet scooted out from the slippery clay, and, with a crash, he tumbled through the brush and came skidding to the edge of the bridge. He turned on his hands and knees and stared through the driving rain at the lynch party.

"There he is, boys! That's Mouse there. Let's get him."

Mouse scrambled to his feet and took a bounding leap toward the creek bank. He shuffled through the ferns and stood at the side of the overflowing creek, petrified with fear, staring at the racing water. Everything inside his guts seemed to suspend him on the edge of the raging stream, unable to move.

The sound of the men trampling over the bridge was soon followed by several shots. Mouse heard the whir of lead balls as they sped past him, then he jumped feet first into the foaming current.

He scrambled under the bridge and grabbed for the motionless legs of Joe Johnston. He could see Tom Whipple still spinning at the end of his rope, his feet dancing up and down, as if riding a ghostly bicycle, but Joe's legs were straight and lifeless. Mouse hung on to the dead man's feet, trying to stay under the bridge. Several of the men on the span strained over the side of the trestle and he recognized the voice of Toby Summers.

"He's down there, hanging on to the old man. You men go on down to the bank and see if you can get a good shot at him. The rest of us will wait for him to come out."

Mouse imagined the line of men on top of the bridge ready to cut loose when he came out from under the bridge. He hung on for a while longer in the icy water, then let go. Moments passed before the shouting started. "He's gone. He must've let go."

When Mouse broke the surface, he heard the shouts of men from the bridge again and saw the torches of others in the posse fan out on both sides of the creek. He gasped for air and struggled in the water. He'd never learned to swim, but found himself racing down the white water, bouncing off boulders, then gouging and tearing his clothing and flesh on sharp deadheads afloat.

From the sound of the men on the shore, he knew full well they were following the fast-moving current on both sides of the stream. He didn't know if he could stay alive for long, but right then he had no choice. He gulped water and tried to paddle like he'd seen other men do.

His knees slammed into submerged rocks and pain was shooting through his entire body, numbed only by the temperature of the water. He knew he couldn't make it much longer and figured if he stayed in the water, he'd either drown, or the stream would pull him right into Volcano. He had to get to the creek bank right away, with or without the know-how to swim.

He began to flail his arms in the direction of the muddy bank. Suddenly, the water slammed him into a large boulder in the current. He felt his wind leave him and struggled to stay conscious in the chilly stream. Pushing against the swift tide, he turned in the direction of the shore. The water swept him away again and sent him headfirst into a snag. His hands could not get a grip on the wet wood, and now his fingers were feeling so numb from the cold that he didn't think he could squeeze them together even if there was a grip to be had.

With his elbows and beaten knees, he fought and crawled his way onto the mass of logs and debris. He lay on the gnarled wreckage for a moment to get his breath. He'd have given all the gold he'd taken from that creek just now for a few minutes rest on those slippery logs, but he knew that if he was still there when the search party arrived, he'd be joining his partners mighty quick. He wasn't fooling himself, either, about expecting any mercy from the people in Volcano. He didn't know who'd organized this murderous gang, but he did know they all came from Volcano. No, his only hope was to get to the road to

Jimtown. Somewhere, there had to be somebody who hadn't lost his mind.

He stumbled and slipped across the top of the snags. Bruised and battered, he reached the shore and crawled up the muddy bank. He'd lost a shoe in the stream and now took off the other one so he could run better. Mouse's leg throbbed with pain—his twisted leg, the leg he'd been born with. His whole life had been affected and even his name had come as a result of that freak of nature. Now, he ran with it in a gimpy lope toward the town of Volcano. He'd have to skirt around it and somehow get to the road to Jimtown.

✦ ✦ ✦ ✦ ✦

As Zac rode all day from Sonora, he tried to piece together in his mind the information the company had given him about the robberies. The lightning flashed overhead and the big bay gelding seemed skittish. He occasionally paused under a tree in the rain to allow him and the big horse to blink the water out of their eyes and pick up their bearings on the road. Now, with an electrical storm brewing along with the driving rain, he didn't want to stay under any tree for very long—it made him just too inviting a target for Thor's hammer strikes. He'd just have to live with the downpour until he could find the turnoff to his Aunt Hat's place.

Hattie Woodruff, Zac's aunt, was known for her cantankerous nature. She bragged about having a seat reserved in hell, just on account of her meanness. No one who knew her dared call her "Ma'am." She kept to herself and few people even in her extended family would have anything to do with her, except Zac.

Why she liked him, he never knew. Maybe it was because she sold some of her precious horseflesh to Wells Fargo, and Zac worked for the company. Maybe it was because he was an outlaw in spirit like she was, or because she believed him to be the last of her sister's surviving children. Zac didn't know why she ever wrote him, but write she did, and now he carried one of her pencil-scribbled letters in his pocket. She needed his help and here he was, wet and tired. The company had endured a number of robberies in this region and they'd asked him to investigate. Visiting his Aunt Hat would be good cover.

A crack of thunder overhead caused the horse to jerk the reins, and Zac looked up to pick out the lightning flash. Suddenly, he unloosened the thong around his Shopkeeper special. He jerked the Colt .45 clear of the holster and pulled back the hammer. Perched above him, sitting in the tree limbs, was the outline of a man.

Zac spoke to the figure in a low and menacing drawl. "Mister, I don't know who you are or why you're there, but you're about to meet your Maker. You better speak up now or if the next crack of lightnin' don't find you, my .45 will. Now, who are you and what the blazes are you doin' up there?"

The voice above him came accompanied by chattering teeth. "Please . . . I ain't meaning no harm. I ain't about to rob or hurt nobody. Just ride on. All I'm doing is hiding up here."

Zac pushed his slouch hat back with the barrel of the revolver. "You must be in powerful trouble to be hidin' up a tree in a lightnin' storm."

A noise on the road ahead caused Zac to look away from the treed and now shaking man. A faint glow of torches peeked between the trees in the road, and Zac could make out the murmur of men's voices coming their way.

"Please, Mister, in the name of God, don't let those men find me. They already done gone and hung my partners. Please, you gotta believe me. I ain't done nothing wrong. Well, leastwise nothing worth no hanging."

"Well, if you're innocent like you say you are, the law will protect you."

"Mister, that's who I'm running from. The law in Volcano is crooked. Just ride on and leave me be."

Zac planted his Colt back in his holster and swung the bay around. He slackened his reins and moved the big horse down the road a few yards to face the men coming up the road. Reaching behind his saddle, he pulled a burlap bag from his bedroll, a bag containing his sawed-off shotgun, and hung it on the pommel of the saddle.

CHAPTER 3

+ + + + + + +

THE WOMEN ARRIVED at the bluffs and began their descent down the sides of the wet, slippery slope. Below, they could see the lighted cabin—the door was wide open, letting out the light, letting in the cold and rain. There was a silent emptiness to the place that told the women what they would find before they got there, but still they scurried down the sloping path.

Maggie's feet shot out from under her skirts and she began to somersault down the muddy path. Emily heard her friend hit the ground behind her and cry out. Each jolt brought a painful bruising thud, followed by a sharp scream. Maggie slid the last few feet to the bottom of the hill and Emily, out of breath, turned and stooped to pick her up.

"Here . . . put your arms up over my shoulder."

Maggie was crying now and the sobs mixed with the wind and rain made talking difficult. "I can't. Please, God, help me, I can't go no more."

"Just get your arms around my neck and I'll take you inside."

"No, I just want to sit here. I want to sit here and die. This is all my fault. If I hadn't told that deputy about the gold, all this wouldn't have happened."

"Don't blame yourself. Maybe the boys got away. Maybe they're okay."

The women shuffled into the cabin and Maggie collapsed on one of the bunks while Emily closed the door and turned the wick up on the burning lamp.

Maggie was still sobbing and shaking her head. "I knew when I saw those men ride out tonight that I had to tell you. That large group riding out together on a night like this, I knew they were up to no good. I just wish I'd kept my big yap shut. I never could keep quiet about nothing. I just never could."

Emily sat close to her and put her arm around her. "Listen, you can't blame yourself. No matter what happens, you had no part in this. Maybe you were wrong. Maybe they weren't coming this way at all. Now let's go find the men. I'll go around to the hillside and out to the privy area and you go across the bridge to the mine. Take the lamp, I'll be all right."

Emily went to the back of the cabin and began calling out for the men. Within minutes, she heard Maggie shrieking. Running to the sound of Maggie's cries, she saw her standing in the middle of the bridge, holding the trembling lamp with one hand as she looked off the edge of the bridge and screamed.

"They're there . . . Emily, they're there . . . Oh, God, they're there."

Emily took the hurricane lamp from Maggie's trembling hands and peered over the side of the bridge. She could see where the ropes were tied onto girders, and looking down she saw two men suspended above the raging stream. She couldn't make out the identity of the second man, but right away knew the sight of Joe's white hair.

"Maggie, quit. There's a third rope here. You take it and follow me. We've got to get those men out from under there."

Emily handed the rope to Maggie and, setting down the lamp, hiked up her dress, pulling it off over her head. She removed the sharp knife she carried strapped to the outside of her right leg, then ran with the lamp to the path leading under the bridge. Still bawling, Maggie followed.

Under the bridge, Maggie held up the lamp and could see clearly that the second man suspended underneath was her Tom. She pushed her hair back and tied it up with the wet scarf she had hanging around her neck, then froze and stared under the bridge, biting her lip.

"It's Tom," Maggie called out behind her. "Oh, Lord, save us, it's Tom."

Emily didn't utter a word. She handed Maggie the lamp, took the rope, and tied one end of it to a girder at the edge of the fast-running stream. Taking the sobbing Maggie by the shoulders, she stared into her eyes.

"Stop, Maggie, stop! I need you now. There's no time for that. There'll be time for it later."

Many times in her life Emily had been forced to deny everything she was feeling and just move on with what she knew needed to be done. She shook Maggie vigorously. "Do you hear me? I need your help. You've got to hold on to this rope and help me bring Tom and Joe in." She shook her hard once again and Maggie quieted down. "Now set that light down and follow me in that water. Get your skirt off and your shoes; we got work to do, girl."

Emily planted the backside of the knife in her teeth and stepped into the fast-moving torrent, gripping the rope, hand over hand. Reaching the first piling, she looped the rope around it, securing a lifeline to the shore. Turning to Maggie, who was still standing on the bank, she yelled, "Stay upstream of the rope." The lightning cracked overhead.

The frightened Maggie waded timidly into the water while Emily hung on to Joe's body and began to saw the line above his head. The men's feet were dangling in the water, their heels pushed out by the stream. Emily held the dead man close to her and continued to cut the thick hemp. The old man's beard was in her face, but she closed her eyes and blindly sawed the knife back and forth.

"Get behind him, Maggie. When I cut the rope, you've got to grab him or I'll go downstream with him."

"Emily, why are we doing this? Let's go back and get help."

"No one will help us. The men in town are cowards. They're all frightened by these nightriders. They'd be afraid if they helped us, they'd be next. Just do what I say and we'll be all right."

She finished cutting the rope and the old man dropped into

her arms. His legs rushed out into the current. Emily tightened her grip and pulled.

"Grab the rope in back of his neck and pull, Maggie."

"I can't do that!"

"Do what I say. He's past caring. Just do it!"

They struggled against the tide and pulled the body close to the suspended lifeline. With the sagging line at their backs, they moved to the shore and dragged the old man onto the bank.

Breathing heavily, they stooped over and put their hands on their knees to rest for a few moments. Emily straightened herself up. "Maggie, I'm going out to Tom now. Give me a minute alone with him, then come on out and help me. I don't know how deep it is under Tom or if I can get to him."

Numb with fear, Maggie could only gaze into Emily's eyes and nod.

Emily made her way back into the stream. The rocks were slippery under her feet and the water was moving fast and rising. She left the line and tried to balance herself on a rock in the stream. She knew that if she stepped forward and the water was even several feet deep, the force would sweep her away. She knew she had to try. She couldn't leave Tom—hanging there, under the bridge.

Tom's body hung near one of the bridge poles. She measured the distance in her mind and jumped for the rock underneath the post. Landing on the slippery surface, she grabbed for the rain-slicked piling. It held her. She reached out and took hold of Tom's legs, pulling him next to her. She held his body close and began to cry.

Maggie called out, "Are you all right?"

She nodded her head and looked into Tom's face. She spoke to him as if he could hear. "I love you, Tom Whipple." Moments passed by and the softness disappeared from her voice. "I don't care what it takes, I'll get back at them. I swear I will, no matter what . . . no matter who did this."

✦   ✦   ✦   ✦   ✦

Zac stood with his horse on the road outside of Volcano.

From what he knew of mob violence and their mentality, he knew anyone who interfered with a hanging could just as well find himself swinging on a rope beside the person he'd been trying to protect.

It was tempting to just stand aside and let what was about to happen, happen. He didn't know the particulars, either. For all he knew, the man might be guilty. All of the very sane logical thoughts a man could think in the situation passed through his head and might have stayed there, had he not seen their faces. The torchlight showed that this wasn't a drunken, frenzied mob—these men were cold-blooded killers. He raised his hand to the men. "What's the problem, boys, you lost somethin'?"

The man riding in the front of the pack walked his horse forward and pulled aside his oilskin, showing the glint of a badge. "You might say that. I'm Toby Summers, a deputy marshal in Volcano. We're looking for a robber—short man with a gimpy leg. You seen anyone like that?"

Zac forced a slight smile. "Well," he craned his neck surveying the party, "this man you're lookin' for must be John Wesley Hardin and Ben Thompson all rolled into one. If you got twelve to fifteen men in the posse, he's gotta be a mighty dangerous man." The thunder clapped overhead and lightning blazed to the ground nearby. The horses stamped and skittered to the side.

The deputy leaned forward in the saddle. "This ain't a posse, it's a hanging party. We aim to rid ourselves of highwaymen hereabouts."

"Then I reckon this man must have been tried, convicted, and done broke jail?"

Fast losing patience, another member of the mob walked his horse forward. "We ain't got all night to stand around in the rain and lightning. Maybe you're part of the bunch we're looking for yourself." He pointed his chin at Zac.

"Well, I doubt that," Zac replied. "I just rode in from San Luis Obispo, lookin' for my aunt. Maybe you know her, Hattie Woodruff."

"Yeah, everybody knows her," the deputy said. "Meaner

than a teased snake that old woman is."

"That's Aunt Hat. Where might I find the turnoff to her place?"

"You go on toward Volcano and when you get to Sutter Creek, move up it about three miles." He smiled. "You'll pass our night's handiwork there and it's about seven or eight miles farther on. You'll cut the trail past there, then turn off north. Follow that and you can't miss it." The deputy hunched his body forward in the saddle. "Now, about our business, you seen anybody pass this way?"

"I been on this road all the way from Jimtown," Zac said, "and nobody's passed me all night."

Just then a large clap of thunder boomed overhead and a bolt of lightning cracked into the oak tree where Mouse had been trying to hear. He screamed and tumbled out of the tree and onto the wet ground.

"There he is." The mob of men spurred their horses forward past Zac and surrounded the dazed little man at the base of the oak. "Tie his hands. We'll string him up right here and be done with it." Several of the men wrapped the shivering man's wrists with cord while the others watched. The torches were brought closer and the men who had fastened themselves to the fallen man hoisted him onto the top of one of the now empty saddles. They scooted a rope over his neck and threw the end of it over a large limb.

They had completely forgotten the stranger they had met moments before. In a booming voice, Zac shouted, "Hold it! That's plenty far enough."

The mob snapped their heads around and saw that Zac held a sawed-off Meteor ten-gauge shotgun in his left hand, the butt resting on his hip.

In plain sight, he cocked both barrels. When he had their attention, he squeezed off one of the triggers and sent flame and thunder into the air. The men's horses stamped and shied. He had their complete attention now, and repeated his demand. "That's as far as you're gonna go."

The deputy swung his horse around and stepped it forward.

"Mister, you're involving yourself in an affair that don't concern you. These boys are wet and tired and if you don't back off, you'll find yourself hanging right next to Nichols here. For all we know, you're in cahoots with him anyway."

"Never seen him before in my life," Zac answered. "All I know is this man ain't been tried and if you're the town deputy marshal, you're out of your jurisdiction even to make an arrest." He lifted his eyes from the deputy to the group of men who had swung their horses around to face him. "That makes you people nothing but a bunch of killers on the highway."

A large man with a dark beard sat on his horse beside the prisoner. His menacing eyes blazed at Zac. "You best back off and not even think of cutting this man down. You mess with us and what we're about to do, mister, and I'll hang you myself."

Zac reached under his slicker and produced a long, sharp knife. He flipped it in his hand and held on to the blade. Looking at the bearded man, Zac let a slight smile crease his face. "Oh, no, I wouldn't think of comin' close to you there. You got me plumb frightened to death. I ain't about to cut that man down . . ." With the quickness of a coiled rattler, Zac slung the blade. The shining knife zipped past the bearded man's chin and straight into the trunk of the oak. "You are!" Zac said.

The mob of men froze, staring at the blade, but the deputy moved his horse closer to Zac. One of the men on the edge shouted, "Toby, let's take him."

The deputy looked at Zac. "Mister, we got ourselves a group here and you're only one man with one load left in that scattergun of yours. I'd say you were well outnumbered and outgunned."

Zac lowered the ten-gauge and pointed it directly at the deputy's head. "I rode with Moseby durin' the War Between the States, so I guess you could say I've been outnumbered and outgunned since I was sixteen."

He looked into the man's eyes and, lowering his voice, spoke so only the deputy could hear his words. "You listen to me careful-like. If you or any of your men so much as twitch without me tellin' you to, I am gonna take your head clean off. It doesn't matter who moves, it makes no difference whose fault it is, you won't live to see another sunrise. Make no mistake about it. I mean what I say."

Zac went on with his soft-spoken instructions. The other men leaned forward to hear, but only Zac and the deputy could hear the words. "Deputy, right now, this is between you and me. No matter what happens in the next few moments, one thing is for certain, I'm gonna see that you lose. Is that understood?" Zac asked.

The deputy marshal sat silent in the rain, paralyzed by a threat from a man he didn't know and couldn't read.

Zac spoke again. "Nod your head if you understand what I'm tellin' you."

The deputy nodded.

Zac went on, "Now, you tell those men of yours to cut that man loose."

The deputy spoke up, "Cut him down, boys."

A number of the men reined up their horses and gave loud protest. "Why? We can take him, Toby—let's us hang 'em both."

The deputy swiveled in his saddled and looked back at them. "Do exactly what I tell you to do. We know where this man is going. There'll be another day."

The men paused. "Do what I said, right now!" he shouted at them.

With that, the burly man with the beard took Zac's knife out of the tree, cut the rope from Mouse's neck, and began to free his hands.

"That's very smart." Zac's eyes were fixed on the deputy. "I'll be into town in a couple of days, Deputy, and we can discuss this a little more. Maybe by then you'll have thought better about what happened tonight."

The deputy shot back, "We ain't gonna ever discuss nothing. If I ever see you in my town, I'm gonna shoot you on sight. And I will be seeing you again. As for that cripple you just decided to die for, we hung two of his partners earlier tonight and I'll see him swing, too."

Zac kept his voice low, but redirected the muzzle of the shotgun at the deputy's face. "Some folks never learn." Zac's patience was gone. He could feel himself boiling over and was trying hard to keep it in check. "You tell those men of yours to unbuckle their gun belts slowly and shuck them out on the ground. Of course, you take yours off first, pays to set a good example. Then tell them to get off their horses and drop the reins."

The deputy looked at him hard. "They won't do that."

Zac smiled. "Oh, they will, if you ask them real nice. I got a powerful confidence in your ability to persuade them."

The deputy took a long look at the muzzle of the ten-gauge, unbuckled his gun, and let the hardware drop to the ground. He craned his neck around. "Men, unbuckle your guns and let 'em drop. This man wants you down from your horses, too."

The posse reluctantly shed their weapons and let them fall to the ground. Grumbling, they dismounted, planting their feet in the rain and mud.

This mob was responsible for the deaths of two innocent men. Corruption always bothered Zac. He had lived with injustice all of his life, and seeing it approved of by the law left him sickened. To see guiltless men die, however, made him plumb mad. He wasn't going to let this night go by without making the men who were responsible pay. It really wasn't his business and to extract revenge went against his better judgment. It didn't go against his nature, he knew himself that well, but it did violate his common sense. He knew his actions might very well interfere with the job Wells Fargo had sent him to do. But the notion of letting the guilty go free, no matter who they were, irritated his soul more than he could stand.

"Deputy, you and I, along with the cripple, are gonna take a little ride," Zac said. He raised his voice so that Mouse could hear his instructions. "Little man, pick up those guns and bring 'em over here."

Mouse wove in and out of the horses, scooping up holsters and firearms. He piled the guns at Zac's feet.

"That's all of them," Mouse said. "But the rifles them men carry are still in their saddle boots."

"We'll take care of that," Zac said. "Pick yourself out a horse, then drive the others off. The heroes here will have to walk."

Mouse gave him a second look.

Zac caught the look. "Oh, don't worry about it. When we're done with it, we'll turn the animal loose. We'll get some proper law to handle this thing." He smiled at Mouse. "Besides, if they catch you for horse stealin', they can't very well hang you twice."

While Mouse chose his mount and stampeded the other horses, Zac fastened a look on Toby Summers. "Deputy, I'll say one thing for you, you got a mighty disciplined crew. Strangest lynch mob I ever saw. They must either respect you somethin' powerful, or fear you." He stopped and looked the man up and down, as if making an inspection. "But, if I had my guess," he went on, "I'd say they fear who you work for, 'cause it's plain to see nobody needs to fear you, man to man."

Hatred flashed in his eyes and the deputy stuck out his chest. "You'll meet the marshal all right, and Judge Harkness too."

Mouse joined them, mounted on the back of a large sorrel, his feet dangling above the stirrups.

Zac relaxed his grip on the shotgun and motioned his prisoner toward the road. "Let's go, mister tin star. We're goin' back to where this man's partners are hangin'. You and this boss of yours have got some graves to dig." Zac fired the second load over the horses' heads, scattering the creatures in all directions. "You men, don't let your horses run around too long in this storm. You better get 'em now or you may never get home."

Later, the three men rode down the slope to the cabin. They saw the light burning brightly in the window. Inside, the two women had bathed the two miners and laid them out on their bunks in fresh clothing. The women were sitting beside the stove under blankets and warming their hands when the three riders stepped inside.

Mouse scrambled up beside the women, wringing his hands. "Emily, I'm sorry," he said. "I couldn't stop them. They come in here whilst I was working the claim."

Emily raised her gaze from the floor. Her look was expressionless until she saw the deputy. She sprang to her feet and walked directly to the man. "Toby Summers, you aren't fit to call yourself a man. I know Breaker put you up to this and you just didn't have the backbone to say no to him. You don't have the backbone to say no to anything or anyone." She paused, then added, "Except your own conscience."

Zac took off his hat to the woman, "Ma'am, I'm sorry about this, sorry to crowd into your grief time."

"Who are you?" she asked.

"My name's Zac Cobb. I was just passin' through to visit an aunt of mine. I'm sorry about your menfolk here, but we ain't got much time. The deputy here and this Breaker feller, whoever he is, are gonna dig some graves. They seem to be the ones who are behind this. It's only right the town should see them deal with the problem. You can come along and watch, if you've a mind to."

"I'll do that. Breaker Morgan is the marshal," said Emily. "He's also my brother," she paused, "though I'm not proud of that. If he's going to dig graves in a storm like this, then I'd be pleased to watch."

Zac turned to Mouse and delivered instructions. "Make us some travois for these two bodies here. We'll hitch them to the deputy's horse and what you're ridin'. We can then put the ladies on my bay and find an undertaker. Let's go latch on to this Breaker Morgan."

CHAPTER 4

+ + + + + + +

THE BURIAL PARTY SLOSHED into the dim streets of Volcano. The rain pelted the mud, thunder exploded, and the electrical storm cracked overhead. Because of the downpour, the streets were deserted, but the numerous honkytonks were filled to capacity and music blared out, interrupted only by the thunder.

Mouse ran ahead to a barbershop on the corner and banged on the windows. He circled to the side of the building and yelled at the upstairs lighted window. "Olson, Olson, come on down." He flung several small stones at the shaded windowpane and continued to call out to the owner."

A large man with a white beard pried open the upstairs window and stuck his head out in the rain. "Who is zis making all the racket?"

"It's me, Olson, Mouse Nichols. I got me some friends down here who need your help. Come on down to the shop and open up."

"Mouse, Mouse Nichols? Come back in the morning. My wife and I are in bed."

"Olson, you got to come down right now. Breaker Morgan and Toby Summers are going to dig some graves in the rain." Without another word, Olson closed the window. The lights inside the barbershop went on downstairs and Olson came to the door in his bedclothes, holding a lamp. The burial party stepped inside.

The old man held the lamp high, surveying his visitors,

while his wife went around the shop lighting several lamps. "Goot evening to you, Miss Emily. Vat is all zis about a burial on a night like zis and why can't it wait till morning?"

Mouse shook his coat free of the rain. "The nightriders have been at it again, Olson. They done gone and hung Joe and Tom and would have got me too, if this fella hadn't happened along." He motioned toward Zac, and for the first time the barber could see the shotgun held at the deputy's back. The old man's eyes grew wide.

The barber gulped, then turned his attention back to Mouse, "Vat is all this about the marshal and the deputy here digging graves?"

"We don't have much time," Zac said. "I'm just here to make sure that the people who are responsible for these men hangin' share in the work."

"Vell, I'll be switched. I ain't never seen the like. The marshal is over to the St. George, gambling."

The old man pulled Zac aside and spoke in low tones outside the hearing of the deputy. "Just the marshal is in town, the other deputy, a man named Evers, rode out this morning. You vatch out for the marshal now, ya hear. He's mean that one, just as soon poison a dog to watch him die. He's big too, big as a house. You best think twice about taking him on. He don't get the name "Breaker" for nothing—he gets it by breaking men in half."

The red-cheeked Swede paused and scratched his whiskers. "The judge is over there, too. He's the tall hog at the trough around here."

Olson muttered an oath that must have been in his native tongue. None of the men could understand him. Without thinking, he raised his voice. "Zis is sure going to be quite ze show. I enjoy my vork as barber, but I've never liked making coffins till tonight."

Olson saw the deputy look in his direction. He thought of how dangerous his tongue might be with the lawman standing there and how inappropriate his comments were with the women nearby. He never seemed able to develop an undertaker's mentality and poise, no matter how hard he tried.

Embarrassed, he turned to Emily. "Miss Emily, I am sure 'nuf sorry about Tom. I find him a nice box, though, and we'll get him and old Joe buried good and proper." Turning to Mouse he said, "You bring ze bodies in here and I'll keep ze vemen folk and hitch up the carriage. My wife vill drive them and I'll take the deceased in ze wagon up to the graveyard. You can have ze two spots near the corner of Emigrant Street, across from the church."

Zac snapped open his shotgun, extracted the spent shell, and dropped a fresh load into the open chamber. "Mouse, bring two shovels. We're gonna take this tin star and look for his boss. They've got two holes to dig."

They wheeled around and left the barbershop, the deputy in the lead, followed by Zac and his shotgun and Mouse with two shovels. As they crossed the street, the mud squashed under the men's boots. They mounted the boardwalk and Zac called a halt in front of the saloon's open door.

"That's far enough." He leaned forward and, in a menacing but quiet voice, spoke to the deputy. "Tomorrow may be a beautiful day. If you want to see it, you'll do exactly what I say."

The deputy stood erect and tense, his eyes stone cold, facing the door. "You're welcome to brace up to me on any day of your choice," Zac said, "but tonight you've got only one druthers open to you, dig or die. You foller what I'm sayin'?"

The deputy nodded. "Let's just walk in. You walk up to where the marshal is seated and just stand there, I'll do all the talkin'."

Hurdy-gurdy girls ran from the bar to the tables, carrying customers' drinks along with their own glasses of weak tea. A piano player sat in the corner banging out a lively rendition of "Yellow Rose of Texas." Beside the far wall, Zac spotted a well-armed faro dealer "bucking the tiger" with a number of miners.

A young woman, Gypsy-like in appearance and strikingly beautiful with dark, doe eyes and raven black hair, danced on a small stage. She spun around on one leg, flashing a bare foot with a row of gold charms on her ankle. She smiled at the miners, but when she saw Zac walk by with his shotgun pointed at the deputy's back, her smile disappeared. She stopped her dance and stood gawking at the men.

Every head spun around and the young woman's stare was joined by the gapes of the miners and townspeople who had been watching her. With each step the men took, a hush grew in the loud saloon, until the silence was broken only by the loud piano player in the far corner, obliviously pounding away at his keys.

Zac and Mouse herded the deputy to a poker game in the back of the room. Cigar smoke curled up from behind the cards, and the men seated at the table refused to notice the newcomers standing beside them until the piano player, who had now become aware that he had lost the attention of his audience, turned his head and froze in midsong.

Zac stood behind the deputy with his sawed-off Meteor in the man's back. Mouse stood his distance with the shovels. The first man to look up from his cards sat across the table from where the men stood. A thin man in his fifties, he wore a sweaty undershirt that was topped off with a black broadcloth dress jacket. He had a salt-and-pepper beard and small beady eyes, black and expressionless, that looked past the panicked deputy Summers and straight at Zac. "Marshal Morgan, I do believe you have some company."

The marshal was sitting with his back to Zac. He was a huge man, even when seated. Letting out a puff of cigar smoke, he grunted and continued to stare at his cards. With his extended right hand, Zac pushed the deputy aside, exposing the sawed-off shotgun. He pressed the barrels of the weapon to the base of the marshal's skull. "I assume you are Marshal Morgan," Zac said.

The big man froze and dropped his cards. The bearded man across the table continued to stare at Zac, but kept speaking to the marshal. "I do believe, Breaker, that this man intends to interrupt our game. From his appearance, I think I'd take him very seriously."

The other men at the table placed their cards down and kept their hands visible. With mouths gaping open, they scooted their chairs back from the table, trying to stay out of harm's way. Everyone moved except the marshal and the man with the gray beard, whose appearance seemed calm and cool.

"If you're Marshal Breaker Morgan, unbuckle your gun belt and stand up." The saloon was silent, except for the sound of the marshal's gun belt hitting the floor. The chair squeaked. Breaker painstakingly rose from the table and stood with his back to Zac. Then he turned and faced the room, his large, menacing brown eyes blazing.

"Who the blue blazes are you?" His whole face seemed to flush with blood as he delivered the question.

"I'm a man with a job for you to do. I thought you and the deputy here might want to finish what you started this evenin'."

"Now what might that be?"

"Your deputy here led a group of self-appointed jurors with ropes. They hanged two men tonight."

"What has that got to do with me?"

"You sent them. The men you hung are on their way to the cemetery and we're gonna have a little service for them."

"Well, whoever you are, you can go about your service without me." The big lawman turned his back on Zac again and started to sit, but before he could, Zac shot out his own right foot and swept the legs of the chair out from under the man. The move sent the marshal crashing to the floor.

With the quickness of a cat, Zac drew his short-barreled Colt off his left hip and swept the muzzle of the belly gun around the room, pointing it at the deputy. In the same instant, he planted his left foot firmly on the marshal's throat and with his left hand stuck the barrel of his shotgun directly on the big man's nose.

"You misunderstood me, Morgan. Nobody wants you at the service. You and your deputy are comin' with me to dig graves."

The room was silent. Zac's action had spurred those at the table back from any possible danger, all except the man with the gray beard. Cold and expressionless, the bearded man sat across the table, his gaze riveted on Zac's every move. He spoke to the marshal, whose face had begun to perspire. "Marshal Morgan, I believe this man means exactly what he says. If I were you, I'd follow his instructions—to the letter."

Zac turned to the people in the saloon. "When the graves of these two miners are dug, you all are welcome to come to the service. If there's a parson nearby, somebody get him."

One of the men at the bar spoke up. "Pastor Young is close to hand. I'll get him."

Tipping the edge of his hat lightly with his six-gun, Zac looked at the women who were next to the bar. He nodded politely to them. "Ladies, I know many of you must have beautiful voices. If you know some sacred music, I think these folks would love to hear you."

A tall redhead whose face looked hard as flint spoke. "Mister, it's the worst storm of the year, but I think you can count on a whole choir. Besides my own funeral, this is one I ain't a gonna miss."

Zac looked down at the sweating man on the floor. "Okay, Morgan, you're gonna get up nice and slow. Don't bother to get your coat on, 'cause you're gonna be workin' real hard. We're goin' out that front door and straight to the cemetery. Don't let anythin' else even enter your mind, 'cause we'd just have one more grave to dig and one less gravedigger to do the work."

Zac took his foot off the big man's neck and backed away, holding the shotgun. Everyone watched silently as the marshal got to his feet. The men headed out into the storm.

Miners and townspeople followed them to the door and out into the rain. They didn't want to miss whatever was going to happen. They knew this would be something to write home about, something to tell the grandchildren.

As they followed along, the people poked their heads into noisy saloons telling each establishment in succession what was happening. "You gotta come see the show in the cemetery. A stranger is gonna make Morgan and Summers dig graves." Within minutes, the darkened street was filled with people following the little burial party to the cemetery. Darts of lightning lit up the curious faces in the growing crowd as thunder boomed and the rain poured relentlessly.

CHAPTER 5
+ + + + + + +

WHEN THEY REACHED the graveyard, Mouse ran to
the two selected grave sites. "Right here, this is the place." He
put the shovels down, one on each location, and filtered back
to the front of the crowd.

Zac pointed with the shotgun. "There they are, gentleman.
You make us two holes, four feet by seven feet, and six feet
deep."

The two lawmen stood staring in disbelief while the rain
pelted their faces. Lightning struck nearby, making the crowd
gasp and Toby Summers flinch.

"Get at it," Zac said.

The men began to dig in the pounding rain. Each shovelful of
mud was placed beside the graves. The men stepped into the
growing holes and continued to spoon out the mud and rocks.
Time passed, but no one left. Zac motioned to Mouse to come
closer. "Get back to town and keep a sharp eye out for that posse.
You get our horses, too. I want to make sure these graves go to
who they're intended for and not us. Savvy?" The little man left
the churchyard and ran down the hill to the main street.

From behind the church, Zac noticed a tall, gangly man am-
ble out from a house. He stuffed his nightshirt into his pants
and carried an umbrella over his bare head. He stopped at the
edge of the crowd and questioned several of the onlookers. The
men explained the situation to him and all pointed to Zac.

"Hello, Parson," Zac said as the man came closer. Zac was
a good judge of people, it was his business to be. The man looked

37

a little like every preacher he'd ever known. "I can see you got the word and I appreciate you comin'."

He blinked at Zac and stuck his hand out from under the umbrella, testing the intensity of the downfall. "I don't understand this," he said. "Why are we doing this . . . uh-hum . . . in the middle of the night and in . . . uh-hum . . . the rain?" The young man had a high squeaky voice and a tendency to clear his throat, midsentence.

"Well, Parson, you ever heard the sayin', 'Don't look a gift horse in the mouth'?"

The man nodded.

"You got the whole town here, Parson. I'd say a crowd like this gathered at any time and for any reason was just such a horse for a man with your callin'."

"I 'speck you're right. My congregation is small. I hear Joe Johnson and Tom Whipple have been hanged. I . . . uh-hum . . . never met old Joe Johnson, but . . . uh-hum . . . his young partner Tom would come from time to time."

The tall, hard-looking redhead Zac had seen at the saloon joined the two men. "Mister, I got over a dozen girls here who can sing." She glanced at the minister, almost apologetic. "These girls ain't been a part of any service in years, but they'd be right pleased to do the music."

Before the parson could answer, Zac said, "That'd be fine."

"They know 'Shall We Gather at the River?' and 'Amazing Grace' real well." She looked at the minister and attempted to explain, "Parson, most of these girls were good girls back home. They went to church where they came from and would give anything if they could honestly write their mothers and tell them they had sung at a service."

The parson's eyes brightened. "Ma'am, I'm sure anythin' you ladies could do would be honoring to our Lord . . . uh-hum . . . and it would be pleasin' to us as well."

The woman flushed with pride. At a loss for words, she turned on her heels and ran back to the bevy of young women standing nearby.

"You know . . . uh-hum . . . that's exactly who the Lord came to save," the preacher said.

"You don't need to explain to me, Parson. There was a time in my younger days when I never missed a Sunday. All these folks are your customers." Zac looked at the gathering crowd. It now had grown larger. "From the looks of things, I'd say the whole town has turned out."

The minister surveyed the crowd. "Well, I can understand why they're all coming . . . uh-hum . . . given who's digging the graves. I know why I'm here . . . uh-hum . . . but who are you and why would you be doing this? Seems like a mighty dangerous thing."

"I don't reckon it would be smart, if I was plannin' on stayin', but I'm just passin' through to see my Aunt Hat."

The minister's mouth dropped open. "Hattie Woodruff?"

"My mother's oldest sister. Came to California in '48 and been here ever since." Zac watched the preacher's face lengthen. "Preacher, don't bother to be polite about Aunt Hat. From what I know about her, I know she's not a member of your congregation. She and my mother loved each other, but they were miles apart, spiritually speakin'."

"Then your mother must have been a very honest and godly woman," the preacher said, tightlipped. "I've had some business dealings with your aunt."

"What'd she do?" asked Zac. "Sell you a blind horse?"

The minister stuck out his jaw. "No, I was trying to breed some pigs and your aunt sold me a blind boar."

Zac couldn't control the laugh. It exploded and was loud enough to attract the attention of several people standing by. "Hard to breed 'em, I guess, when the old man can't even find the sow." He laughed again.

The parson tried to explain his actions. "I'm pretty ignorant about such things. I'd turn the boar into sausage, but it just don't sit right with me, being taken in like that."

"Don't feel bad about that, preacher. Old Aunt Hat could hoodwink the merchant of Venice." Zac was sympathetic. "It seems you and I, Preacher, have some of the same stuff swimmin' around in our innards. I don't like to see people robbed, plundered, and taken advantage of. When I do see it, I poke my nose into where it don't belong. By profession, I bring thieves to justice and interfere with some pretty hardened sinners hereabouts. So I 'speck you've got a right to be a bit put out with old Hat."

The crowd separated and the wagon carrying the bodies of the two miners rolled up to the cemetery, followed by the carriage with Emily, Maggie, and Mrs. Olson. Zac and the preacher moved forward to the graves and watched the men continue to dig.

The lawmen dug quickly, anxious to finish. The harder they worked, the less they had to look at the faces of the gathered townspeople, people who for the most part lived in fear of these men and now were watching their humiliation.

Mouse Nichols made his way through the crowd, leading Zac's big bay. His feet were out of the stirrups and he was kicking the sides of the horse he was riding, trying to gain authority over it. Zac noticed him right away. The posse! Zac knew what he had to do. He spoke to the lawmen in the holes. "All right, gentlemen, let's see you get out of there."

The two men tossed their shovels out of the muddy graves and looked around for someone to help them. Several men approached to offer assistance, but Zac put up his hand. "No, no, these are big men," he said. "They don't need any help."

The would-be rescuers backed away and the two men scrambled up the muddy sides. They began by jumping, only to slide back down the pits, much to the amusement of the crowd. The deputy scrambled out of his hole first and stood to offer Marshal Morgan his hand. The two men stood and looked at Zac without saying a word.

"Gentlemen," Zac said, "you've been very helpful tonight and most entertainin'. We'd invite you to stay for the service, but you're a mess." The crowd broke into uncontrollable laughter.

Morgan had reached his boiling point and he bellowed at the surrounding people. "All right, that's enough. You've had your fun tonight and you'll have your service, but me and my deputies will still be here in the morning, and this man will be gone, or dead." He peered coldly at Zac. "You've had your little sport, fella, but I'm going to kill you. I'll kill you with my bare hands."

"You're a real scary man, Marshal," Zac said, "but right now, you're a real dirty man. I suggest that you and your deputy here go take a hot bath. Then my advice to you would be to go find a different town to ply your trade in, because these people have seen your real line of work tonight, and they'll never respect you again. With a little thinkin', they may not even fear you. I'm sure the U.S. Marshal will also be interested in what brand of law you're sportin' here. Now get!"

The two muddy lawmen began their walk back to the main street and Zac turned to the minister. "Parson, I'll turn this here proceedin' over to you. Mr. Nichols and I are gonna follow the same advice I just gave those two." Zac mounted the big bay and turned on the road that led out of town. He felt a hand tugging on his chaps. It was Emily.

"Mister, I want to thank you for what you did tonight. No one that saw it will ever forget it, and years from now there'll be many people who will claim to have been here that weren't. You've helped me bury my man and I'm grateful, but there's more goin' on here than you know." Her lips quivered and she shook in the cold rain. She bit her lower lip. "That man you humiliated tonight is my brother. You've made an enemy for life. He'll do just what he says. He won't wait for you, though, he'll hunt you down and kill you."

Zac pulled at the front of his hat in farewell. As Emily stepped back from the horse, he touched his spurs to the animal's sides and the big bay quickly caught Nichols on the road north.

Emily called out into the falling rain. "Keep riding, and don't stop till you're out of the territory."

Beautiful female voices sang out, "Shall we gather at the river, where bright angel's feet have trod. . . ."

* * * * *

Judge Ruben Harkness pulled up his chair to the potbellied

stove in the St. George Saloon. With his boots on the circular rail that surrounded the glowing heater, he sat thinking, sipping on a glass of whiskey. Beside him sat the young Gypsy dancer, curling her finger into the old man's gray hair.

Morgan and Deputy Summers entered the saloon. The men each grabbed a glass and a bottle from the top of the bar and walked over to the warmth of the glowing heater. They were swearing and muttering when the judge looked up at them and raised his hand. The men quieted down and held their hands up to the heater.

"What we saw here tonight, I ain't never seen the like of," the judge said.

"Judge," the marshal said, "I'm gonna kill that man with my bare hands and I won't be alone when I do it. Every man, woman, and child who saw what they saw tonight are going to watch that man die."

The deputy chimed in. "The man said he was here to visit his aunt, Hattie Woodruff."

The judge's eyes grew wider.

"If he's there," the deputy said, "me and the men can take him and bring him back here for Breaker in the morning."

The judge was momentarily distracted by the young girl curling the locks in back of his head.

She looked up at Summers. "Did you get the quick deed signed by those men before you hung them?"

Summers reached into his inside pocket and handed the paper to the judge. "We only got Joe and Tom to sign. Mouse Nichols got away."

"So I saw," the judge said.

The marshal had a faraway look in his eyes. "The thought of killing that man would make me crawl through hell itself. I can promise you, he is going to die."

"Don't be so quick, Breaker. I think I know who this man is."

The two lawmen were riveted on the judge.

"Wells Fargo has an agent hereabouts, I've heard of him. He's a bandit-hunter, a man-killer. They send him out when their losses are particularly high and when they can't get results from the law." He stroked his gray beard. "Zachary Taylor Cobb. That's the man's name, and he's dangerous. If he's old Hattie's nephew, that's got to be him. I talked with the old gal a couple of times about two of her nephews that I had in the prison camp, the one I administered during the war. Their names were Cobb."

Morgan threw his glass against the wall, held the bottle to his lips, and took several swallows. He was boiling mad and would listen to no amount of caution, even if it came from Judge Harkness. "I don't care if the man is Custer and the entire Seventh Cavalry come back from the dead. The fact that you had his brothers in prison and that he works for Wells Fargo ain't going to erase the taste of yellowness in my mouth. If I don't kill that man, I might as well put a bullet in my own head."

"Oh, we'll kill him all right," the judge shot back, "but after we break him. We've got to be careful. Wells Fargo wants these robberies stopped. If Cobb is killed, they'll send others and the U.S. Marshal to boot. I mention his brothers, too, because these were very competent men. I don't want them riding down here to avenge their little brother."

He sat for a moment, remembering. "One of those boys was a man named Julian. He had one eye gone and cannon had taken his left arm off at Gettysburg, but he's the kind of man that if he had both arms missing would ride three thousand miles just to kick you to death, I reckon. This man tonight appears to be cut from the same bolt of cloth."

The judge leaned back in his chair. "Where's your other deputy? The sharpshooter, the hardcase. Evers, is it?"

The marshal dropped his head, remembering what Judge Harkness had said moments before. "He's out on a gold shipment job. The Jimtown to Columbia route."

The judge looked at Marshal Morgan and Deputy Summers as he took a slow sip of whiskey from the glass. "Wells Fargo," he said. "Lucky thing for them they got a man already here." He paused. "I suspect Zachary Taylor Cobb isn't in Volcano just to visit his aunt."

CHAPTER 6

+ + + + + + +

ZAC WATCHED MOUSE kick the sides of the horse. The stirrups were far too long for his legs, and the fear he obviously had in riding the animal made him hold the reins tight. Zac rode up beside him. "Nichols, nobody's going to ever mistake you for a cowboy. You're confusing that animal. Kicking the bejabbers out of his sides, he thinks you want him to go faster, but you're pulling up on his reins too and that won't do."

"I can't ever get this right," Nichols said. "I was born in Pennsylvania, not Texas. My Pap done reared me to go down in a hole and dig, not ride a horse."

"Well, you stick to what you know, but for now just let up on those reins or that roan's going to put you on the ground. When we get to Hat's place, we'll turn that animal loose and let him find his own way home."

"Hattie's ranch is just through the trees up ahead. It kinda sits down in a little valley, prettiest place you ever did see."

"You know Hat?" Zac asked.

"Everybody round here knows old Hat. She sticks pretty much to herself, but when she does get to town she whoops it up with the best of them. She can out-drink and out-spit any man in town, and don't get her to cussing you. I ain't never heard such words out of a woman before. If you really want to hear her give out a string of blue blazes, just call her 'Ma'am.' You'll get it!"

"Sounds like you know her pretty well."

"Well, I can't really say why, she'd skin me, but let's just say

44

I do a little business with her from time to time."

"From what I hear, anyone who does business with Hat winds up not speaking to her."

Mouse laughed. "Yeah, I reckon that's so. She's a sharp one, she is. I don't do that kind a business with her, though. I'd never buy anything from the woman. I just handle some of her affairs."

They rode their horses to the top of the ridge and looked down into the valley at the cabin. It was a log dugout built into the side of a mountain. Logs were reinforced with rocks and small slit windows gave the appearance of a fort. It could only be approached by riding the length of the valley in full view of the gunport windows. Lights were on and smoke curled out of the stone chimney. The men rode down the middle of the valley toward the house.

Approaching the dwelling, Zac's big bay stepped into a rope that stood only a foot off the ground. It was suspended by line, and bells were hung on it that gave out a clamor of noise that could be heard even in the storm.

Mouse called out to Zac. "That's Hattie's way of knowing someone's coming. She don't like no surprises."

Zac pulled up the bay and grabbed the reins on Nichols' horse. "That's far as we go," he said. "I think we ought to walk the rest of the way. I don't know what we're going to run into, but I don't want to take these horses into any more of my aunt's surprises."

The men dismounted and began a slow walk toward the house. The storm had finally begun to slip over the mountains to the west and both of the men held their hats in place. The wind picked up in irregular gusts.

"Hello in the house!" Zac yelled out. "It's Zac Cobb, Aunt Hat, with Mouse Nichols. You in there?" He put his hand to the latch and lifted it. Pulling it toward him, he noticed a string attached to the inside of the door. Suddenly, as if by an unseen hand, another gust of wind blew the gray hat off his head. He leaned over to catch it and an explosion shattered the air in front of him, tearing part of the door off he had in his hand. He lay at the open door on his belly, facedown in the mud.

The smell of gunpowder was everywhere and smoke drifted over him. Slowly, he lifted his head and peered into the now open door. A double-barreled shotgun was bolted to a table just inside the door. A series of strings that led from the door and around a support post in the house were attached to the weapon's trigger mechanism. Zac got to his knees and peered around the room, pushing the door farther open.

"Hee-hee-hee." He heard the cackle first. It came from directly behind him. He got to his feet as Hattie came sliding down the muddy hill on her backside. "Hee-hee-hee." She was laughing and started clapping her hands when she hit the bottom of the hill." She drew a black powder Colt Navy from her waistband and, without missing a beat, ran to the front entrance of the cabin. "I got you," she said. "I got you, you miserable sons a . . ." She stopped midsentence when she saw Zac. "You!" She came to a dead stop, still pointing the pistol, and stared at him. "Zachary Taylor Cobb, is that you, boy?"

Her dress came down to the tops of her heavy shoes and the old hat she wore was pulled down over her ears, hiding most of her gray hair. She spat a stream of tobacco juice on the ground and wiped her mouth off with the back of her hand. She stuck the pistol in her belt and embarrassed Zac, kissing him quickly on both cheeks. Holding him at arm's length to get a better look, she said, "Boy, you sure get better lookin' ever'day. I ain't never seen the like of you for handsome. You take after your pa. Your momma would have been right proud, boy."

Zac stepped back and dusted the mud off of his pants and shirt. "Aunt Hat, you just about blew my head off with that booby trap of yours. Who are you trying to kill?"

"Oh, nobody special," she replied. "Just anybody snooping around, putting their nose into business that don't concern 'em." She paused and cut off a slice of chewing tobacco from a wedge she carried in her apron. She put it in her mouth with the edge of her knife, squinted her eyes, and started chewing feverishly. Cocking her head, she said, "You didn't write me you was coming, boy, you could have gotten yourself hurt."

"I could have gotten myself killed," he said. "I came here with Mouse Nichols; he says he knows you." He turned to where Nichols had been standing, but instead saw only the horse the little man had been riding. Mouse was gone. "Well what do you know," Zac said. "Nichols, Mouse Nichols!" Zac yelled. "It's okay to come out. It's just Hat." He waited. There was only silence. Turning back to Hat he asked, "Well, what do you make of that? He was right behind me when I got to the door. Did he know the darn thing was rigged?"

"I 'speck he did," the old woman replied.

"That don't figure," Zac said. "I just got finished saving the man's life and burying his two partners."

"Joe Johnston and Tom Whipple? What happened?"

"They got strung up by a lynch party."

The old woman chewed and thought. "Come on in the house," she said. She busied herself with straightening the chairs around the fire and loading more wood into the flames. "Set yourself down," she said. "I'll go out and take care of your horse." She stopped at the door. "Yep, the Vindicators have been at it, shore 'nuf. That's what these nightriders are calling themselves. They are supposed to be protecting us and the gold shipments from highwaymen, but it seems the only people getting suspected and hung for being a part of this supposed gang of road agents are those whose claims are showing good color. Makes a body think and makes 'em take precautions too."

She spat on the floor and, wiping her mouth, pointed in the direction of the table with the shotgun. "That's why I got me that there welcoming device. 'Cause I'm likely as not to be drinking a little too much some night and not hear folks sneak up. That thing over there will wake me up for sure." She started to go out the door and in an afterthought turned back to Zac. "But it'll put whoever's sneaking up on me to sleep . . . forever." She gave him a big wink and, with a deep rumbling giggle, went out the door.

Zac reached into his jacket pocket and removed his dark briarwood pipe. He knocked loose the remnants of his last smoke from the bottom of the bowl and loaded tobacco into it,

packing it with his thumb. He reached out and got a splinter of
kindling to start the flame in his pipe and, puffing it to life, surveyed the room.

Hard rock mining tools were stacked in the corner, along with
lanterns and torches. Hattie had always communicated to people
that she raised horses and mules and wouldn't touch a shovel. Zac
thought maybe that was a smokescreen after all. Zac knew the
old woman approached life as if it were the enemy. Each day held
a potential horror for her that she was prepared to endure and con-
quer. He kept glancing at the picks and shovels in the corner of
the room and wondering why she'd want to keep her digging
equipment in the house. The tools themselves were interesting.
They were caked with dirt, red and dry.

Walking back and forth across the floor, he noticed it
squeaked and had a slight give and sag toward the far corner containing the tools. Something else was unusual about the floor—
a Persian carpet lay in the corner, covered by a bearskin rug.

The door swung open and Hattie stepped in and hung up her
coat on a pegboard beside the door, exposing a bandoleer of ammunition slung over her shoulder and around her waist. "Didn't
see hide nor hair of your Mouse Nichols. He musta lit out like
a scalded pup."

Zac puffed on his pipe and shook his head. "It doesn't make
sense," he said.

"Nothing makes sense if you don't know somebody. That
boy's been runnin' all his life. Ain't likely meetin' you and having you save him is gonna change that." She curled her riata and
hung it up on the rack. "The storm's passin' on now. Shore hit
us something terrible. Got your horse all put away." She hung
Zac's inlaid bridle on a peg beside the coats. "That blood bay of
yourn is a right smart, pretty animal. What you want for him?"

"Hat, I couldn't sell that horse. That gelding carries me all
day without even needin' a blow. Besides, you need brood stock
for your operation."

"You're plumb right there; still, he's right pretty to look on.
I gave him some hay, no oats. You don't want to spoil these animals." Hat threw open the grate on the stove, lifted one of the

lids, and poked at the kindling. Moving to the fireplace, she removed a burning piece of wood and took it back to the stove. Stirring the flame inside, she dropped the lid back on top with a loud clang. "If you've done gone and crossed your sword with these nightriders, you've got yourself into a heap of trouble."

He walked around Hattie and stood near the fireplace. He knew enough about her to know that if he asked her direct questions, all he'd succeed in doing would be to make sure she never talked about the subject again. She was a contrary woman and if you wanted to know something, you'd better not ask. He stood quietly and puffed.

"The last thin' a body would want to be in this town is a successful hard rock miner. If you bring in placer gold to have it assayed, they'll leave you be, since it comes from the creek bed and all." She stopped and squinted into his eyes. "But if'n you takes quartz type hard rock stuff into that town, that's a sure sign of deep motherlode mining and I figure it makes you a candidate for those killers masquerading about pretending to be the people's protectors." She shrugged and took out a plug of tobacco from her pocket and cut off a slice with her knife. She rolled it into her mouth. "Don't make no never mind to me, though. I'll just keep jingling horses hereabouts till I die."

Zac stood near the fireplace and puffed on his pipe. The smoke curled up and into the open log rafters. He watched the old woman stoop over and pull a skillet out of a box. "Hat, when did you take up hard rock minin'?" he asked.

The old woman swung around suddenly. She squinted an eye at him. "Boy, mining is a fool's errand. Only way to make money round here is to shear those miners like you'd do a sheep. They grow the wool and you take it off."

"I've heard you talk about that often enough, Hat, but it doesn't agree with the facts."

"What do you mean?" she asked.

"Well, Hat, don't stack your diggin' tools in the corner. Keep them out of sight." He paused and puffed a column of smoke in the air. "I'd have to say also that it appears your cabin is sittin' right on top of your mine."

"Boy, you're too dang smart for your own good."

"You don't have to be smart, Hat. A blind man could stumble across the truth here. You only got two rugs in the whole house and somebody would be mighty curious about why they're sittin' in the corner, away from furniture or anyplace useful."

The old woman stirred up a fire in the stove and tried to ignore him. "I reckon you'll be hungry. I'm gonna start up some bacon and get some grits a goin'." She poured water in another pan and set it on the stove to boil. "Your momma would be right proud of you, boy, being as you turned out so smart and all." She continued to work and talk to him from over her shoulder, afraid to face him. " 'Course, speaking for my own self, you'd be right smarter if you stuck to your own business and left other folks be."

"Aunt Hat, I don't mean to butt into your affairs," he said. "I'm just tryin' to do my job. Wells Fargo asked me to look into the stagecoach robberies out here. I wanted to see you anyway, so I figured it made pretty good cover to be visitin' an aunt of mine." He puffed on his pipe. "In any event, I best be gone before mornin'. Those nightriders and that Marshal Morgan know I'm stayin' with you; they think Mouse Nichols is here too, for that matter." He paused, still watching the woman's backside at work. "I hadn't planned on stirrin' up the hornet's nest quite the way I did, and I am truly sorry for bringin' trouble down on you. I suppose I just can't abide heavy-handed, might-makes-right injustice when I see it."

She finally turned around to look at him. "You still got too much of that lost-cause-of-the-South thinkin' floatin' around in your head. Forget it." She wiped her hands on her apron. "I loved that sister of mine, but sometimes I believed she read you children too much of the Bible combined with all those stories of the knights of the round table. It made your thinkin' plumb addled, caused you to see right from wrong too blame good and fooled you into believin' you could do somethin' about it. Well, you can't. A body best go about featherin' their own nest and stayin' out of people's way." She turned to stir the grits into the boiling water and slice the bacon.

"You'd best stay here," she said. "Got me a fort here. I can hear people comin' and I got a free field of fire with that Spencer rifle of mine. People round here know it's a crazy thing to try to ride up on old Hattie Woodruff."

"Hat, I'd be too comfortable here. I'd get to sleep and never wake up. No, I'll take my bedroll and that Sharps Creedmore of mine and get to the other side of the valley. If those boys do come and get in between my Sharps and your Spencer, I think we can put some learnin' into them."

"I 'speck so," she said.

+ + + + +

Mouse huddled under a tree near the mouth of the old mine. The tailings were scattered throughout the trees and he sat in the wet earth and watched the cabin. *Maybe the man was who he said he was, and maybe he wasn't,* Mouse thought. *If he was a claim jumper, that was going to be old Hattie's lookout, not his.* He had seen the old woman leave the cabin, however, and had heard them both call his name. He just felt better knowing that he was the one who was in control of his own life. He hadn't lived this long by throwing in with strangers and he wasn't about to start changing his ways now.

He watched the smoke curl out of the stone chimney and wanted to be warm and dry, same as anybody. He watched Zac leave the cabin with his bedroll and rifle and disappear into the trees at the far end of the valley. *That man is smart and gutsy,* Mouse thought. *Maybe he might be safe enough. Still, with him stirring up that trouble with the law in Volcano, he probably don't have long to live. For that matter, the same could probably be said about me.*

Mouse moved along the tree line and watched Zac filter through the trees. He wanted to make sure where the man lit before he bedded down. He had strung along with this Cobb fella earlier, mostly out of curiosity. Now, though, it was just him. He had no partners anymore and he knew it was probably his fault they were dead. He'd gotten his cut when he took Hattie's gold into town, but the word got out that it belonged to him. Now Joe Johnson and Tom Whipple were dead and buried.

51

CHAPTER 7

+ + + + + + +

EMILY SLIPPED IN THE MUD and caught herself against the rail. She knew it was early enough in the morning to be able to find Maggie alone in her crib house. These poor, tiny one-room shanties were the last stop for any prostitute. Maggie would be alone, though. She didn't like any of the men well enough to let them stay all night. Maggie had done badly. Going from a hurdy-gurdy girl to a woman of the cribs was the end of the line, and Maggie herself knew it best.

The constant sadness in Maggie's eyes made it difficult for Emily to talk to her. A body had to keep eye contact with someone when they talked, and for Emily that was getting harder and harder to do with Maggie. Emily had lived with pain a long time in her own life. She knew Maggie lived with a scar in her soul, one that Emily would never know, the pain of trading away who she was as a person for money.

She knew Maggie blamed herself for Tom's death. She had passed on information about what a customer of hers had told about the men's gold strike. Everyone in town seemed to know under their breath that the stagecoach robberies had become an excuse for stealing successful hard rock claims. Maggie must have known the secrets passed would be relayed to this gang of hangmen, and now she felt guilty.

Emily had to talk to her. She had to find out who she had told about the mine and who she got the information from. She knew Tom wouldn't have been her customer. *It must have been Joe or Mouse*, she thought. She rounded the corner and raked some of the mud off her shoes.

Knocking lightly on the door, she called, "Maggie! Maggie?" There was no answer. *Maybe she had a rough night*, Emily thought. No, something was wrong. Emily could feel it in her bones. Something was very wrong. She turned the old knob and reluctantly pushed open the door.

As she stood in the doorway, the morning light filtered around her and settled about the disheveled room. The dust from the burlap curtains mixed with the kerosene of the still burning lamp and hung heavily in the air. Emily stood with her hand still on the doorknob, eyeing Maggie.

Maggie's body lay on the old narrow bed. Her arms drooped straight down and the tips of her fingers rested lightly on the bare wooden floor. The knife in her chest had a large blade and several inches of shiny surface under the wrapped hilt glinted at Emily in the dawn sunlight.

Emily's stomach turned over. She felt like retching but was compelled to inch toward the bed. A yellow scarf was stuffed in Maggie's mouth. Emily took the corner of the scarf hanging below the girl's chin and slowly pulled it out. She thought she recognized the scarf and, wadding it up, pushed it down into her apron pocket.

Maggie's eyes were open. Emily read the same sadness that she had always seen, a sadness that now lingered in the girl's lifeless pupils. She shut Maggie's open mouth and took one last look into her eyes. Reaching up with her fingers, Emily gently closed them. *She is resting now*, Emily thought.

A large shadow fell on the room, darkness blocking the morning sun. Slowly turning around, Emily saw that the light in the open door was being shut out by a man standing there. She couldn't see the facial features of the man because of the sunlight at his back, but the size of the figure meant it could be only one person. Anger roared from within her, but Emily knew she had to conceal how she felt and what she knew, especially from her brother.

"What are you doing here?" he asked.

"I might ask you the same thing," she said. "She was my

friend, but I wouldn't expect you to be one of her gentleman callers."

"What I do with my time is nobody's business but my own. What happened? Did you two girls have a spat and you push that toad sticker into her?"

"No, I think you know who killed Maggie."

"I know nothing of the sort. Far as I can see, you're my only suspect, but since I know where to find you, I'm going to release you. Be kind of embarrassing for the marshal to have a murderer for a sister."

"Breaker, all of my life I've known you to do cruel things. I'd watch you chop the wings off baby birds. I'd cry to Momma about you. She'd just look at me with tears in her eyes and say that that's the way the menfolk are. She'd say you were just like Daddy, and you are."

Breaker slapped Emily to the floor with the back of his hand. She fell backward and landed with her head near the edge of Maggie's bed. The dead woman's cold hand rested on Emily's right cheek. Its light touch shocked her.

"Girl, you don't know what you're doing. I'm protecting you. You keep snooping about in my affairs and you'll wind up like that friend of yours there."

Emily sat up and put her hand to her bruised cheek. She looked up at Breaker. "You are like Daddy. He hit me just as hard as you just did." She got to her feet and stood in front of him. "He hit you something fierce, too. I know he used to beat you something awful. He'd say how he was going to whip you till you cried, but you never did cry. You've still got Daddy's buggy whip marks on your back, though. I think that whip of Daddy's left other marks, too. You've got marks on your soul, Breaker. They've twisted you." She stepped closer to him. "Now you think you're going to beat me till I cry. Well, I won't do it." She stepped past him, twisting him sideways, then stood in the sunlight facing back at her brother.

"Girl, I don't know if I can protect you. What's happening here can't be stopped, not by me, and certainly not by you. It's out of my hands."

Emily thought about the man she had seen the night before and looked up at the graveyard on the ridge overlooking the town.

Breaker saw the look. "That man last night can't help you. When he came here and shamed me and Toby Summers, he gave you even less protection. The only way I can help you is to be as strong as possible. The slightest notion people have that I can be buffaloed, and I'm a dead man." He stepped forward and down off the wooden walkway. "That man last night put you in great danger. Besides, he'll be dead by nightfall."

"What happened last night was something the whole town has been waiting for," she said. "Justice; justice came to Volcano. Someone I loved got buried and someone else I love, you, Breaker, got the whipping of his life. You were shamed and you had it coming."

She whirled on her heels and plodded back to the hotel. The breakfast crowd would be walking in soon and she had to be ready. She also had to make plans for another funeral. There wouldn't be many people at this one. She wasn't even sure if they would allow Maggie in the cemetery. Poking her hand into the apron pocket, she felt the scarf. She wadded it up into her fist and squeezed down hard.

* * * * *

The fog had settled in the valley that morning and Zac watched the floor of the grassy plain. He knew that in all likelihood the men he had embarrassed the night before wouldn't take a chance on him living out another day. They'd want him dead and they'd want to cart him or his body into town. Last night was a mistake, he knew that. He'd let his own inner sense of justice get in the way of doing his job.

He worked for Wells Fargo. The company trusted him to put a stop to the robberies, but to do that meant that he had to conduct an investigation. That involved going into town. It also mandated the cooperation of the law and now that was impossible. Zac had never quit a job in his entire life, but he thought it might be best for the company if he did just that.

His aunt had also been placed in danger. She was in big trouble now and all because of him. Her life was wrapped up in this place, and even though much of the trouble was her own doing, Zac knew he had exposed her. That fact alone kept him there. To pull out now meant leaving Hat alone, exposed without him to protect her. He couldn't do that. *Besides*, he thought, *the next agent, if the company could find someone else to do the job, wouldn't have any reason to care what happened to Hat, and he'd simply let the law take care of it, even if there was no law.*

Never before had Zac gotten himself into the fix that what was best for him and his might not be best for the company, might prevent him from doing his job. Maybe he'd learn his lesson from this. He had risked everything just because he wanted to make somebody pay for some injustice done to somebody else. Next time he came upon somebody about to be hung at the hands of a mob, he was just going to leave it alone. He'd just do his job and that'd be it. *Let the devil take the hindmost*, he thought.

Behind him, he heard a twig pop. He turned his head around and watched the two men come down the hill. They sounded and looked like misplaced buffalo. They bounced down the hillside and came off the leafy slope to his right without casting a glance in his direction.

Zac lay still. His buckskin jacket and gray slouched hat offered little concealment, but these men weren't looking for anyone out there. They hit the ridge he was lying on and moved off in the direction of Hattie's cabin. Each of them clutched a Winchester, and Zac could only guess what they were up to. They lay down on the ridge to his right, their backsides pointed in his direction, and took up a watch of the house.

Zac had put on his moccasins during the night. He always carried a pair in his saddlebags. There was much less chance of stepping on and breaking a branch when you wore the soft Indian shoes. Every twig and branch could be felt before putting your weight down on it.

He slowly got to his feet and, carrying the heavy Creedmore, moved silently toward the men. They were sitting now, their backsides still toward him, and rolling smokes the way the Mexicans took their tobacco, sprinkling the stuff on paper and twisting the ends together. He'd seen it done hundreds of times. They talked loudly and popped a flame on the end of a match.

"Hope you boys aren't lookin' for me," Zac said. The men turned their heads and the man to Zac's right reached for a side arm. Zac came forward with the butt end of his rifle. It landed with a hollow thud on the man's forehead. The man's body dropped to the ground like a log. Zac snapped the muzzle of the big gun forward and leveled it at the face of the remaining bush-whacker. "Don't even twitch. This end takes no prisoners." The man shot his hands straight up in the air. "Knowin' that bunch what little I do," said Zac, "I don't expect they sent you and your friend in here all alone."

Zac spotted the men in the floor of the valley. Ten of them rode their horses down the length of it. They were in a ground fog but made little effort to otherwise conceal themselves. Zac turned to the man in front of his gun. "They were supposed to get me out of the house while you and your friend here were gonna bushwhack me, I suppose." The man nodded in agreement. "Turn around," Zac said. "I'm gonna tie your hands."

He pulled out a leather strap from his jacket pocket and made a locking loop. Placing it over one of the man's wrists, he looped it around his other hand and pulled it tight. He made a knot and pushed the man to the ground. "Set there," he said. "You can watch quietly like you are, or be quiet like your friend."

The man glanced down to his right at his companion, who lay there stiff and quiet. His mouth was open and the cigarette was burning on the ground. He whispered, "I'll just sit here and be quiet. I got no truck with you, mister."

"Smart gent," Zac said. "You just watch and keep your mouth shut."

The horses the men rode stepped lightly through the fog, making their way through the field quietly, until they tripped Hattie's alarm string. The bells on the string tinkled and clanged, moving the line of horses back. The men stepped their horses back and forth until Hattie's Spencer carbine cracked a shot from the slit in her window. The bullet echoed in the canyon and the men froze.

Hattie's shrill voice shot out the portal. "Stop right where you are. Don't move a step. I'll empty the saddle of the first one who does."

Zac turned to the man sitting at his feet. "She will, too."

The old woman called out again, "What do you want?"

One of the men in the line stood up in his stirrups. "We're here for your visitor, Hat. Send him out so's we can talk."

She screeched back at them, "He ain't here. He's probably lookin' down his rifle barrel at you right now."

Zac spoke to the man by his feet. "I 'spose this is the point where I was to come out while you and your partner here sighted down those Winchesters of yours." The man remained mute and Zac stepped back to a small tree.

He removed his jacket, exposing a bandoleer studded with large-caliber cartridges. He tied a scarf around the small sapling next to him and stuck the barrel of the heavy Sharps through the loop. Spinning the rifle, he tightened up on the slack and sighted down the heavy barrel. He watched the men on the ends of the line begin to fan out to the sides and work on flanking the cabin. Other men in the group twisted their heads, looking for the two men Zac had intercepted.

Zac sighted down the Creedmore and set the hair trigger. When he squeezed the trigger, the big gun roared and the round bounced off a rock in front of one of the horses. The animal bolted and, jumping and kicking, tossed its rider. Zac broke open the single shot rifle, ejecting the spent shell. He slid another round into the chamber and brought the stock forward, locking the gun into place. He yelled down at the men in his booming voice, "Hold it right there. You make another move and I'll put one into you. Your choice." He spoke quietly to the man tied up below him. "You better tell them I mean what I say."

Zac's prisoner yelled out at the top of his lungs. "Boys, it's me, Stretch. He's got me and Luther. You best do what he says."

A number of men in the group swung their horses around and faced the hillside. They seemed to be talking among themselves and trying to decide what to do next.

Zac yelled out, "Toby, Toby Summers, is that you down there? It's wonderful to see you again, Deputy, especially fixed in my rifle sights. Did that big ox of a marshal send you out to do his dirty work again?" He paused. "You make a fine target down there, trespassin' and all. You're also well in Hattie's range with that Spencer of hers. You hear me, Hat?" Zac's voice echoed through the canyon.

The old woman screamed out through the open door of the cabin. "I got them boys in my sights. We can empty plenty of saddles." She followed up her scratchy voice with laughter. "Hee-hee-hee." When she returned to her window, two shots rang out and landed in front of the line of riders in the valley. Several of the men's horses bucked and one of the animals shook its rider loose.

Toby Summers rode a black that seemed spooky and the shots were spinning him around. He pulled up on the reins to steady the big stallion. Zac took careful aim. His shot cut the reins from the deputy's hands and the black began galloping back to town at full speed, with Summers hanging on to the saddle horn. Zac broke down the big gun and chambered another round. He called out to the men below, "Stay right where you are. Just let the deputy go. That horse has got some run left in him." The men stiffened in their saddles, afraid to move.

Zac recognized one of the interlopers below as the man he had forced to cut Mouse Nichols down the night before. He seemed to be spoiling for a fight. He spoke to the other men and looked up the hill in Zac's direction. "We'll go," he called out, "but we'll turn around and come right back and we won't be standing down here being targets."

Zac yelled down at the men. "I'll let you go, all right, and you may come back, but it ain't gonna happen today."

"And why not?" the man's voice fired back.

"Because," Zac said, "you won't have any guns and you'll be walkin' like you were last night." Zac took careful aim and ripped a shot at the big man, catching his hat and sailing it into the air. He ejected the shell and reloaded the big gun.

"The next one comes down two inches," he said. "Now all of you, unbuckle those side arms from where you sit and let them drop. You're all trespassers here and trespassers can be shot."

Each of the men in the group loosened his holster and, one by one, let them slide to the ground. Zac yelled out, "Now, shuck those saddle guns and step down off those horses." The men complied. The sight of their friend's hat flying off his head only moments before had convinced them that Zac meant business, and that he was highly capable of shooting anyone with great accuracy. The thought of the old crazy woman with the rifle at the window didn't settle well with them either.

When the men had laid their rifles on the ground, Zac called out to Hat. "Aunt Hattie, put some rounds at those horses' feet." The old woman sent a burst of gunfire at the ground, surrounding the horses, and the animals began a panicked gallop in several directions out of the valley. Zac could hear the old woman's cackling laughter as the animals ran.

Zac lifted his voice to the stranded men on the valley floor. "You men have a long hike. Remember what you've seen here. Those tin stars of yours are no good outside of town. Next time we see any of you around here, you'll be goin' back to Volcano tied to the back of your horse like a dressed out deer." The men listened and absorbed the meaning of what Zac was saying. He went on, "Now, you tell that no-account marshal of yours that I'm comin' into town to see him. If he wants to talk to me, tell him to wait by the fire."

The men began their trek out of the valley. Zac pulled out his knife and cut the rawhide on the man's wrist in front of him. "You go back and tell those fellow travelers of yours that this isn't a healthy place for any of you. I'm gonna stop embarrassin' you people and start inflictin' some real pain. You would do better to get rid of that pack of dogs you're runnin' with and find some real lawmen."

The man rubbed his wrists and looked up at Zac. "This sort

of thing has been going on ever since Grant appointed Judge Harkness to the bench. We just go along with it and figure to get ahead."

"Well, you can trust me or not as you choose, but this house of cards is goin' down," Zac said. "If I don't do it, somebody else will, but it'll get done, and you can take that to the bank. I'm lettin' you and your friend go in spite of the fact that you were gonna ambush me. Cart him on out of here and back to your horses." Zac tossed the cut rawhide aside and fixed his gaze on the man. "You can be assured, though, that the next time I see you on this property you won't get the chance to leave it."

The man scampered to his unconscious friend and loaded him over his shoulder. He started over the hill, then turned and watched Zac go.

Zac gathered the men's firearms and started down the hill to where Hattie was gathering the scattered guns that lay on the valley floor. The old woman was laughing as she scooped up the new bounty. "Hee-hee-hee. We sure showed them boys. They ain't comin' back here ever agin."

"They'll be back," Zac said. "They'll be more careful. They won't come ridin' into the valley, and they won't have just two men in ambush, but they'll be back."

Hattie stared at him. Her face drooped. "How you figure?" Her eyes looked up at Zac while he watched the troop of men walking toward town in the distance. "What you reckon we should do?" she asked.

Zac continued to watch the retreating figures. "I'll have to go into town first. I got to get to the belly of the beast."

CHAPTER 8

+ + + + + + +

"DID YOU STAY THE NIGHT in the hotel? Angel's Camp is such a noisy place, I hope you slept." The young woman smiled at Jenny.

The brightness of the girl's face radiated the inside of the stagecoach. There was an innocent cheerfulness to her that Jenny instantly liked. "Yes, I did stay at the hotel last night. It was noisy outside, like you said, but I've been traveling for several days, and I think I could have slept on the roof."

"I was scheduled for the trip last night, but I'm glad the storm gave me an extra night." The girl giggled and stuck out her hand. "I'm Sarah Lewis and I'm going to Volcano where I'm to join my new husband. We were married here last month and he's there setting up a place for us."

"Congratulations. You seem quite cheerful about it. No misgivings or second thoughts?"

"Oh my, no. Merriweather is a perfect gentleman. He's a doctor, but he's digging in the dirt around Volcano for gold too, like the rest of the men in that town." She blinked her sparkling eyes at Jenny. "I didn't get your name."

"I'm sorry. Jenny Hays. But please just call me Jenny. Volcano is my destination as well."

The door to the coach opened and a burly man in a buffalo hide vest stuck his head inside the coach. "'Scuse me, ladies. I'll be joining y'all." He reached for his hat and lifted it momentarily from his head. "Name's Chester Dobbin. If'n both y'all could sit in the front seat over there, then I'll take the back next to the window. I chew 'bacca and find it best to spit out the window to where's it won't land on other folks."

Jenny moved awkwardly around the large green strongbox bolted to the floor of the coach. She settled into the seat next to Sarah and watched the man take her seat. "Normally, Mr. Dobbin, I'd insist you sit up here and put aside your nasty habit for the duration of the trip. Passengers who ride bumpy roads in the front seats are normally tossed about. But with the strongbox here on the floor, I think we can successfully stay out of your lap."

The grizzly bearded man grinned and straightened out his brace of pistols as he settled into the seat. He showed a set of tobacco-stained teeth to the women in a broad smile. "Well, ladies, I'd sure be plumb pleased to have either one of you in my lap, should the occasion arise."

Jenny felt the young girl press closer to her and saw the smile disappear from her face. She looked at the man in cool deliberation. "The occasion will not arise, Mr. Dobbin, and a gentleman would never have suggested such a thing. Of course this self-centered habit and nature of yours has already shown you *not* to be a gentleman."

The burly man grunted and turned his face to the window, spitting out a spray of brown liquid. He kept his face out the window, choosing to ignore the women.

Jenny continued to stare at the man, not content that she had made her point. "I'm sure your mother would be very proud."

A heavy silence fell and Sarah broke the tension by turning to Jenny. "Why do they have such a large strongbox bolted to the floor, and one with such a large number of locks?"

"I have a friend who occasionally works for Wells Fargo. He says that the robberies in the gold country have prompted the company to secure the box, especially when it's carrying gold."

"Oh my! I hope we'll be safe. Perhaps we should have gone on last night through the storm. I shouldn't think bandits would be out in a storm like the one we had last night."

Suddenly, the door was flung open. A black-bearded man in

a crushed beaver top hat stuck his head through the door. His
buffalo robe went clear to his knees, and he wore bright red suspenders on top of a faded green drover shirt. The man's entire
face looked weathered and gray. "Pardon our delay, folks.
Name's Charlie Halperen. I'm gonna be your driver here on out.
We'd a been long gone afore now, but we'ze trying to scare up a
shotgun messenger that ain't drunk. Y'all sit yourselves still a
mite and we'll get one or somin' else." With that, he slammed
the door shut and stomped back into the hotel.

"They'll need a guard for sure," Sarah said. "There's been so
many holdups on this road." She glanced down at the golden
ring on her finger and nervously fingered it.

"Don't be concerned," Jenny said. "Women can travel anywhere in the West unmolested. There's so few of us, the men,
even bandits, treat women with respect." She cast a glance at
the man across the strongbox and wrinkled her nose. "Of
course, there are a few ill-bred exceptions."

The man grunted and spit another stream of tobacco juice
into the street.

"A man who would put his hand to a decent woman would
be hunted down and hanged," Jenny said.

"There's already been quite a few hangings in the Volcano
area, from what I overhear," Sarah said. "In fact, at breakfast I
heard several men discussing a hanging that took place in Volcano last night. I'm amazed at how fast the news of such things
travel. Of course with citizens like that—people who are willing to execute justice on such a night as last night—we ought
to be safe."

"Well, personally speaking, I don't put a lot of stock in vigilantes. I'm much more comfortable with the law, but I'm well
capable of protecting myself, should the need arise."

"How is that?"

Jenny reached her hand into the small purse she carried on
her wrist and pulled out a fist-sized spinning revolver. "This is
an Allen Pepperbox. It'll do the job."

"Here, let me see it," Sarah said. She grabbed the smooth-
handled weapon and swung it around.

The man on the other side of the coach swallowed his plug of tobacco. He wheezed and coughed. "Me . . . huh . . . haw . . . uh . . . here now, that be far enough. That thang's dangerous. It may not get what it's aimed at, but it'll always fetch somethin' else, and I don't want to be that somethin' else. I seen a man shoot at a barn once wif one of them things. He missed the barn, but kilt the cow in a pasture next to it. I ain't gonna be no dead cow, so y'all put that thing away."

Jenny reached for the revolver and took it out of Sarah's hands. "This time, Mr. Dobbin is perfectly right." She smiled at the man as she held the gun in her lap. "More men have been killed in the West from accidental shootings than gunfights. This weapon is very unstable, too. I've known all six barrels to go off simultaneously and that's horrifying." She smiled at the panicked man as she placed it in her purse. "I shudder to think of what might happen should I bounce around in the coach and wind up in Mr. Dobbin's lap with this thing in my purse."

Terror spread across the man's face and he quickly stuffed the plug of tobacco into his vest. "Here, ladies, y'all both sit over here and I'll move over there and give up my 'bacca till we get to where we're going."

"How considerate of you, Mr. Dobbin," Jenny said. "We'd be delighted to change places with you."

The driver emerged from the hotel with a gentleman in a black suit, white shirt, and tie. The driver placed the man's valise on top of the coach and stuck his head in the window.

"Folks, we're goin' to be moving out now. Sorry for keeping you sittin' here. You hang tight now and I'll try to make the time up."

As the new, well-dressed passenger climbed into the stage, Dobbin craned his neck out the window to yell at the driver. "Charlie, you take it easy there. There's womenfolk in here that don't sit too well wif bouncing up and down. Just go easy, ya hear?"

The new passenger removed his flat brim hat and smiled through a well-groomed black mustache at the women. He circled the green strongbox and took his seat next to the far window. "Pleased to meet you, ladies. Name's Sam Frazier." The man spread his coat to get more comfortable, and Jenny caught a glimpse of the pearl-handled revolver he carried in a shoulder holster. She immediately sized him up as a man who knew how to use it.

The driver shouted a curse at the horses and swung his whip, lurching the coach forward. It thundered down the busy street, sending people scurrying in every direction. Dobbin clutched the windowsill to keep from bouncing forward into the women's laps, an event he now saw to be certain death.

"I wonder why the driver didn't find a messenger to go with us," Sarah blurted out. "Everyone says these coaches need protection these days."

Jenny patted the young woman's arm and smiled at the man in the dark suit across from her. "I wouldn't worry, Sarah, I feel sure we have some protection."

The newcomer twirled one end of his mustache and winked at her.

+ + + + +

The men had waited in the rain all night. All six of them sat by the fire, warming their hands and drinking what little coffee they had left. The barricade erected the night before was still there, lying across the muddy road.

"It ain't coming. I say we ride on. Fer all we know, that coach is in Columbia or Angel's Camp. They's dry and having breakfast, and we'ze out here drippin' wet and hungry."

"Well, no matter where it is, it's got to come this way, can't go round nowhere's else. Far as I'm concerned, ever' stop it do make, it picks up more'a what we're after. Let 'em stop all they wants ta, jes' so they're loaded down when they gets here. Ain't that right, Roman?"

The dark-eyed man peered down at his coffee and said nothing. His sharp features were emotionless and cold.

"Roman, ain't it right, what I say? They'ze still got to come through here, right, Roman?"

Without responding, the lanky man by the fire rose to his

feet and walked toward the road. He looked down the road and continued to sip his coffee. His eyes were dark brown, almost black. He was clean shaven, with a chiseled face, high cheekbones, and a hawklike nose. The scar across the left side of his face showed him to be someone who'd been in scrapes before, been in them and walked away.

"Well it's right and Roman knows it's right. He'd a said so if'n it weren't."

A third, older man, spoke up. "Roman Evers don't say nothing, less it's absolutely necessary. Offhand, I'd say that'd be a good rule for you to follow, Hank. A man can't think and talk at the same time. If I had my druthers, I'd have Evers over there thinking, not answering your fool questions."

The other men in the group nodded their heads and looked at the nervously pacing man. He seemed visibly upset. "You got no call to talk to me that way. I'ze jes' trying to tell Frank here we got to wait. I don't wanna, but we gotta. We don't have to worry 'bout no new locks either, not with what I'm packing in them saddlebags."

"I'm just tired of settin' here, that's all," Frank broke in and got the men's attention. "Us just being idle here bothers me. What if some pilgrim comes along and wonders who we are and why we're here. What we gonna say then?"

The older man with the gray beard looked back up from his coffee. "We tell 'em we're part of a posse." He glanced over at the dark-eyed, silent man who had returned from inspecting the road and was now watching them talk. "Roman Evers here is a lawman. We just tell 'em we're with him, looking for someone."

The lanky lawman held the steaming cup to his lips, then swallowed. Lowering the cup, he grimaced. "We don't tell nobody nothing. I don't want no witnesses. Anybody sees us, we kill 'em."

+ + + + +

Jenny smiled as she listened to Sarah talk about her wedding. In vivid detail, the girl described the bridal party's dresses and what the guests wore. What made Jenny smile, however, was the way Sarah described the groom. It was obvious she was in love.

"You'll like Merriweather. He's a little rough-talking, being from Texas and all, but he has a heart of gold. I suppose that's what led him to practice medicine."

"He sounds wonderful."

"Oh, he is, he is." She caught herself blushing and laughed.

Jenny looked up at the well-groomed man in the dark suit. He had been paying close attention to the conversation for the past ten miles, silently watching and smiling. "You've traveled this road before, Mr. Frazier?"

"Many times," he replied.

"Then I suppose our delay last night was necessary in your opinion."

"I'd say so. Even though it did allow the shotgun messenger to find the wrong bottle, it kept this coach out of the worst of the storm."

"These things handle adversity pretty well, and the road seems straight and level."

"Yes, indeed, you're quite correct. But unlike the last ten to fifteen miles we've covered from Angel's Camp to Monk Hill, this next stretch is pretty treacherous. With creeks flooded and the possibility of a wheel breaking and leaving us stranded on the road in the rain, I'd say you spent a more comfortable night in Angel's Camp."

"Why are we slowing down?" Sarah asked.

The man leaned his head out the window, then bringing it back inside the coach, replaced his hat and straightened the brim. "Don't be alarmed, ladies. It appears to be some obstacle fallen across the road in the storm last night." He reached under his arm and extracted his pearl-handled, shiny Smith and Wesson. Breaking it open, he reached into his pocket and planted another cartridge into the empty cylinder under the hammer. He snapped the revolver closed and stuck it back in the holster under his arm. He closed his coat and smiled at the women.

"Don't worry, ladies. I don't think there's anything to be

alarmed at, but I like to be careful." He paused and saw the young bride's astonishment.

"I never travel with a round beneath the hammer. Too many accidents."

Jenny spoke calmly. "I'm sure you are the soul of caution, Mr. Frazier. Do you think there is any danger up ahead?"

"Well, there have been a rash of robberies on this road, and up ahead would be a likely spot. It's probably nothing, but if something should go wrong, you have no fear. I will not let anything inconvenience you two ladies in the slightest."

CHAPTER 9

+ + + + + + +

ZAC HAD SPENT THE NIGHT curled up on the hillside in as cramped a spot as possible. Keeping watch alone, a body had to be restless, ready to get up at the slightest noise. Squatting down on his feet next to a tree kept him from falling into a deep sleep, kept him alive. Now, though, his muscles were aching and he massaged his legs. His belly button was also rubbing down his spine; he was a hungry man.

They stacked the guns the men had been forced to discard in a corner of the log house. Hattie stirred the coals in the stove and tossed in some wood. "Nephew, I knowed you must be powerful hungry. Set yourself down whilst I rustle you up some fatback and grits. I'll turn some bacon fer ya too. I keeps hogs, you know, along wif my utter enterprises."

"Yeah, I met one of your unsatisfied pig customers last night."

She turned from the open stove and smiled. "Ha, you must be talking about the preacher man," she laughed. "He's dumber than dirt."

"He's probably smart about the Bible and such, but I'll grant it to you, he knows little about hogs."

"Well then, I jes' gave him a liddle bit of education." She smiled broadly, showing blackened and missing teeth. "Them preachers needs edgy-cation 'bout real life."

"Hat, everybody knows you're a sharp woman." Zac took out his pipe, thumbed tobacco into the bowl, and lit the mixture. "I'd say most people hereabouts look over every deal made

70

with you twice." He puffed the pipe to life. "But a man of the cloth, they trust people. To cheat somebody who trusts you, I'd say that was wrong."

Without answering him, Hattie put the skillet on top of the stove and, skirting to the corner of the room, opened a dusty, bright red steamer trunk. She pulled a burlap bag out and sauntered back to Zac, holding the bag behind her back with both hands.

"I'm a gonna tell you why I cheat and steal from every preacher I kin, but fust you gotta do sumpin' fer me."

"Nothin' that comes from you is ever free, Aunt Hat. A body always has to pay. What do you want from me?"

"Promise me now; y'all can't say no."

"Hat, if I can do it, I will."

She brought the bag from around her back and, reaching in, pulled out a brightly polished, cherry-colored violin and bow. "You recognize this, do ya?"

"My mother's."

"That's right, your momma's. The most saintly woman ever lived. I got cheated, you got cheated, the world got cheated, when she passed on. I was there when she went. You've probably wondered why I write you and keep up with what you're doing."

"I have wondered that, quite a lot."

"I do it because of this thing here. It reminds me of her. I know you were the closest to her and I also know she taught you to play it. Now, afore I tell you any more or feed that there face of yourn, I want you to play it."

Zac put down his pipe and, taking the instrument, turned it over, gently rubbing his hand across it. He held the violin lightly, as a father would his newborn baby. With the stroke of his hand across the polished wood, his mind raced backward in time, to a time by the fireplace on his family's farm, a time of sweet music, a time when his mother would play the beautiful violin, the only luxury the family could afford.

She played it with a sweet smile on her face, almost as if each note were a babe in arms. She had taught Zac to play it when he was just a small child. She had worked with him patiently and with a great deal of love. When he would play, she'd wrap her arms around him and rest her cheek on the top of his head, listening to each note and helping his fingers press down on the strings.

She'd say to him, "Zachary, just relax your little fingers on the strings, and let Mother play through you." Even now, when he put it to his chin, it was just as if she were there, holding him, and listening softly. He twisted the strings tight and listened to each note, carefully tuning it.

"What would you like to hear?"

The old woman took out a handkerchief, dabbed her eyes, and began to wring the dirty cloth nervously in her hands. "You knows the one, boy. Play your momma's special song."

Anguish shot though his heart. It was what he feared she'd say. His face remained deadpan, but inside, the thought of once again playing the tune made him wince. "Hattie, I don't know that song was her favorite. She just said so because I liked to play it for her, and I played it 'cause it had her name in it."

"Play it, boy."

His nervousness increased and he tried to be talkative and change the subject, ever so slightly. "You know, it was Jeb Stuart's favorite song. He'd throw back his head and sing it lustily at the top of his lungs every time we rode into battle. He'd always sing it at too fast a tempo." He smiled faintly at the thought, then turned sober. "The last time I heard it was while we were riding into the Battle of Yellow Tavern, the place where the general was shot and killed."

"Hush up 'bout the war. I jes' want to hear you play that song."

Zac reluctantly put the violin up to his chin and drew the bow across its strings. Tuning the instrument, he played a few notes and ran his fingers over the strings. Then he began the sweet, soft melody, *Dear Evelina, sweet Evelina, my love for thee shall never never die. Dear Evelina, sweet Evelina, my love for thee shall never never die.*

A tear began in the corner of his eye and rolled down his

cheek. He drew the bow back and stopped. "Hattie, I can't." He shook his head. "I can't play it no more."

"I know, boy." With that, the woman turned back to the stove and stuck some more kindling into the flame. She took out a sharp knife and began to cut the bacon.

"It ain't fair in no way that I'm alive cooking fer ya and Evelina ain't. It ain't right, it ain't fair, and it ain't just."

Zac set the violin on the table and picked up his pipe to relight it.

The woman shook her knife in his direction. "There ain't no loving providence of God on this here earth atall. He don't know who to take and who to leave, and all them preachers wif all their spoutin's can't never make no sense out of it no ways."

She hacked the bacon angrily and, tearing it into shreds, flung it into the hot skillet. "Why God took your pa, as good a man as ever drew breath, and your ma, an angel on this here earth, and left me who was a wicked woman that deserved to die, I'll never know in a thousand years. Hadda be sheer meanness on His part, I'm a figured."

She stopped midthought and banged a pot on the stove, then poured water into it. "I'll burn in hell for saying that, but it's so, jes' the same."

She scooped up the fried bacon and placed it onto a blue tin plate, then opened the stove and poured the grease into the fire. The flames shot up with a roar and the old woman beat out several sparks that landed on her dress.

Zac smiled and puffed on his pipe. "Hattie, if you don't watch what you're doing, you're gonna burn before you get to hell."

She began a string of talk would make a sailor blush, and concluded with "Serves me right." Then turning back to Zac, she waved the knife. "Boy, I'm a gonna tell you how your folks done died."

She paused and stared at him, her hands on her hips. "When I'm through, you're never gonna want to see me again, and then I'll have no kin atall hereabouts. That'll serve me right, I guess, but it's gotta be done all the same. I'm plumb tarred o' carryin' this curse 'bout my neck."

Zac puffed on his pipe, sending blue smoke into the rafters.

"I paid your folks and some of my other kinfolk a visit during the war. I'd done been out here in the diggings and had gotten some ahead, soze I figured to go back home fer a spell afore the whole place got burnt down by the Yankees."

The woman dug into her apron pocket and took out a tobacco plug. She cut off a slice and popped it into her mouth. "Y'all wants some, boy? It'll help your appetite something powerful."

He held up his hand. "No thanks, Hat. It would plumb cure mine."

She began to chew and work the plug. "You wuz done gone to war when I got there, boy. Fact is, ever' man over fourteen and under sixty wuz gone. Twern't no fun fer me atall."

She spit some fresh juice into the fire. It sizzled.

"Well, I dun come down with the sickness and nobody wanted to ketch it. Didn't have nobody who wanted to keer for me, none atall. They was all skeered o' the sickness and didn't want to take me in. Cain't says where I blamed 'em none. Well, your pa found out 'bout it and drove his wagon twenty miles to fetch me over to yer place.

"Him and your momma watched over me like a hawk. They cleaned me up on one end and fed me with a spoon on t'other. One of 'em wuz up all night wif me. Your momma, bless her heart, read the Bible to me, and they both prayed their hearts out fer me to get better."

She opened the stove and spit a stream of tobacco juice into the flame. Banging the lid back down on the top of the stove, she reached around to her cook box and pulled out a jug. "This is gonna call fer some drinking." With that, she hoisted the jug to her arm and lifted the thing to her mouth. She spat out her plug onto the floor and put her lips to the jug. Several swallows washed down her throat.

"To get down to plain-speaking, chile, God heard them prayers in His own wicked way. I lived and they done ketched the sickness and died days later. I brung it to 'em and I'm gonna haf to pay fer thet the rest o' my sorry miser'ble life."

She perched the jug on her lips and drank hard. Swinging it down off her arm, she wiped her mouth with the back of her hand. "There, that 'bout does it, boy. Them graves you done found when you got back from fightin' the Yankees wuz all my doings. If'n I'd a never come back, or if'n I'd a never been born, you'd a come home to your ma and pa, 'stead of graves and an empty farmhouse. Why God takes the good and leaves the miserable and mean is beyond any fair-minded person's sense of justice and right doing. There ain't no sense of it."

Zac puffed on his pipe and looked at the woman. Another tear rolled down his cheek. He wiped it off. It embarrassed him and surprised him at the same time. "Hattie, I spent a couple of years on the cold ground of northern Virginia with people dying for someone they hated. We didn't own no slaves. We didn't even believe in the whole secessionist nonsense. We were fightin' and dyin' because we hated the Yankees. We hated them telling us what to do. We hated them for marching on our homes. The very idea that they wanted to force us to stay a part of the Union at the point of a bayonet filled our craws with hatred. And I suppose they had every reason in the world to hate us too."

He leaned forward in his chair and looked the woman straight in the eye. "Seems to me, my ma and pa both died for somebody they loved. It sounds just like them. They both lived their lives for the people they loved, understandable for 'em to end it thataway too. It ain't often a body gets to die for someone they love."

He reached for the violin on the table and started to put it under his chin. "Ma gave this to you before she died?"

"Yes, boy, she said to give it to ya when I could. She said it reminded her of you, that you were God's own instrument to make beautiful music, but you just had to be picked up and held just so. I ain't had the heart to give it to ya till now, 'cause I couldn't bear to tell ya the truth."

Zac held the violin on his shoulder. "I ain't no Bible

thumper, but I know what I was taught as a boy. If God heard my ma and pa's prayers and saved you and then took them, it was for the same reason—because of His love."

He drew back the bow and again began to play the familiar tune, "Dear Evelina." There was a stillness in the cabin. Zac could feel his mother's presence in the room, pressing his fingers into the strings with each note. He looked up at his aunt and put down the violin. "Hat, when I do my job, I have to face death quite often, but I gotta tell you this right now; when I die, I want it to be for somebody I love."

CHAPTER 10

+ + + + + + +

JENNY HEARD THE DRIVER call out, "Got some company on the road; rest easy, folks." He began to tug on the ribbons to slow up the team.

Sarah nervously fingered her wedding ring and looked at Jenny. "These roads are so bad. Why won't these people just leave decent people alone? I don't understand it."

Jenny watched Sam Frazier. He seemed cool, yet she could see his mind was racing. Chester Dobbin, on the other hand, was wringing his hands. He removed the poke of gold he was carrying and shoved it into a rip in the seat. Carefully, he stuffed it under the upholstery and, shifting his weight, sat down on it. "You're armed, Mr. Dobbin. Besides, being the man you are, they won't dare bother you."

The look of panic in his eyes made Jenny feel sorry for him, and sorry she had been sarcastic to him. "I'm sorry, Mr. Dobbin. Don't do anything foolish with those guns of yours and I'm sure everything will be all right."

"Don't worry, ma'am. Momma Dobbin never raised such a foolish child. I'm a gonna do 'zackly what they say and just disappear in plain sight, and I'd hypothesize y'all to do the same."

"I don't care what they take," Sarah said, "just so they leave my wedding ring alone. It's precious to me. It belonged to Merriweather's mother and I just couldn't bear to part with it. You don't think they'd take it, do you?"

Jenny patted her hand. "Rest easy, Sarah. They've got plenty to attend to in this big green box bolted to the floor. They won't bother with a ring."

"Sorry to disappoint you," Frazier spoke up," but there's nothing in there today but the U.S. Mail, and if it's tampered with, it's a federal offense."

"How do you know that?" Dobbin blurted out. He took off his hat and began to wring it in his hands.

"Well, there been so many robberies hereabouts, they just decided to let this one go through dry. And if the mail is tampered with, then it's a federal offense, and that's where I come in. I'm a United States Marshal." There was a slight hesitancy in his voice. Exposing himself like this was a dangerous thing to do, and he knew it, but he also saw the extreme nervousness in at least two of his fellow passengers, and he didn't want them doing anything foolish. He drew aside his dark suit coat and exposed his badge. "Don't worry, there won't be any gunplay. I'm just here to witness this. Just relax and do what you're told, and I'll see to it that no one gets hurt."

The coach had come to a complete stop. Peering through the windows, they saw men with shotguns and drawn revolvers approach the Concord. One of the men yanked the door open. "Please step out, folks, with your hands raised high. Just stand aside and you'll not be hurt."

The man who opened the door seemed polite, but the masked man who seemed to be the leader was cold and emotionless. Jenny watched him gesture instructions to the gang without saying a word. He pointed to one burly masked man in the front of the coach, who responded by growling at the driver. "All right, ribbon-handler, tie them reins up and climb down off a-there."

As the driver climbed down, the silent leader of the group pointed to two more men, who began to unharness the horses. "Here now," the driver said. "Whatcha all doin' that for? How we gonna get to where we're goin'?"

"You wouldn't want them horses in harness with what we got to do here," one of the bandits replied.

One of the men emerged from the coach. "It's here all right. It's heavy and huge and with more locks on it than you kin find in a hardware store. Got a little sumin' else too. Musta fell outta someone's pocket." He bounced the poke in his hands that Dobbin had tucked into the seat.

"Now here. Just a carn sarn minute. That there's my road stake. You can't take that. I'll have nothing to live on."

The man's smile could be seen from behind his mask. He pointed his gun at the miner's belly. "Get back in that line and keep your hands in the air."

The bandit with the poke walked off, and Jenny watched in horror as Dobbin fumbled for the pistols he carried in his waist-holster. The leader of the bandits didn't miss a beat. From his vantage point at the side of the road, the cool shootist pointed his revolver and fired, drilling their traveling companion twice through the midsection. *Boom. Boom.*

As Dobbin clutched his wounded belly, the coldblooded killer sent a final round into the man's forehead. *Boom.* The bullets ripped into Dobbin before he had the chance to remove either one of his pistols. He dropped to the ground where he stood.

Sarah jumped back in panic. Two of the bandits who were carrying shotguns leveled them and began to shout, "Stand still! Don't move! Keep your hands in the air!"

Jenny stepped forward toward the silent man who had coldly killed the miner. "Sir, it wasn't necessary to kill him or even to take his money. He wouldn't have touched those guns if you had warned him."

The man looked at her coldly, with eyes like a snake charming a bird. He pointed the smoking revolver toward her. She froze in her tracks.

"Here, ma'am. It'll do you no good," Frazier said. The marshal slowly stepped forward and put his arm around Jenny. He whispered to her, "Don't do anything more. What's done is done."

Jenny was not to be quickly silenced. She looked at the killer and said, "I think what you did was cowardly, sir. You might be very proud of yourself right now, but if you have any conscience at all, you need to know that you'll be judged for what you just did."

Frazier pulled on her shoulders, trying to bring her back to the others. "He's not listening to you, ma'am. There'll be another time for him."

"There certainly will!" She was upset. Jenny felt badly for how she had treated Mr. Dobbin on the stagecoach, and now she didn't want to see him die without a protest. She turned back to the silent bandit with a last look of disdain. "Mark my words, sir, you'll be judged. It may not be in this life, but you'll be judged in the next."

The bandit leader motioned with the pistol for the two of them to rejoin the others. Then he picked up a burlap bag and handed it to a little man with red long underwear tucked into canvas pants.

The man sauntered past the passengers and held up the bag for them to see. "Wells Fargo can't keep us out of their strongboxes by bolting them to the floor of no stagecoach. Hee-hee-hee. Ain't no lock gonna work, neither." He shook the bag. "This here is giant blasting powder sticks. It'll do the job on that there strongbox."

Jenny now understood why the bandits had mercifully freed the team of horses. *They're compassionate with animals, even if they aren't with people,* she thought. The men with the shotguns motioned for them to step back while the man in the red climbed into the stage.

Several minutes went by before the man emerged on a dead run. "Get back now; it's all set to blow. Better get behind a tree and cover your faces."

Jenny dropped to the ground along with the others and put herself on top of Sarah to protect her. "Cover your ears," she screamed to the girl.

The explosion ripped open the stage, sending splinters of wood flying through the air. The people lying on the ground were instantly covered with dirt and debris. They could hear the sound of falling rubbish for some time as they continued to lie facedown in the dirt. "They could have allowed us to get our suitcases at the very least," Jenny muttered.

Jenny raised her head to watch the bandits comb through the skeletal remains of the coach. Its top had been blown off and now rested beside the road; the coach itself was now in two major sections, and the wheels were off of the back half of the vehicle. All over the road and for some distance to either side were the personal effects of the passengers' suitcases. Jenny could recognize some of her own garments. Scattered among the wreckage was also what remained of the mailbag.

"Thar ain't no gold in there, jest mail. That's all it was carrying." Several of the bandits that were scouring the wreckage were now shouting at each other and then back to the silent leader, who was still watching from under a massive oak beside the road.

Jenny turned her attention to the tree. Clothing of all description was hanging from its branches, and the force of the explosion had driven several spears of what had been the door of the coach directly into the trunk like arrows from an Indian attack. Jenny was thankful they had sailed over her head, and yet sorry they had not found their mark in the silent leader of the pack. Jenny wanted very badly to see him sent to his ultimate judge.

They got to their feet. Several of the bandits had braced the driver between them and were asking him questions. "Why ain't there no gold? What'd ya do with the stuff?" The man looked full of fear and unable to answer. They slung him to the ground in disgust.

The man in the canvas pants and red underwear was not about to leave things as they were. "We can't just go. What we got ain't even gonna pay for that dynamite." He reached for the driver and pulled out the pocketwatch from the man's vest pocket. Pulling it sharply, he broke the chain from the man's pants. "Come on, boys, let's find out what them passengers is carrying. We done been here in the rain all night and I ain't about to go back with nothing to show for my time and displeasure."

"Don't let them take my ring." Sarah scooted close between Jenny and Frazier and placed her right hand over her ring finger.

"Here now, let me see that thing." The man pulled Sarah out from between them and held her left hand in the air. "Looky here what I got me. I'll take this thing back to my wife."

"No, no! Let me go!"

The man ignored her and, looking at the masked leader, continued to plead his case. He held Sarah's hand high to allow the man under the tree to see the ring. "This might make my wife forgive me for a being gone from her last night. Okay if I get this?"

The masked man nodded, then walked to where the group was beginning to assemble around the driver and passengers.

Sarah looked back at Jenny and Frazier with wild eyes, then swiveled her head to the man with the red undershirt, pleading her case. "That's my wedding ring. It's sentimental, please don't take it."

The man began to wrestle it from her finger. "It'll be sentimental to my missus, too, lady." He twisted the ring, but the tension of the moment had frozen it on Sarah's finger, so he pulled out a sharp knife from his waistband and held her hand tightly. "Lady, if I can't get this off, I'll have to take the finger."

Sarah screamed and Frazier stepped forward to try to grab her. "You men let that woman go. This is barbaric."

Suddenly, from behind, one of the bandits clubbed the marshal senseless with his heavy revolver. He hit the ground on all fours and let out a soft groan before passing out. The bandit turned him over and went through his pocket, searching for a purse.

"Hey, I got me something here." He held up the marshal's badge. "We done got us a U. S. Marshal here, Mr. John Law, his own self."

The bandit watching Jenny stepped up to the masked leader. "I don't like this atall. What if he's got a posse following the coach? This whole thing is a rigged deal. We better get onto them horses of ours and hightail it outta here."

"Not till I get this ring. I don't go home without this ring for my wife, even if there's a finger attached to it."

The bandit leader spoke up. "Get the blazes outta my way! I'll cut it off myself. Hold her tight." He holstered his revolver and took the knife.

"Wait a minute, don't do that!" Jenny yelled.

She walked toward the three men hanging on to Sarah, her hand in her purse, giving the appearance that she was about to produce some valuable find. "Before you take that poor girl's ring, I have something here for you to take instead."

The men turned and stared at the approaching woman.

"It's not gold and it's not silver." She stepped closer, pulling her hand out of the handbag, wrapped around the butt of her Allen Pepperbox, her finger frozen on the trigger. "It's lead and plenty of it. Now drop that girl's hand."

The masked leader pulled Sarah's hand away from the other bandits and dropped it. He pushed them away. Jenny approached him, pointing the revolver directly into his midsection.

"Sir, your cowardice and bad manners will get you killed and this might as well be the time. I've seen enough of your hooliganism," she said as she reached up and with her left hand jerked down the man's mask, "but I haven't seen enough of your face."

His eyes showed surprise and his dark heavy eyebrows arched upward. He dropped his hand to his holstered six-gun and froze in midmovement, staring at the six barrels of Jenny's Pepperbox revolver.

"Sir, you move one more inch and I promise I'll wipe you off the face of this earth."

Sarah was sobbing and holding on to her left hand. "They were going to cut my finger off," she cried. "I can't believe anyone would do such a thing."

"Roman, let's get outta here for somebody else comes."

The bandit leader shot a cold look in the direction of the man in red. When their eyes met, the man knew instantly what he had done. He'd used a name. *His leader's face had been seen and now his name was known.*

"I'm sorry, I wasn't thinking," the man blurted out. "All the same, we can't stay around here any longer. That explosion was heard, you can be sure of that. We gotta go."

"That's right, Mr. Roman, whoever you are, you gotta go," Jenny joined in. She held the gun up higher. "This thing is awful unpredictable. Send those men of yours away first."

"Lady, you're not fooling anybody," he said. "You shoot me and my men will kill you." He paused, then added, "Ain't no telling what they'll do first though, before you die."

Jenny didn't flinch. "Be that as it may, you'll be very dead." She paused. "And for good reason, I have a feeling that death for me will be much more rewarding than death for you."

He studied her, trying to determine her capacity and resolve.

"Don't think I won't shoot you," she said. "I've never killed a man like you did today, but I have killed plenty of varmints." She looked him straight in the eye and didn't blink. "I killed a charging cougar last year and believe me, I was much more frightened of him than I am of you. I've still got his hide on my wall to remind me to hit what I aim at."

He needed no further convincing. "All right, boys, clear out. Wait for me at the top of the ridge over there. I'll be along shortly."

The men mounted their horses and began to ride down the road. Jenny smiled at the bandit. "That was probably the first time you've showed good sense in years. Now, take out your revolver by two fingers and drop it right where you stand."

He paused and looked at her, not moving a muscle. "I didn't want to embarrass you by disarming you in front of the men. Menfolk do such irrational things when their pride's at stake. But I'd urge you to do what I say right now."

He slipped the six-gun slowly out of his holster and dropped it to the ground. Jenny waved the revolver in the direction of his horse. "I'll walk you to your horse. When we get there, I'll take that saddle gun of yours and you can ride on." She smiled slightly. "Remember, if you're tempted to ride back, I've got that cougar's hide. I do hit where I aim."

The man mounted his horse without uttering a word and rode to the top of the ridge, joining the disheartened renegades. Together, they waited and watched the stagecoach survivors below as Jenny moved around tending to their wounds. Deputy Roman Evers watched her carefully. She was deliberate in everything she did. He watched her and knew he'd give up everything to have her. He would have her, then he'd kill her.

CHAPTER 11

+ + + + + + +

THE SOUND OF IRON HORSESHOES carried into the valley. They were followed by the nicker of Hat's horses and the restless stamping of the whole corral outside the window. Inside, it brought Hattie to a dead stop and she listened carefully. "We got us some company, nephew. People jes' won't leave a body be. Last feller that come here afore you was a drummer selling pots and pans. A body could hear him a comin' fer miles and miles, all that tinware clanging and banging round." She reached up above the door for the Spencer rifle, mounted on wooden pegs.

"Well, before you go to shootin', Hat, let's find out who it is."

They opened the door and walked out into the afternoon twilight. It always got darker sooner in the valley. The shadows began to cover Hattie's place around midafternoon. They could see the man riding over the rocky shale and coming down the slope. He was a tall, gangly man, riding a mule and leading a large hog by a length of rope.

"It's that danged scarecrow of a preacher." She put down the Spencer and planted her hands on her hips. "He's bringin' my boar back to boot. Dag nab busybody, helpless, good-fer-nuthin' 'scuse fer a man." She started a string of curse words and stomped the ground. "Nephew," she said, "why cain't they take their medicine like anybody else and jes' learn somethin'? What makes 'em think they deserve some kinda special treatment jes' because they is so all fired stupid?"

"Hat, your problem ain't with Parson Young, you got a war going on with God. Sooner you recognize it and come to peace, the sooner you can get on with what's left of your life."

The woman squinted and looked at him. "Don't reckon I needs no sermons from you either."

Zac pulled out his pipe and stuffed a whisky-soaked mixture into the bowl. He struck a match and cupped his hand over the flame, touching it to the tobacco. "You won't get no sermons from me. I violate at least one of the Ten Commandments for a living."

The minister pulled up outside the alarm bell line and Zac and Hattie walked out to meet him. He got down off the mule and stepped over the line. He held up a burlap sack. "Don't mean to bother you none."

"Well you is!" Hattie shot back.

"My missus baked some cornbread and I brought you some buttermilk to go with it."

"Why, that's your favorite, Hattie," Zac said.

She shot the parson a look that would have stopped a clock. "You ain't gonna be gettin' into my good graces with that there bribe of yourn." She paused. "And you ain't gonna be gettin' that there thirty dollars back neither. You bought you a pig an' you kin keep it."

"Oh, I don't want my money back, Mrs. Woodruff. I just consider that part of my ongoing education out here in the West. I do want to return your boar, though. I have no use for him in his condition, and I thought you might know something better to do with him." He pulled the rope, and the hog stumbled over the alarm bells. The preacher stooped down to untangle the ropes around the animal's legs. "Poor old fellow's blindness does him in every time. If I had some smaller pens he might work out, but he just gets himself lost as it is."

"Only thing better I gots to do fer him is to smoke him fer the sausage, and y'all could have done that."

"Well, I guess I'm just not much of a butcher. I'm trying to raise a few hogs to make ends meet, but I don't do the butchering."

"Well, then, why'd you bring me this sack of bribes if you didn't want your money back?"

"Oh, I bring a little something to anybody I invite to church, and Mrs. Young and I would like you to come as our guest."

Hattie began to cackle and laugh. "Preacher, you sure is a green one, you surely is. Last time I was in church, I was standing up to marry Will Woodruff, worst fool thing I ever done in my life. No sir, I ain't got no use fer yer church—nor yer God either fer that matter." She latched on to the rope that held the pig and pulled the animal toward her. "I will take the pig back, if fer no other reason than to teach you to mind yer own business." With that, the woman began towing the blind boar toward the pens that held her other pigs, leaving the parson and Zac to watch her.

"I'm sorry, Parson. Sorry you went to all this trouble for nothing. My aunt is a bitter, cantankerous woman. She's got nothing against you, it's God she hates." He looked the man in the eye. "You see, she feels responsible for my parents' deaths and just won't put the thing behind her."

He puffed on his pipe and took the bag from the preacher's hand. "Thank your wife for me, though." He held the bag up and looked back at Hattie, retreating toward the cabin, then lowering his voice, he turned back toward the preacher. "She will eat this and she'll be forced to think about your kindness with every bite."

✦   ✦   ✦   ✦   ✦

Mouse reached Volcano's streets well into the night. He couldn't tell the time. A watch was something he'd never owned. Still, he could tell that the time was right for doing what he needed to do. The shops were long since closed, and the lamps hanging from the balcony of the hotel were glowing brightly. For some distance now, he'd been able to hear the piano music that clanged through the night air. One tune sounded the same to him. He'd never been able to tell the difference, so even though each saloon and hurdy-gurdy house banged out their own entertainment, to Mouse Nichols, they were all playing the same music.

He hobbled along the outskirts of the town, moving along beside the creek. The waters were swollen. They were always high these days, with or without rain. The judge's company was doing hydraulic mining, washing away the sides of the hills, washing the soil into the creek and down to God knew where. *The early days were better*, he thought. *More people, more tin-panners, more money to be had by the common folk. Now you have ta have a big operation to get rich. Lotsa money to start with, lotsa pull. That's what it takes to assume other people's claims and wash 'em away through your own durn sluices.*

He skittered from shadow to shadow. Stopping across from the hotel, he peered through the windows at the brightly lit dining room with its crystal glasses and clean tablecloths. The chandelier was ablaze with light, and he could see several of the diners cutting meat on their plates. He thought Judge Harkness was in the group at the back of the dining room, but at this distance, he just couldn't be sure. He was hungry and paused to watch them shove forksful of meat into their mouths. *Some day*, he thought. *Some day that'll be me. When I get what's coming to me, I'll be in Sacramento or even San Francisco, then I'll live like that—rich food and nighttime ladies, no more crib women and jerky.*

Only a few days ago he had thought he was well on his way. They were digging high-grade ore out of their claim, and he was selling Hat's rose quartz and gold and splitting it with her. He didn't even have to dig that. She'd been afraid to come to town and tip people off as to where there were such rich diggings, so he'd been a convenient gold mule. *The old woman shore likes her privacy*, he thought. *Likes it enuf to pay dearly for it*. That was all right with him. He'd lie for her. He'd lie for anybody to add to his poke.

That was all over now though. Now he was a hunted man, hunted for something he hadn't done. He was broke too. The claim had been stolen. He hadn't signed any papers, but it was gone nonetheless. Old Hat had been pretty smart all right. Nobody knew about that mine of hers; if they did know where those spider webs of gold that colored the quartz had come from, he still would have had his place and Hat would have been out of hers. Since he'd brought it into the Wells Fargo office and sold the stuff, though, people thought it came from his, Joe's, and Tom's place.

She musta known it all along, he thought. *The old woman has a sixth sense about her. She can see around corners*. He had to get the claim papers back. Maybe Hat would buy the claim. She didn't have any group of nightriders visiting her place with a rope; she'd seen to that. He might have to sell it to her at ten cents on the dollar, but at least he'd have the ten cents. He knew everything would be kept in the judge's office—he might even get lucky and find some gold the old man had squirreled away.

Volcano had no courthouse. Anything presided over by Harkness was carried on in the saloon or in the livery stable, all depending on how the man felt about it on the day. The judge had an office on top of the Jug and Rose. Mouse stood at the bottom of the outside stairs and watched the office window.

A faint light glowed behind the curtains, and Mouse watched the windows for any movement in the room. The light burned steady with no shadows. He started up the stairs, placing his shoes carefully on each step, his eyes pasted to the window, looking for any sign of life. Quietly, he turned the brass knob on the door, slipping into the dark hallway. The office doors lined the walls of the hall on his right. He knew the judge's office took up the whole left side of the upstairs. The man even had a balcony that looked out onto the street. He would often sit up there and watch the traffic and people on the street.

Several times, Mouse had come into town with Hat's gold and looked up to see the gray-haired man watching him. There was something about the judge's look that made him think the man knew everything about him—where he came from, where he was going, and even what he wanted. The judge had always given him the heebie-jeebies—something like a man would feel if he were walking past his own open grave—just to see him sitting up there, not smiling, not frowning, just eyeing him, rocking in that rocking chair and looking right through him.

Mouse held his ear up to the door, then gently turned the knob. He knew it would be locked, but he turned it anyway. It was the only way he had of being sure the judge was not there. If it opened, he knew the man was inside, maybe sleeping, maybe working, but inside all the same. *It was locked!*

Reaching into his coat pocket, he took out his lock pick. It was a skill he'd learned as a boy. While other children were going to school or more than likely working in the sweatshops of lower New York City, he'd been acquiring some skills as a second-story man. It got him into big trouble as a kid, but tonight it was going to get him a grubstake. He felt the tumblers and moved them ever so slightly. *There!* He pushed the door open and closed it.

The office was furnished in red velvet with green tassels hanging along the borders of the curtains. Mouse thought it looked like something out of a Jackson cathouse. The lamp on the desk flickered and its etched-glass globe glowed, making the cut crystal shards that hung along the edges of the glass shade sparkle with color.

No use looking in the file cabinet—his reading wasn't good enough to even look in there! He deciphered a little and read enough to make out some simple words and his own name, but education was only one of the things he was lacking.

He looked across the desk and began to shuffle through some official-looking documents. There it was! He couldn't read it all, but it had his name on it along with that of Joe Johnston and Tom Whipple. He took it and stuffed it down his shirt. Swiveling his head around, he spotted the small safe in the corner of the room. He'd been shown how to open one back in New York, but that had been a long time ago. His mind raced. He had what he'd come for, he had what was only rightfully his, but the safe looked mighty tempting. If he could have what was in that, then he could light out for San Francisco tonight. He wouldn't have to wait around, contest his claim, or stay one step ahead of the Vindicators.

✦   ✦   ✦   ✦   ✦

Judge Ruben J. Harkness sat with his chair tilted against the wall. He always chose the seat facing the front of a room. He'd move toward the back of any room he walked into and perch himself where he could see everyone and everything. Even while talking to him, one had the feeling he wasn't missing anything that went on, and when he did give his full attention, you'd wish he hadn't. His black eyes would auger into your soul.

Right now, Deputy Roman Evers had his full attention. The three lawmen had arranged a meeting with Judge Harkness in the dining room of the St. George Hotel. "Now, why don't you explain to me why you thought it was necessary to kill the man."

Roman Evers was a man not easily flustered. His exterior was always cold and hard. He was a back-shooter with very few scruples, and his ability to remain calm was one of the elements that made him a deadly shot. "You know I always have a reason for doing what I do. I don't go off half-cocked," he said. "The man was reaching for his pistol. I killed him to make a point to the driver and the others on that coach. When word of this gets around, we won't have to tell people to hold up their hands more'n once."

He reached into his pocket and pulled out a long black cheroot. He ran it through his lips and curled his tongue around it to firm up the dry tobacco leaves, then he bit off the end.

Judge Harkness continued to stare at Evers, and Breaker Morgan spoke up. "Yeah, but you were seen. You also got yourself backed up by a woman. Afore too long, your face will be all over the territory."

Evers took the match and, with his thumbnail, popped a flame on the end of it, puffing the cheroot to life. "That's where I'm counting on you, Marshal," he said through the billowing smoke. "When those people come in, I want you to take their statement and prepare the handbills. You leave the woman to me; I want her."

"I'll bet you do at that," Toby Summers grunted. "I've heard plenty about your wants and desires." The deputy looked around at Judge Harkness and Breaker Morgan to make sure he had their attention. "Our fellow deputy here enjoys mixing his pleasure with a woman's pain."

"I don't care what you do to her," the judge said. "I just want to be sure there's no one left who's able to identify you. There's more to be had here, and I don't like the way things are shaping up. You robbing a stage with a U.S. Marshal on board, being seen, and then killing a passenger. Meanwhile, your two fellow lawmen here rubbed up against a Wells Fargo special agent, who shamed 'em in front of the whole town."

"I heard about that." Evers smiled with the thin cigar clinched in his teeth. "I 'speck that story will get all the way to the coast by week's end."

"Well that's our biggest problem," the judge spoke up. "That's also where you come in, Evers. This here Zac Cobb is staying out at Hattie Woodruff's place. He's like a ghost, too, and won't be easy to eliminate. I've heard a lot about him. I had two of his brothers locked up during the war; they're about as tough as they come."

"Yeah, I've heard some stories about him," Evers said.

"Well, whatever you heard ain't half the truth," Summers broke in. "There's somethin' about him, somethin' serious in his look, his eyes. He faced me down and that whole group of nightriders I was with the other night, and even though he had only one load left in that shotgun of his, I knew he intended to use it."

Marshal Breaker Morgan had been sitting quietly, but he was seething at every mention of the man who had shamed him in front of the town. His eyes blazed. He spoke quietly through grinding teeth. "You just got to get him back into town and leave the rest to me." He held out his huge paws. "I'm going to kill him with these hands."

"The survivors from the stage is coming in; they's pulling up right now." The desk clerk had stuck his head in the dining room and alerted everyone to the latest news about the story they were all talking about. A dozen or more diners put down their knives and forks and were going out to see up close.

"Evers, you better go out through the kitchen. Stay out of

sight until I send for you. Meanwhile, the rest of us will greet those poor unfortunates and see if there is anything we can do."

Deputy Roman Evers got up and moved toward the kitchen door, brushing past Emily Morgan on his way out. She shot him a look and, putting down her tray of dishes on a suddenly empty table, moved out the door toward the lobby.

"Shall we join them, gentlemen?" Harkness asked.

Charlie Halperen had placed a burlap bag on the hotel counter with what was found of the mail and was leaning on his elbows watching the people pour out of the hotel dining room. He turned to Jenny, Sarah, and Sam Frazier, and then cast his eyes at the high ceiling and the staircase.

"This be the place, folks, the St. George Hotel," Halperen announced. "The last two hotels that were on this here spot both burnt clean to the ground, so when they built this one they took special care. They named it the Saint George. I guess he was some kind a English knight or something that kilt fire-breathing dragons. Well, whatever he was, it worked. The St. George is still standing."

He cast a proud look at the polished wood counter. "Well, old St. George done killed the dragon that lived in this place; ain't had no fire since they renamed it. This'll be where y'all will stay, till we kin fetch your loved ones to come get ya, or till we kin find ourselves another coach."

Sam Frazier slapped the dust off his black broadcloth coat. "I believe this is the end of the line for all of us, Charlie. We'll be staying right here for a while."

The two young women approached the desk clerk, who was opening the large black registration book. He grinned and held the pen out for Sarah to sign in. "Here, ma'am, if'n you'll just place your name on that line right there, I'll see to your things."

The lawmen walked into the lobby from the dining room and stood watching the passengers, trying to place which one had braced Roman Evers with her pistol. Judge Harkness carefully surveyed the two women. Whoever it was had to be quite a woman.

"No, thank you," Sarah said. "My husband lives here in

town. Merriweather Lewis. Dr. Merriweather Lewis. If you could just send someone to fetch him for me, I'd be very grateful."

Jenny approached the man behind the desk. "I'll be needing a room, sir, at least for a night or two. I'd be obliged if you could get me a horse for tomorrow as well. I need to find a friend of mine who is visiting his aunt. Perhaps you know her—a Miss Hattie Woodruff."

The lawmen's jaws dropped open and Judge Harkness's eyes grew wider and brighter. He straightened his coat, stepping forward. "Pardon me, ma'am. I'm Judge Ruben J. Harkness. I know Mrs. Woodruff very well and I'd be happy to show you to her place. I could drive you out there tomorrow. Perhaps I've even seen your friend. Might I ask his name?"

"His name is Zachary Cobb. He is Mrs. Woodruff's nephew."

"Tall fella with brown eyes and a big mustache?" he asked.

"Yes, yes, that would be him. He smokes a pipe. When did you see him?"

"He came through the other night," the judge replied, "and the strangest thing happened." The man's eyes flashed. He looked at Jenny to see how she would react. Judge Harkness enjoyed toying with people, especially women. "He breezed into town with barely a fare thee well and had two men buried. Men he felt had been wrongfully hung."

Jenny smiled broadly. "Yes, that's Zac. He's a man who gets very concerned when he sees things that aren't the way they should be." She paused. "And generally he sets them right."

"Well, ma'am, I'd say we were all impressed with his ability to do just that. I'd be happy to take you to him in the morning."

"Thank you, Judge."

"May I introduce you to the law in our town. This is Marshal Breaker Morgan, and his deputy, Toby Summers. I know they'd like to get your statement on the robbery and a description of the bandits. We've been after this bunch and have already brought some of their confederates to justice, but as you can see, our work is just begun."

Jenny noticed that Sam Frazier retreated a little during the introduction of the city lawmen. From the corner of her eye she could see him watching the men with silent interest. If he wasn't going to introduce himself, she wasn't about to say anything. She'd learned that much in her dealings with Zac. If a man didn't say anything, he had a good reason, at least one that was good in his own mind, and that was all that mattered.

The judge turned to the lawmen. "Gentlemen, you can take the good lady's statement. Perhaps she's too exhausted this evening to talk, however, and if so, you can get her description of the event tomorrow morning. I'm going back to my office now." He tipped his hat to Jenny. "Ma'am, I look forward to the pleasure of our ride on the morrow."

CHAPTER 12

+ + + + + + +

MOUSE SPUN THE TUMBLERS on the safe. He had to keep trying, and each try became more frustrating. The more frustrated he became, the more intent he was on opening that safe no matter how long it took. He knew he could do it, he just had to keep trying.

With each attempt, he paid less attention to what was happening out the window on the street below him. He had started by watching each person come out of the hotel, trying to stay alert as to when or if the judge might be returning to his office. He knew that the man often worked late into the night—that was, if he wasn't watching Delia dance. Mouse knew Delia ran the trade for the crib women in town. He sighed. *She sure can dance*, he thought, *and when those dark eyes look at you, a body is ready to sell his soul to have her.*

He had glanced out the window a few moments before and watched the wagon pull up to the St. George. He had already heard a little about the holdup, but didn't place the wagon and its cargo with it. He watched them go into the hotel and went back to his frustration with the safe.

+ + + + +

Pat Wallace was a large man with a bald head and red muttonchop whiskers that stood out from his already pudgy cheeks. Heavy eyebrows with flecks of gray dominated his small blue eyes.

He had seen to the needs of the passengers at the hotel and taken the mail in the makeshift burlap mail sack with him. He was anxious now to get home to his fireplace and whiskey, and wanted to do as little as possible to make things right before he went home. What was making him rich by the standards of a Wells Fargo agent had little to do with hard work.

He crossed the street to the stone house with the green shutters that had become Wells Fargo's trademark. He had left the light on when he went to the hotel, and while he did notice the large and rather expensive-looking horse tied up outside, he paid little attention.

He opened the door and stopped in his tracks. A man with shotgun chaps and a buckskin jacket sat with his chair tipped back against the wall, his feet on his desk. The man's dark brown eyes looked up at him. He was smoking a pipe that hung below a large, brown, drooping mustache, and was whittling on a piece of wood with a sharp knife. "Step in and close the door," the man said.

"Who in blazes are you and what are you doing in my chair?" Pat Wallace questioned, stepping in and standing beside the door instead of closing it. "We're closed and we won't be open till nine o'clock tomorrow morning." He motioned with his hand toward the open door. "You can come back then." He paused as a thought came to mind, a thought that frightened him. "I don't carry any money here . . . if that's what you're after."

"I said . . . close the door." The stranger's deep baritone voice had an authoritative ring to it, and in spite of Wallace's fears he obeyed.

Bringing the chair forward with a thud, the stranger pushed back his gray hat with the edge of the knife. "My name's Zachary Cobb." Reaching into his pocket, he produced a badge with a "Wells Fargo Special Agent" insignia and dropped it onto the desk. "The company sent me," he said.

"How can I be of help?" Wallace asked.

"First of all, you can help by keeping our caucus private."

"Oh, of course, that goes without saying. Far as anyone else is concerned I've never seen you, don't know who you are."

Zac surveyed the man carefully and wasn't so sure. His nervousness and the way he started to wring his hands caught Zac's attention. "Tell me what you know about these robberies and especially the hangings that have been going on."

"Well, Mr. Cobb, it's a pure puzzlement, it surely is. The stages are being held up and gold shipments are being taken right and left. I don't know how these highwaymen find out about when the gold is due for shipment. Near as I can figure, some of the small-time mine operators are in cahoots with the bandits and pass on whatever information they get ahold of."

Zac listened to the man and then nonchalantly turned his attention back to the whittling, adding to the pile of wood shavings on Wallace's desk. "It's these small-time operators who are bein' hung by this gang of nightriders, I assume."

"Yes, the citizens around here are outraged. When someone who shouldn't have all that gold starts flashing it around, they lose their heads."

Zac started fine smoothing the wood piece and puffed on his pipe. He drew the dark briar out of his mouth and used its stem to point outside toward the street. "Mr. Wallace, those folks out there are not outraged, they're frightened. They all seem to know what's going on around here. In fact, everybody seems to know, but you."

The man seemed startled and jerked his head back, blinking furiously, his bushy eyebrows flapping on his forehead like the wings of a bird. "No, I don't know everything about it, I just do my job. I didn't know the stage from Jimtown wasn't carrying gold yesterday, either." He paused and swallowed. "I guess the bandits were as unaware of that fact as I was; they hit the thing and one of the passengers was killed."

Zac showed no emotion. He leaned his chair back, parking the top of it against the wall. "There are some things you do know, Mr. Wallace. The miners come in here to get their gold assayed, don't they?"

"Why yes, they do."

"You pay them for their nuggets and the presmeltered gold they dig up, am I right?"

"Yes, that's part of my job."

"Then, when these small operators are hung, you'd be in a position to know how valuable their claims are, wouldn't you?"

The man's bushy eyebrows arched up and his face flushed. Zac could see he had hit a nerve. "Yes, I suppose I would," the man replied, "but I resent the suggestion that I'd have anything to do with these lynchings."

"I s'pose you do. Somehow, though, I don't think you resent it near as much as the men who get hoisted up."

"Looky here, Mr. Cobb, I like my job and I do it right well. The bandits blew the coach up today trying to get to gold that it wasn't carrying. I just came back from settling the passengers down at the St. George." He looked down at the list he was carrying. "One of them, a man named Chester Dobbin was killed. Three more—a Mr. Sam Frazier, a Miss Jenny Hays, and a Mrs. Merriweather Lewis—are at the hotel."

Zac's eyes were wide. "Who was that again?" he asked.

"Chester Dobbin, he was the man who was shot."

"No, not him. Who were the others?"

Wallace looked back down at the list. "A Mr. Sam Frazier of Sacramento, Miss Jenny Hays of San Luis Obispo, and Mrs. Merriweather Lewis." He looked up at Zac. "Her husband is a doctor here in town and she just came to be with him."

The chair Zac was sitting in came forward to the floor with a loud thud. He scooped up his saddlebags and grabbed the sawed-off shotgun that was underneath them and walked past Wallace. Wheeling at the door, he drilled Wallace with his eyes. "You like this job, and if you want to keep it you'll keep our conversation and my presence here in town to yourself."

✦　✦　✦　✦　✦

Judge Harkness stood at the bottom of the steps outside the Jug and Rose. As he grasped the handrail, he turned back to the street and watched Zac leave the Wells Fargo office. Harkness was a good gambler, always hard to read. A body couldn't tell if he was holding a royal flush or a pair of deuces; he surprised people every time he laid down his cards. He watched Zac cross the street with the same cold emotionless study he always used.

Nothing could surprise the man, not even the sight of someone that his deputies wanted desperately to kill walking toward the hotel. Breaker and Toby Summers were still there. He smiled and started his climb up the stairs. He'd hear about it soon enough.

Mouse had finally managed to open the safe in the judge's office. He had no interest in any of the papers, though he did notice a stack of official-looking quick claim deeds that looked like the one with his name on it that he'd removed from the top of the judge's desk. *There! That's more like it!* He lifted out a roll of double eagle gold pieces and swept out several pokes of gold dust. Peering deeper into the safe he saw a large nugget of pure placer gold. It must have weighed five pounds!

From the bottom of the safe, he pulled out a large leather bag and began to stuff his booty into it. With what he had here, he could live off the fat of the land for a long time in San Francisco, and he intended to enjoy every minute of it. He'd go on to Hat's place tonight and try to sell his claim, then get one of her horses and be long gone before morning.

Judge Harkness had reached into his coat pocket for a cigar and stopped at the door to strike the match when he heard a noise inside his office. The cigar dropped from his mouth. He leaned his head forward and put his ear to the door to listen. There was someone in there! Reaching into his coat pocket, he grabbed the 32-pocket pistol he always carried. He'd be careful—there might be more than one person inside.

+ + + + +

Zac had walked into the hotel just as everyone had retired from the lobby into the dining room. He walked to the counter and perused the large black guest registry. Beside the book, a quill stood sentinel in a jar of black ink. There she was—room 201.

He took the stairs two at a time, never bothering to look around and not slowing down until he reached the landing on the second floor. He expected to find 201 next to the stairs, but instead saw the numbers 212. He walked the length of the hall and finally came to 201, next to the back stairs. He rapped on the door lightly.

"Yes, who is it?"

Her voice was sweet, yet right now it was stirring up anger inside of him. The fact that she came without telling him what her plans were bothered him, and the notion that he had one more thing, one more person to worry about, infuriated him. He knocked lightly again.

"Who is it, please?"

"It's me," he mumbled. "Open the door."

Jenny unlocked the door and threw it open, a smile across her face bigger than all of Montana. It quickly disappeared when Zac stepped in and she saw the scowl on his face. He closed the door behind him, trying to stuff his feelings inside. Try as he might, he couldn't hide his anger.

"What's wrong, aren't you glad to see me?" she asked.

He dropped his saddlebags and placed his shotgun in the chair next to the door. "What in blazes are you doing here?"

She backed up, feeling a little defensive at his tone. "I had some time. The restaurant is being handled well, and I just wanted to see this aunt of yours, the one that writes you . . . wanted to talk to her about your family . . . your home."

Zac wheeled around and stared into the corner of the room. He was angry and didn't want to say something he'd be sorry about later. "My job's dangerous enough," he said as he whirled to look directly at her, "without having to look after somebody else."

"Oh, I won't be in your way."

"You're in my way already." His voice rose with emotion. It startled her and made her blink.

"I'm sorry, I thought you were only visiting your aunt and buying some horses. That was what you told me."

"I know what I told you." He edged up to her with an intimidating closeness that he used often in conflict, but never before with Jenny. "But I don't tell you everything. I still got a job to do and I still got my own life besides."

He shuffled his feet closer to her. "That's why I live alone.

My job gets even more dangerous if I've got to look over my shoulder every time I get into a scrape. This is my job, woman. If you wanna have any part in my life, you got to stay outta my job."

She wanted to fire her immediate thought right back at him: *Your job is your life—a lonely, solitary life, which you can keep!* But she held her tongue. She also held her ground and cleared her throat, which she was prone to do when nervous. "I'll just stay out of your way. I'll stay right here in this hotel until your job is finished."

"You don't know what you're about, woman." Zac could see that the distance in his tone was hurting her feelings, and he didn't like talking down to her, but he went on anyway. "The people I'm up against are in charge of this town and everybody in it. You being here has just given them another weapon to use against me. They'll do anything and use anybody to stop me."

"I didn't know," she said softly.

"That's right, you didn't. When I leave San Luis, I can give you all the details and worry you to death, or I can leave you be in ignorance and jes' trust your judgment to stay put till I get back."

"Is that the way you see me?" she asked. "Someone who's comfortable in ignorance? A fragile little glass knickknack that needs to stay on the shelf and be protected? Well, I'm not. I'm not Daddy's little girl anymore. You may think you're doing me a favor by not telling me about what you do, but you're just lying to yourself."

"What do you mean?"

"You don't want to deal with people that care about you. You like to be lonely, Zachary Cobb. You keep your distance from folks and lie to yourself by saying you're protecting the people that care about you, but all you're doing is protecting yourself."

Zac seemed flustered. He paused and took a breath, allowing the air to slowly escape his lips. He looked at her carefully and cocked his head to the side as the slight crease of a smile crossed the rim of his mouth. "I know women don't think men notice much about them," Zac said. "But I've noticed something about you."

Jenny was on a tear now. She didn't want to stop telling him what she thought, but Zac always had a way of changing the mood at the drop of a hat. "What's that?" she asked.

"Whenever you're frightened or nervous, you get angry." He smiled. "And when you get angry, those blue eyes of yours flash white hot and the roses bloom in your cheeks."

She softened slightly, but still refused to calm down. "You're trying to change the subject."

Zac ignored her and took her in his arms. "I know." He squeezed her tightly. "You make me nervous, Jenny. When I think about you and me I get scared—scared for you and scared for me, I guess." He continued to hold her. "I heard about the stage being hit that you were on today. If I'd known you were on it, I'd a been pretty useless round here."

"The marshal wants a statement and description from me in the morning. I saw one of the men's faces."

"Then that's all the more reason we got to leave right now. Those outlaws work for the marshal; they're his men. Now gather up your things. I'm taking you to Aunt Hat's."

+ + + + +

When the door to the judge's office creaked open, Mouse snapped his head around. He sat down on the floor and watched the revolver slide through the crack in the door, followed by Judge Harkness's salt-and-pepper beard. He was unable to move, paralyzed by fear.

Stepping through the door, the judge spotted the frightened man on the floor, in front of his open safe. "Mouse Nichols, as I live and breathe. I see you're continuing in your life of crime." He smiled a wide smile. "Anybody that didn't think Tom Whipple and Joe Johnston shoulda been hung is going to learn better now. You're their partner, a sneak thief." He cocked the revolver. "We can hang you later after a trial in my court, but I don't think anybody would care," he said, extending his arm to full length and looking down the barrel at the cowering man, "if I just shot you where you sit."

CHAPTER 13

✦ ✦ ✦ ✦ ✦ ✦ ✦

EMILY ATE HER LATE DINNER after the customers had left the St. George's dining room. It galled her to see Breaker sit there with Judge Harkness and listen to him alternate between laughter and seething anger. She knew him to be a volatile man with no control whatsoever of his emotions. She knew him well. He was her brother and, more importantly, he was his father's son. Everything about him reminded her of her abusive father, the man who crippled her mother with a beating and came close to doing the same to her. His brand of fathering had made her hard inside.

Tom had tried to change all of that. He'd been a gentle man when she didn't think such a man existed, but now Tom was dead, murdered by the men she watched laugh and talk at the judge's table, murdered by her brother and his lackeys.

When she'd had time to eat, she sat and watched them. She knew she'd be willing to do anything to put a stop to those men. She was alone now, though; Maggie was dead and buried. Emily had nothing left in her now but her hatred. It bothered her because it reminded her of how much she, too, was becoming like her brother in her own way, of how much she was like her father, something she never thought was possible.

She knew how hatred and abuse were like the cockleburs she picked up on her stockings when she walked through the fields in the summer. They stuck her and gave her pain, clung to her, became a part of her. They weren't easily removed either. It took time to stop, sit still, pick them out, one by one. *Better to leave them*, she thought.

With each mouthful of supper, she resolved to pay whatever price it took to get to the bottom of the lynching, to find out who'd given information to the nightriders. Somehow she knew that Maggie's murder had to be a part of it. Somebody didn't want her to talk. She thought she knew who, she just had to find out for sure. She couldn't expect any help from the law. The very word "law" left her mouth dry and made her want to laugh. She was growing more cynical. Everything Tom had done for her by his innocent sweetness while he lived, she was allowing his death to undo. She knew it, she just didn't know how to do anything else.

Power. The need for power in a situation where she felt totally helpless dominated her thinking now, night and day. She'd felt protected by Tom, and she knew that with him a day would have come in which she would have felt safe. Now he was gone and the feeling of being protected had gone with him. She'd have to live without it, and live without him.

There was a power to be had by young, attractive women. She could have that power if she wanted it. She'd seen the way men watched her when she served them. She listened to the way they talked and bantered with her. She felt their strength when they grabbed her at the tables. She'd kept herself from them. The thought sickened her. To become a woman like that meant being handled by men that her heart couldn't and wouldn't ever belong to, men like her father.

Delia was a woman of great power. Men watched her. Men wanted her. They'd do any silly thing to have her, pay any price. Emily hated her and everything about her, but she respected the power she had over men. They hung on her every word and held nothing back from her.

Emily quietly finished her dinner and rose to wash the dishes before she quit for the night. She gathered up the plates and knew what she needed to do. She had to talk to Delia. She had to find out what Delia knew about Maggie's murder. Neither one of them liked or trusted the other. Delia never liked Emily for the purer-than-thou airs she carried around and the tone of condemnation Emily communicated whenever they saw each other. Now Emily knew the whole reason she'd never liked Delia. She envied her mastery over men.

Emily felt out of place in a saloon. She slunk around to the back door of the Jug and Rose, where Delia danced, and turned the brass knob. Cigar smoke belched out into the night air, and Emily quietly slipped inside. She walked lightly to Delia's room and gently knocked on the slightly open door.

"Door's open for you, honey; come on in."

Emily pushed the door open and stepped inside. Delia's back was to the door as she sat in front of her mirror applying heavy makeup. She saw Emily and froze.

"Can I help you?" she asked coldly.

Emily wrung her hands in front of her gravy-stained dress. "Yes, I hope you can. I apologize for interrupting you like this. It isn't often someone can find you alone."

Delia turned on her stool and looked at Emily, fullface. She spoke with disdain, a tone that made Emily feel small and out of place. "I make myself alone for the right person."

"Yes . . . and I know I'm not that person."

Delia laughed. "You got that right, little sister. Whatcha want with me, anyway?"

"First off," Emily said. "I want to say that I'm sorry for the way I've acted toward you. You do what you have to do and I should know that. I suppose you're just doing with what God gave you."

Delia looked surprised. "And it's no more than you've got yourself, sister. It's just that you think you're too good to do what I do. You've got some dream that a man on a white horse is going to ride in here and save you, and that ain't never gonna happen. He'll ride in here to use you, but he won't save you. You've got to save yourself."

Deep down, Emily hated everything that came out of Delia's mind. She was beginning to believe what she said, but she hated it all the same. There was a note of resignation to the worst life had to offer, and Delia built her existence on it. But at least the woman had a life, a life free from dependency. Emily didn't like Delia's life, but she was envious of it nonetheless.

"I know I haven't acted very civil toward you in the past," Emily continued, "and I'd like to apologize to you for acting that way. I suppose it'd be fair to say that in a way I admire what you do to men. You're not beholden to any of them, they're beholden to you." Emily swallowed hard before admitting, "And I like that." Every word hurt, but she said them.

Delia put her foot up on a stool and waggled her legs back and forth. She studied Emily up and down, as if surveying merchandise. "Well, I suppose I got all the attention I need and then some. Maybe I can send a little business your way." A smile crossed her painted lips. "Would you like that?"

"What would I have to do?"

"Honey, you just gots to be pretty and close your eyes tight and pretend the first few times. You can make an extra double eagle, too, by keeping your ears open and letting the men talk to you about what they're digging out of the ground."

Emily knew that was what she had come to hear. She had played in her mind with the rest, but she had to know how Maggie died, how the nightriders got their information. "What am I supposed to hear?" she asked.

"All the boys like to brag. Darling, the way to a man's heart is through his ego, not his stomach. They all want to know how good you think they look, how great a lover they are, how much you just love to see them, and how rich and successful they're going to be. That's the way all men are from the time they crawl out of the crib."

She got up and moved a chair closer to Emily. "They got eyes too, honey. When they see you're a beautiful woman and that you're with them, they feel good about themselves. It's not your beauty, it's their pride that's the point, and don't you ever forget that."

Delia poured herself another brandy. She was on a roll now, teaching Emily and feeling good about herself for doing it.

"What could they possibly tell me that would earn me a double eagle?" Emily tried to sound naive. She'd never been a babe in the woods, but she'd become one if that's what it took.

"They all take pride in what they're taking out of the

ground. They'll all lie, because they want to impress you with how important they're going to be, so you got to see some samples. Try to do it by buttering them up. They'll have placer gold; that's what's in the creek. It's the quartz hard rock gold we're interested in."

"We?" Emily asked.

"You just tell me and I'll pass it along and pay you the extra money. These water miners with their powerful spraying machines need more hills to wash. If we can find them fresh claims, then how the big boys get them is their business."

"Do the other women tell you this type of thing too?" Emily held her breath. She didn't think Delia knew about her friendship with Maggie, but she couldn't be sure.

"I know everything, baby sister. All the girls from the hurdygurdy types to the ones in the cribs come to me. They tell me and it goes to Old Rube and the water miners. They all need the money. Money is the only reason we do what we do." She laughed. "It isn't love, sis, it's money. Your days of doing it for love are all over."

The last statement out of Delia's mouth sent a look of anger across Emily's face. She couldn't control it. Delia saw it and suddenly stopped—stone still.

+ + + + +

Two floors above the women, Mouse Nichols squirmed, with his back pressed against the open safe in Judge Ruben Harkness's office. He was desperate. "Don't shoot me, Judge, I can make it worth your while to let me live."

"How? What you gonna do, give me my own gold back?"

"No, but I can tell you where to find the mother lode, rose-colored quartz with a vein of pure gold the thickness of my arm, laced all the way through it."

The judge lowered the revolver. "I already got your claim, Nichols, if that's what you're talking about." He raised the gun again and took aim.

"No! No!" Mouse raised his hand, putting his outstretched palms between his face and the muzzle of the old man's weapon.

"None of the samples I brought in to sell came from our claim. We didn't find nothing but placer stuff down by the creek. This stuff, the stuff I'm talking about, is socked away in a hill close-by, and you can get it too, real easy."

The judge relaxed his grip on the revolver and lowered it to his side. He spun his desk chair around and sat down facing the cowering man. "All right, you weasel, I'm all ears."

"How do I know you won't go ahead and shoot me if I tell you?"

"You don't."

Mouse knew he had one hold card left that wasn't seen, and with all the courage he could muster he was determined not to play it. He gulped. "Give me a drink at least, will you?"

Reaching over to his desk, the judge took a decanter of whiskey and poured it into a glass of Irish cut crystal. He handed it to the man. "This is the best stuff you've ever had, and it's all you're getting from me besides a bullet."

Mouse clutched the glass and slurped the whiskey down. He thought long and hard about what he needed to say next. He knew it might be his last words and wanted to get as drunk as humanly possible before he went into eternity. "More please," he asked, holding out the empty glass.

Judge Harkness grimaced. "All right, but that's the last." He poured another half glass of the warm, brown liquid.

Mouse drank it all down in several swallows, looking up from the rim of the glass to study the judge as he gulped. He was stalling as long as he could, giving the liquid a chance to work on his brain. "This here strike is rich," Mouse said, "the richest I've ever seen."

Harkness once again cocked the pistol. His patience was at an end. He pointed it at the man's forehead. "Nichols, the next word out of your mouth better be what I want to hear."

"You can check the stuff I sold at the Wells Fargo office and see what it looks like. It's nothing like what's in our claim. The truth will bear me out to that. You'd have to admit that I brought in some mighty rich stuff." He could see the judge was thinking it over. At least he wasn't pulling the trigger just yet.

"Now if I tell you everything you want to hear, with your money in my pocket, and the safe open, you'll just kill me and that'll be that." He paused and gulped. He'd have given anything for one more drink, but he knew he'd be pressing his luck, especially given what else he knew he had to say. "I don't want much, I just want to live. I want to live and get outta Volcano."

"You tell me what I want to hear and I'll let you leave town. I'll let you leave and take some of that money with you. I wouldn't want you to be a vagrant out on the open road now, would I?"

"Well, Judge, you're being more than a fair man. This is my deal though, and if you don't buy into it, then I guess you'll just have to shoot me, 'cause the way I figure it, it's the only chance I got."

The judge scooted forward in his chair. He was becoming restless, Mouse could see that.

"You arrest me, Judge, and take me to jail. I'll tell you where to find the mine I got that rich ore out of when I'm all locked up. Then you and the marshal can let me escape. I don't figure you can kill me in jail, leastwise not as easy as you can right here and now."

Sweat was beading up on the man's dirty forehead as he watched the judge think the proposition over. Several moments ticked by and with each one, Mouse thought he might be taking his last breath.

"Nichols, you're a no-good vagabond and I'll probably live to regret this"—the judge smiled—"but you just called me and I'm folding on this one. I've seen that ore you sold and it's the richest I've ever seen. I know you didn't get it outta your claim, 'cause I looked that over today myself. For once you're probably telling the truth." He wheeled his chair back. "You put that stuff back you took outta my safe and we'll go see the marshal."

The judge stood up and watched the man put the contents of the safe back in place and they both turned to the door. "You know, Nichols,"—he looked him in the eye before leaving—"your lying ways cost your partners' their lives."

✦   ✦   ✦   ✦   ✦

Two floors below, Delia knew she'd said too much, and saying too much was dangerous, even for her. She had taken such a delight at watching Emily leave her pretense of purity and crawl to her for help that she'd let her mouth run away from her. It irritated her. She lived on the pride of men, and now she had succumbed to the same thing herself. She tried to change the subject and get back to the topic at hand, but her composure was gone. "I'll get you started as soon as I can, but right now I think you better get, I got a show to do."

Emily rose to leave, still shaking inside with a rage that she was trying to control. The pieces had all fallen into place and weighed on her like a team of oxen. She knew that if she said any more, what had been gained might be lost, but she couldn't help herself.

Reeling at the door, she pressed her luck and asked, "Do you just let any man with money come to you?"

"What do you mean?" Delia asked.

"I mean dirty, unshaven men like"—she paused, trying to think of any name to go along with the one she had in mind—"Robert Parrot or Mouse Nichols."

"Never! not even on my worst day. I send those types to the women in the cribs. I got a reputation to protect." She hadn't realized what she had said. "You just go and get ready. Get a nice dress that shows off your real virtues, the ones men pay for."

Emily stepped outside the door into the alleyway and froze as she saw the men on the steps above her. She stood under the stairs and quietly watched them. It was Mouse Nichols with Judge Harkness, gun drawn. She watched the men walk across the street to the city jail.

CHAPTER 14

✦ ✦ ✦ ✦ ✦ ✦ ✦

DEPUTY ROMAN EVERS had left the dining room out
the back way when the survivors of the stage pulled up outside
the hotel. He'd been seen at the robbery sight, and the thought
of being identified by one of them galled him. The thoughts of
what he'd do to the woman who had jerked down his mask had
become a fixation with him. Standing in the shadows, he
smoked several cigarettes and thought about the woman now
in the hotel. He would wait till later, then find her there and do
as he pleased with her before she died. His mind tumbled over
the act many times, leaving him excited and impatient.

He patted out the cigarette with the toe of his boot and took
out another paper. Opening his tobacco pouch, he shook a line
onto the paper and ran the edge of it over his tongue. His hands
were steady as he rolled it together and twisted the ends. He put
it in his mouth and was taking out a match to light it when he
heard the side door open on the landing above him.

Zac and Jenny hurried down the landing stairs. They carried
her few remaining belongings in a couple of flour sacks. He was
thankful that Jenny was a woman of the West, not prone to fuss-
ing about how her things were situated. She took things as they
came and made the best of it. Zac liked that.

Zac strapped the flour sacks onto the big bay gelding. The
blood bay was more than a beautiful animal. Her stockings were
black, and although she had a blaze on her face, it didn't make
an easy target in the dark. She stood over sixteen hands high and
could go all day and night if needed, so for both him and Jenny

to ride her to Hat's place would be no problem. They mounted up, not knowing they were being watched from the shadows underneath the staircase behind the St. George.

Evers knew at a glance where they were going. He walked toward the livery at a quick pace. Killing them would be a matter of timing for him, only timing. He just wanted to make sure the woman didn't die too quickly. She had done something to him no other woman on earth had done—she'd shamed him. He didn't put up with that from anyone, much less a woman. Her being attractive and proud to boot would only add to the pleasure. When he finished with her, she would be humiliated also, too ashamed to ever again want to live. Killing her would be an added enjoyment for him, and a mercy for her. He knew how proud people thought.

He slapped his saddle onto his sorrel horse and spurred to the road out of town. He cantered past the church without a glance and spotted the two fresh graves as he sped by the cemetery. He had heard all about the man the woman was with. He respected strength. Whoever this man was, Evers knew he was good, not someone to be trifled with. He'd have to die with a clean shot.

"I don't know how hospitable my Aunt Hat's going to be when she sees you," Zac said. "She's not your ordinary matronly aunt."

"I wouldn't expect any relative of yours to be ordinary." Jenny's arms were around his waist as they trotted up the road. She squeezed him playfully. "I 'speck there's no woman I know that likes her kitchen invaded by another woman."

"Hattie won't mind you in her kitchen. It's her life she'll resent you for buttin' into."

"She sounds like your family," Jenny said.

"She's that all right, sprinkled down with sheer cussedness."

Zac craned his neck around to get some form of eye contact. "I can't figure it out. Knowing everything you do about me, why'd you really come all the way out here?"

Jenny paused, thinking how she could respond in a way that told the truth but didn't drive him further away. "Just a feminine notion, I guess," she said. "I feel so . . . removed from your life, you out there at the ranch and me in town; you seeing me only when you got nothing better to do; just a foolish female feeling I s'pose." She threw back her head. "I just thought that if I could talk to another woman who knew your family—where you came from, what you were like before the war, before you got involved with all the hunting and killing you do, then I might feel a little closer to you, that's all. . . . It was a foolish thought, I admit it."

Zac listened. Women's thinking never ceased to amaze him. He appreciated their tenderness and the way they seemed to feel what other people felt without being told. His mother had been like that. As a boy he would lift his head and see his mother watching him. She'd smile and go on about her work, but it was as if she knew exactly what he was thinking, knew it and loved him for it anyway, no matter what it was. Women amazed him and scared him at the same time.

They rode on quietly, the sounds of the creek lulling them and the mare into a steady pace. On reaching the path to Hat's, Zac turned the horse and stared back down the dark road.

"What's wrong?" Jenny asked.

"Maybe nothing," Zac said. "Just a queer feeling, I s'pose. I been at this a long time and can kinda get a feeling about things. I usually keep a careful eye on my back trail." He watched the ears of the big bay horse cock forward, as if she were listening for something. Reaching down, he patted her neck. "You can feel it too, can't you, boy."

He motioned off the road to the trail that led up the hills. "We head off here, and without the creek maybe we can hear better. 'Fore we get to the top of the ridge, though, we'll have to stop and take a look-see. Way that moon is up there, I wouldn't want to be skylighted against it."

"You're such a suspicious man, Zac Cobb."

"I'm alive!" he said.

Zac slapped his spurs to the big bay and they bounded up the trail in the moonlight. They weaved in and out of the black oaks that dotted the hillside and stopped the horse beside a rocky outcropping. The two of them blended in perfectly on the blood bay next to the dark rocks. They sat silently, listening and watching the trail below them.

"What are we waiting for?" Jenny whispered.

"Maybe nothing," Zac said. His sharp eyes peered below them, reaching out in the darkness, reaching out for something he hoped he wouldn't find.

"There he is!" Zac breathed. "Coming up from the creek. See him? That's what I'm waiting for. There's only one way into Hat's valley. If anyone had seen us in town, he'd a known where to come and when we'd get here."

"How'd you know?" Jenny asked.

Zac didn't answer her question. He just shot her a look as if she'd asked something anyone ought to have already known. He slid the Sharps Creedmore out of his saddle boot and reached into his vest pocket. He took a second bullet out and placed it between the fingers of his left hand.

"If we'd a ridden on toward the top of the hill, we'd be in his sights now," Zac whispered. "Whoever it is, we'd be in his sights, with the moon at our backs." He lifted the Sharps to his cheek and sighted down the barrel."

"Don't shoot the man, Zac. We don't know who he is."

Zac looked up at her. "I ain't gonna shoot him, just gonna give him some learning." With that, he drew the rifle up to his cheek again, carefully sighted down the barrel, and squeezed the trigger.

The explosion ripped through the darkness and bounced off the rocks near the approaching figure below. Zac's horse jerked with surprise as he ejected the shell and loaded the round between his fingers.

The man's horse reacted even more violently as the shot sang by the animal's ears and crashed into the rocks beside him. It vaulted forward and stopped violently in his tracks, somersaulting the man forward and onto the ground.

Zac heard the man's cry of pain as he hit the rocks, and he raised the Creedmore for a second shot. It blasted the dirt near the panicked horse's feet and sent the animal scampering down the hill and back toward town at full speed. Zac looked back at

Jenny. "When I can de-horse a man, I don't need to kill him."

He slid the rifle back into the boot and pulled the reins around, hunching forward as they climbed the hill in the moonlight. Near the top, he reined up and turned to look back down at the man, who stood, staring up the hill, hands on his hips. Zac clicked his cheek several times, and the signal sent the big mare scurrying over the top of the rise and away from the moonlit valley below.

Riding into Hat's valley made Zac admire the old woman even more. Her layout was one that was efficient and easy to defend. The rocky shale and granite outcropping that led into the valley made it impossible not to hear someone approach, and the walls of the valley itself carried the echo of any noise a rider laid down. Besides the several alarm bells strung along the trail, Hattie kept her horse corral right next to the fortress-like house she had built, insuring the added warning given by her animals. *The old woman was pretty smart*, he mused.

They pulled up short of the alarm line and Zac sang out. "Hattie . . . it's me. I'm coming in . . . and I'm bringing a friend."

The old woman's screechy voice pierced the darkness. "Come on ahead, dag nab it . . ." There was a pause, then, "and you ain't got no friends."

Zac stepped the gelding over the line, but the animal kicked his back leg into it despite the caution. They rode the last hundred yards up to the house in silence and, reining up outside the low-profile dugout, got down, and tied up the animal.

"Well, go on in and I'll introduce you," he said, "then I'll 'throw you to the wolves' and leave you with her while I give the bay some hay and a rubdown."

From inside the cabin, the woman's voice squawked, "I heard that."

Jenny and Zac exchanged glances and pushed open the door.

The disheveled woman was pouring water into a coffeepot on the hot stove. She turned around and wiped her hands, surprised at the sight of Jenny. "Well, my stars, chile, you didn't say nothin' 'bout no female-type friend." She walked toward Jenny, scanning her up and down. "She's a real looker, this filly is! You done real good boy, putting a loop over this one."

Jenny was beginning to feel like a horse just purchased at auction, but she politely stuck out her hand. "Nice to meet you, ma'am. I'm Jenny Hays."

Instead of shaking her hand, the old woman laughed and stooped over, putting her hands on her knees and staring straight at Jenny's full bodice. "This one's built too, honey. . . . Yessir, you done real fine."

Jenny left her hand in the air, extended in the direction of the woman, determined not to move an inch until politeness overtook the woman.

"Oh, pardon me," Hattie said. She took Jenny's hand and shook her arm like a pump handle. "I don't gets around many women in these parts and seldom, if ever, any decent ones." She stopped pumping on her hand for a moment and then squinted into Jenny's eyes. "You is a decent one, ain't you?" She turned and looked hard at Zac and then back at Jenny. "'Course you is, an ab-so-lute igit could see that. I'm plumb flattered to meet you, missy. Name's Hattie Woodruff, but you kin jes' call me Hat."

"Hat, Jenny here needs to stay with us till we can get her on the next stage. It ain't safe for her in town. She was on the stage today when it was held up and saw the face of one of the men involved."

"I'd like to stay, ma'am,"—Jenny glanced back at Zac—"until I'm ready to leave."

Zac frowned.

"Of course you can, chile. You can stay as long as you like. Don't make no never mind to me, none atall."

Hattie started to brag, still clutching to Jenny's hand. "You'll be safe here chile, place is built like a fortress. Nobody comes in or out that I don't see. What with my Spencer and this here big bad Wells Fargo agent, I'd like to see 'em try anything, I'd jes' like to see 'em try."

Zac dropped his chin and stared at the floor, then shuffled his feet toward the door. "Well, I'm gonna let you ladies visit while I give the bay a rubdown and some hay."

Jenny looked plaintively at him, her hand still firmly in the grasp of the old woman's mitts. She said nothing, but Zac could see she was rethinking her desire to establish a relationship with one of his relatives. He playfully smiled and doffed his hat. "You ladies can talk to your heart's content and I'll just go on about my business."

He walked out the door and took up the bay's reins, leading him to the corral. He closed the gate and proceeded to strip off the saddle and blanket. He watched the light filter through the cracks in the window and could clearly hear the sound of Hattie's voice as he picked up some straw and started to rub down the big mare's back.

Women, he thought, *I wonder what makes them want to be with other people all the time*. He thought for sure that Hattie would resent the notion of Jenny even coming near her, but she had seem tickled to see another woman. *They are different*, he thought. *I'll never understand them no matter how hard I try*. He paused and looked at the dark hills that surrounded the valley. The high cliffs were his only friends. They stood like a silent sentinel between the valley and whatever enemy lay beyond them. Sometimes that was how he thought of himself—a quiet guardian of the peace, a man who separated right from wrong. When he saw the silent, dark hills, he did think about himself. Would he always be this way? Quiet, strong, alone?

He worried little about himself. He liked operating alone. When he was alone his mind functioned more clearly. He knew his own thoughts and could stop at any time to protect himself, but being in the company and conversation of another person was a distraction to him.

The wind from the creek over the crest of the hill picked up, blowing his dark hair into his eyes. He brushed it aside. He knew that in this valley it was the way the wind always blew. It was good protection, too. The horses would sense any intruder by the strange scent on the wind. They were getting used to his smell by now, but no matter, he always saw himself as an intruder wherever he went.

He shivered slightly in the cool breeze. The thought that he might have ridden on tonight, up that hill and to the top of the moonlit crest without stopping to check his back trail, frightened him a little. He'd been thinking about Jenny at the time, thinking about her and talking to her. One of these days, he'd be doing that at just the wrong time. That would be the day he died.

CHAPTER 15

+ + + + + + +

MARSHAL BREAKER MORGAN was leaning on the
support beam in front of the jail, smoking a cigarette, when
Mouse Nichols rounded the corner, followed by Judge Harkness, gun in hand. He stiffened his back.

"Look at what I found me," Harkness said. "Going through
my safe, he was."

Morgan closed the door behind them and stood eyeing the
small man.

"We made us an arrangement," Harkness said. "I wouldn't
shoot him in my office, and he'd tell me everything he knew
about that hard rock stuff he's been bringing into town."

Morgan flipped his cigarette to the floor and sailed a punch
into the man's midsection. Mouse bent over double and stumbled backward, his face turning blue. "I ain't made no deal," the
marshal said. "You're mine now, little man."

"Don't, don't hit me no more." He grimaced in pain, hands
on his knees, sucking wind. "I know where you can find Zac
Cobb; I can bring him to you."

The marshal lifted his knee sharply under the bent-over
man's chin, sending him to the floor with blood gushing from
his face, then moved quickly to the wounded man's side and put
his roughshod boot on his neck.

"Stop! Breaker, stop!" Emily grabbed her brother and pulled
him back. She had followed Mouse and the judge at a distance
and come through the door just as Breaker had unleashed his
fury on the badly mismatched prisoner. She slipped into the jail

in time to watch the eruption. "You've got no right to do that," she said. "Leave him alone."

The huge man pushed her away with one arm and glared at her. "This badge gives me a right." With that, he swung his boot toward the helpless man on the floor, sending a crushing thud to his ribs.

Mouse grabbed his sides and groaned in pain. "Don't hit me no more. I'll tell you whatever, just don't hit me."

"The man is quite right, Breaker." Harkness had been sitting on the edge of the marshal's desk, his hands neatly folded in his lap, his revolver tucked away behind his belt, watching the mayhem passively. Breaker Morgan belonged to him. The man was like a big dog. Harkness took pride in his brutality and could watch him carry out violent acts on others with a degree of detachment that lied about his own accountability. The marshal amused him, and frightened him at times, too, by how out of control he could become.

"Breaker, we both know this isn't the man you want to do that too, he just reminds you of him. We'll find the man, though, and this little man can help us do that. He knows where to find him, and he knows where there's a fortune in gold besides."

Harkness cast his glance down to the groveling Mouse Nichols and in a condescending tone remarked, "Besides, he's not worth your sweat. Look at him there—worthless as a man—a cripple, a dirty thieving cripple. He'd turn on his own mother right now for a chance at money and a fast horse."

Mouse groaned, "I'll tell you, I'll tell you what you want to know."

"See." Harkness lifted his hand out, palm up, motioning toward the cowardly man. "He's not worth your effort." The judge had learned over time that even though he had Breaker Morgan in his fold, the marshal could become a liability when he lost his head. That was why he made sure Roman Evers handled the operations with the stage robberies and why Toby Summers directed the Vindicators. Everyone in town was deathly afraid of Marshal Breaker Morgan, and as long as he occupied the place of power, none of the townspeople would dare lift a finger to stop what was going on. Harkness relied on the man's ability to intimidate everyone, but still, he knew that Morgan had to be held in check.

The judge looked at Emily. "Take the man back to a cell, your brother and I have to talk."

Emily lifted the still prone Mouse Nichols from the floor and, putting her arms around him, helped him toward the cells in the back of the jail.

Judge Harkness looked at Morgan. "You got to get control, man. I've seen the ore samples that no-account brought in, best I've ever seen. I don't want to lose what that man knows."

The marshal jutted out his jaw. He didn't like to be corrected.

"Now you mark my words, I know those no-account types. If you show them a little mercy after a beating like you gave him, he'll come back to you like a whipped dog, with his tail draggin' between his legs. He'll be just as loyal to you as one of your deputies."

"People do what I tell 'em to do 'cause they know I'll kill 'em if they don't."

"That's right. I just don't want you killing the goose with the golden egg. Besides, the man you really want to kill may show up to rescue him—he's saved his skin before, God only knows why."

Emily returned to the office and took a pitcher and basin from an oak stand, along with a towel. "Breaker," she said, "someday you're going to tangle with someone who will kill you, shoot you straight through the heart." She then hurried back to the cells while the marshal took a step in her direction.

"She's right, Breaker. You may be beating the pulp outta someone while they fill their hand with something you didn't see. Pays to be careful. Remember how Hickock got his—in the back of the head by a man he didn't see coming." The judge scratched his beard. "Come to think of it, you did have your back to the door the other night when that Cobb fella came into the saloon."

Emily helped Mouse, who was writhing in pain, into an empty cell and then stretched him out on a bunk. She took the towel and, dampening it in the pitcher, began to wipe the blood off of his mouth and chin.

"Why you wanna help me?" he asked.

"Because Tom was your partner. I'm treating you just like I'd treat him."

He blinked his eyes at her in disbelief. Tom had talked about Emily often, about how soft she was and how strong she was too. Often he'd thought about what Emily and Tom had together. He knew he'd never have that. He'd sought it, though. He'd looked for it in the cribs, among the women there. He'd looked for it in the eyes of the hurdy-gurdy girls as they danced or drank with him. He'd looked for it among all the women of profit he'd tried to impress by bragging about gold. But in every smile, every sparking eye, he'd never seen love or care; all he saw was greed and he knew that quite well. It was the same thing that gripped his own soul.

"I still don't understand why you're helping me."

"Because," Emily said, "in spite of what you are or anything you've done, you're just a man, a man that needs my help."

Mouse reached out and grabbed her wrist hard. "Don't leave me here; don't leave me alone with your brother. He'll kill me, I know he will. I'll never live to see the sunrise." He was truly frightened, Emily could see that. He was so scared he was willing to say or do anything. His mouth raced on, "I didn't mean to say nothing 'bout the claim. I didn't know anybody would come for us and our claim t'other night, honest I didn't. I didn't have anything to do with it."

"Who did you talk to?" Emily asked.

"To a woman; I talked to a woman and showed her some of my ore samples. Only her and Wells Fargo, they wuz the only ones to see them samples and I only told them I got it from our claim; mine and Joe's and Tom's. I didn't know this would happen."

"Of course you didn't." She continued to bathe the man's face and, reaching into her apron pocket, took hold of the handkerchief she had found in Maggie's mouth. She took out the brightly colored cloth and spread it out on the man's chest. She smoothed it out and dipped it in the water, using it to wipe the corners of his mouth.

He jerked his head back. "Where'd you get that?" he asked.

"You recognize this?" she asked.

"No, I ain't ever seen it before."

Emily looked at him sternly. "Now, Mouse, don't lie to me. If you lie to me, I'll just walk out that door and leave you with Breaker."

"No! Don't do that! I'll tell you. Yes, it's mine. That thing's mine. Where'd you get it?"

"I found it right where you left it, with a young woman, stuffed in her mouth to keep her from screaming."

His eyes began to puddle up and fear raced through his mind. "I knew it wuz her that done it," he said. "It had to be her. She was the only one I was with. It had to be her that done told those nightriders where the gold came from. Only thing is, I never told her the truth, see, it didn't come out of our claim at all." He scooted back on the bunk to get his head higher, looking at Emily directly at eye level. "She's the one who told. She got Tom hung, not me, it was her."

"I won't let Breaker hurt you." She was angry, but hid it well. On the outside she seemed cool, but on the inside she hated the man. He was a sorry creature, a creature who had taken her friend's life. In a way she knew that his need to brag about himself had cost Tom his life as well.

Judge Harkness had reasoned with the marshal enough. He knew when he could press his point with the man and when he couldn't.

"All right, that's enough." Breaker had gotten the point. He was feeling ridden and it irritated him. "You can leave your gold mine back there in the cell and I won't touch him—at least till after he tells you what you want to know. Will that satisfy you?"

The judge got to his feet. "I'm satisfied. Don't forget, there's something in this for you, and if it's as rich as it seems, that something will be quite sizable." He paused and asked, "Where's Summers tonight?"

The marshal smiled. "He's out rounding up some of the Vindicators. Seems we may have found one of the ringleaders of the stage robberies." There was a twinkle in the big man's eye as he said it, an inside joke that even he chuckled about.

"Oh, and who might that be?" the judge asked.

"This Lewis fella, Merriweather Lewis. You know, the doctor who moved in to town last month."

"Oh, yes. His wife came in on the stage. Perky woman, she is, and pretty—dark brown flashing eyes and a good shape. When Toby gets done she'll be needing employment." He chuckled. "Maybe I can send Delia round to talk to her."

Emily had been quietly standing near the door. She had overheard the men talking and knew that somehow she had to get word to this Zac Cobb and had to do it fast. She spoke up quickly, so as to pretend she had just entered the room. "I need some tincture of iodine to treat his cuts."

Breaker laughed. "Yeah, we want him in good shape afore we hang him."

"I'll have to go over to Mr. Olson's barbershop for some. He keeps it handy. I'll be back soon." She scurried out the door and into the night air.

Harkness eyed her suspiciously as she left. "You know, Breaker, I don't know how much she heard." He looked at the marshal. "I know she's your sister, but don't forget,"—he paused— "we just got finished hanging the man she loved."

Roman Evers walked in the door just after Emily left. He stood and watched her scamper down the street. He could tell she had something on her mind she wanted to do real bad. Slowly, he turned toward the men in the jail.

"Where you been?" Breaker asked.

Evers walked to the far side of the room and placed the Winchester on the rack. He surveyed the weaponry and took down the needlegun, one he used for long-distance shooting.

"I said, where you been?" Breaker raised his voice to the lean, dark-eyed deputy. Evers turned to face them, showing a new set of abrasions on his face and hands. "And what the blazes happened to you?"

"That man you been wanting to get?"—Evers walked to the drawer where the rifle rounds were stored—"Now I want him too."

"Show you up, did he?" Breaker laughed.

"I saw him and the woman that seen me at the holdup today leavin' town. From what you said, I figured they were going to old lady Woodruff's place, so I followed them. I intended to spill him when he crossed the top of the ridge and then go take the woman."

"Well, what happened?" Morgan was curious.

"He musta been watching his back trail, 'cause when I came to the bottom of the turn he fired a couple of rounds at me—sounded like a Sharps—and spilled me off of my horse."

"You're lucky his aim isn't what yours normally is," Breaker said.

"No, I think he did just exactly what he wanted to do. He didn't know who I was for sure. If he'd a wanted to kill me, I think he would have. Any man who watches himself that carefully knows what he's doing."

"We may have an opportunity here." The judge had been carefully watching the exchange between his two henchmen. "Breaker, I think that sister of yours overheard what Summers and the Vindicators' plans were tonight. Given the way she lit out of here, I'll wager she's heading straight for Hattie Woodruff's place right now to find Zac Cobb. You know the Lewis woman arrived on the stage with her tonight. She'll find Cobb and try to get him to stop Summers and the boys from hanging Doctor Lewis." He stroked his beard and nodded in the direction of Roman Evers and the needlegun he was cradling. "If she doesn't come back with that iodine then I'd say you could wait by the road and, in the moonlight we have tonight, get off a pretty clean shot."

Evers had heard all he needed to hear. He took a bottle out of the drawer and downed a couple of swallows. It would warm his insides in the night air. Then without saying another word, he marched out the door.

The two men turned to each other. "Let's hope that's the end of Mr. Zachary Taylor Cobb," the judge said.

Morgan grunted and scrunched up his chin. "Personally, I hope it isn't. I want to kill that man in my own way, and in front of everyone." He looked at the still open door and then back at Judge Harkness. "If Cobb kills him instead, I won't be crying myself to sleep. I don't like Evers. He's your man, he ain't mine."

The judge had collected the best men he could find to squeeze the most money possible out of the operation. It wasn't important to him whether they liked or trusted each other, it was just important they do what they were supposed to do. If the truth were known, he liked having Evers around. He was the one man who was deadly enough to take out Morgan, should the need arise. Harkness liked having all the cards.

"Go on back there, Breaker, and bring Mr. Nichols out here. We got a few questions to ask him."

"That'll be a pleasure."

The judge heard several screams and some yelling before Mouse Nichols was thrown from the holding cell area into the main office. As he hit the floor in front of the desk the judge was seated at, a piece of paper flew out of his shirt pocket. "Hand that to me, Breaker; let me have a look at it."

The marshal snatched the paper from the floor, stepping on Nichols' hand as he handed the paper to the judge. Nichols let out a yell of pain.

"Mr. Nichols, this here is the quick claim deed your partners so graciously signed the other night before they went dancing at the end of a rope. You must have got this out of my safe." He looked the groveling man over. "I can see you're intent on being a man of property."

Mouse scooted up to the wall, his back next to it for protection.

"Well, Mr. Nichols, I'm going to make you a very generous offer." He looked at Mouse intently. "You tell me where you got those samples and you cooperate with us in getting the mine, and I'll release you right now." He held up the paper. "Plus, I'll give you your claim back, all legal and all yours."

"Why would you do that?" Mouse asked.

"It's plain to see you want to own property. You won't run off anywhere if you can have what you want, and if you do a good enough job, you'll be working with us." He lifted the pen on the desk to the paper and poised himself to write. "Well, Mr. Nichols, now's your time. You can talk to me now or I'll leave you in the good care of Marshal Morgan here and go home and go to bed."

Nichols lifted his head to look at Breaker Morgan. It was plain to see he didn't like his chances of surviving the night with him. "Okay," he said, "I'll tell you what you want to know." He swallowed hard. "I got it from Hattie Woodruff."

Morgan exploded. "You expect us to believe that! That woman runs horses and hogs. She doesn't have a mine and she hates miners and mining."

"She only says those things to bluff folks," Nichols said. "She's got a mine all right. It's a rich one and it's a deep one, right under her house."

The marshal moved toward the man to kick him again, but Judge Harkness stopped him. "Wait, Breaker, perhaps he's telling us the truth. Her house is situated on bedrock, maybe she's got a mine under there. Might be the perfect spot for one." He looked at Nichols. "How'd she let you in on that?"

"Well, she didn't trust anyone enough to bring ore into town herself. She was afraid people would find out about the mine, so she offered me a share to sell it and say it came from our place."

"Sounds just like Hattie Woodruff," the judge said. "The old woman's shrewd—she lets other people take the risks, and she collects the money."

That remark focused the marshal's attention on the judge. "Yeah! You ought to know 'bout that!"

Harkness ignored the marshal's offhand comment and began writing on the document in front of him. "Here, Nichols, take this and go home. You're working for me now." He pulled out two double eagles from his vest and laid them on top of the deed. "This'll help."

Nichols scrambled to his feet and slowly took one end of the judge's offering.

"I want you back in here tomorrow to see me, Nichols. I'll tell you what to do then." The judge held on to the other end of the paper and looked the little man in the eye. "If you fail to show or you fail me in any way, you'll die a very painful death. Don't think you can disappear from me. Do we understand each other?"

The man nodded, then took the paper and the coins and disappeared out the open door.

The judge leaned back in the chair. "He'll be back. He's too scared to do anything else, and he'll be useful, too." He smiled at Morgan. "We can hang him any time it suits us."

CHAPTER 16

✦ ✦ ✦ ✦ ✦ ✦ ✦

EMILY RODE HARD for Hat's place. She had borrowed a horse from the livery and rode, slapping the animal's withers with the reins and kicking his sides. The moon was high in a cloudless sky and she thought to herself how much like a black-and-white daylight things seemed. She galloped on the road beside Sutter Creek and past the miners' cabins that lined the stream. Each place seemed to have signs of life—lanterns burning in the windows and the shadows of people moving behind the dirty curtains. She thought she knew where the doctor's cabin was located and quickly figured it might be best to head there first. Maybe they'd take her advice and get out while they could.

She rode past the darkened cabin that had belonged to Tom, Joe, and Mouse. The place was now only a shell with no signs of life. The thought of her last visit there ripped through her soul, and the fact that the man responsible for it all and for Maggie's death, to boot, was someone who was saved that night made her angry and bitter inside. She had defended Mouse Nichols, too, and bathed his wounds. *He cost me everything*, she thought, *and I was just being the dutiful woman to him, a man who repulses me.*

She slowed the horse down to cross the creek, splashing across the shallow running narrows. Tom had pointed out the cabin of the new doctor and his diggings on one of their many walks together. She thought she could remember it, although she'd only seen it at night.

130

Seeing the darkened cabin calmed her heart. *Still ahead of the nightriders*, she thought. She reined the horse up outside and tethered it to the stub of a tree trunk. Pounding on the door, she cried out, "Doctor Lewis! Doctor Lewis! Get up, Doctor, get up now."

Wearing his nightshirt, Lewis opened the door. "Here, here, what's the matter? Is somebody hurt bad?"

Emily rushed into the cabin, her heart pounding. Sarah, the doctor's wife, was lighting a lamp. "No, nobody's hurt, Doctor . . . it's you, you and your wife. You're both in great danger."

"Sit here, girl. Calm down." The doctor guided her to a chair, but she kept on talking.

"Doctor Lewis, we don't have time to talk, there's not a moment to lose. They've found out about the color you've been bringing in, and these nightriders are involved with the Whitewater hydraulic mining operation. They're going to hang you, Doctor, and take over your claim."

"Now, I can't believe even *these* people would hang a medical doctor. I'm the only one in fifty miles."

"That may be, Doctor Lewis, but I overheard my brother Breaker talking to Judge Harkness earlier and I know what I heard."

"The marshal and the judge, involved with a group of vigilantes? Impossible!"

"Doctor, they've got everything to gain by it, you must believe me."

Sarah Lewis had poured a glass of water for Emily and now sat beside her and put her arm around her. "You must be mistaken—they wouldn't possibly lynch a doctor."

"You don't know these men like I do. They hung my fiancé two days ago. They can do anything if they think you've struck enough gold. They're trying to get this whole valley and the creek, then they'll wash the whole place out with their high pressure water mining."

"I've seen those things. They're an ugly mess."

"I've seen the men these people have lynched . . ." She began to cry and sob, her face in her hands. Sarah put her arms around her and held her tightly. Emily jerked her head up suddenly, a steely resolve in her eyes. "I'm sorry, please forgive me. I won't cry for the dead, there's too much to do here and now." She looked Sarah in the eye. "Please believe me, your lives depend on it. They have plans for you, too, after your husband is hung."

Sarah looked up at Merriweather, an anxious look on her face. He had heard enough. "All right now, don't worry about us." Walking to the door, he reached up and removed a revolving shotgun. "We are from Texas, ma'am. That, and this here Colt revolving scattergun will be more than enough to keep us safe. You can rest easy."

Emily got up from the bench. "You don't realize how dangerous these people are. They've lynched several men at one time and all of them were armed, too. No,"—she shook her head— "your only chance is to get out of here; get out now, and lie low."

She walked over to the couple. "I don't think you understand. These people want all of the claims along the creek; they've got to have them to bring in their water cannons, and they'll have yours, too."

"I'm sorry, but I don't intend on dragging my wife into the woods to hide. I'll just stay right here and woe be to whoever comes down that road for us."

"If that's the way you want it, then I've got to go." Emily scrambled to the door and pulled her shawl tighter around her shoulders. "There's only one man who can help you, and if you won't leave I'll have to go and find him." She looked at Lewis. "You won't be able to last long against that whole outfit, from Texas or not. They'll burn this cabin down around your heads. They aren't interested in acquiring cabins, all they want is your claim—they'll leave the rest in ashes and leave you on the end of a rope, just like my Tom."

+ + + + +

Zac found surprising pleasure in watching Jenny try to talk to Hattie. The fact that she had followed him to the gold country goaded him no end, but now he was smiling and just watching the two women.

"Honey, we wuz jes' simple folk from the hills of North Georgia. T'weren't no school 'n' such. I still ain't found out hows to read. Cain't never make no sense outta them chicken scratchin's no ways."

The gray-haired woman looked over at Zac. She grabbed Jenny's shoulders and turned her toward him. "Boy, this here is shore a fine weddin' woman. Look at them hips, chile. She'll bring out some fine Cobb chillin."

Zac's face flushed. What had been a detached amusement had now become a personal embarrassment. Jenny subtly moved her shoulders and stepped aside, putting some distance between her and Hattie. Jenny's face had turned a bright red, and she tried to change the subject. "Well, then, how did Zac learn to read and write?" Jenny turned to him in an aside. "Although he doesn't write often."

The old woman spat a stream of tobacco juice into a tin pan on the floor. Most of it landed in the pan. "Zac's ma and pa were self-learned people. Never could figger out why Evelina wanted to bother, her havin' the looks 'n' all. Still, she was a determined woman even as a youngun. Kept at it and kept at it, reading the Bible mostly, but any book she could get her hands on. His pa was like that too, even quotin' poetry 'n' such. Never could figure, never could atall."

Suddenly the woman lifted her head. "You hear that, boy?"

"Yes," Zac said, "I heard it. Sounds like only one horse, though."

"Heard what?" Jenny asked.

The frumpy woman reached for her Spencer carbine that she kept by the window.

"Heard what?" Jenny asked again.

"We'll wait for 'em to hit the bell line." Hattie's voice was calm. She turned and put her hand on Jenny's shoulder. "I gots me a couple o' bell lines; cain't nobody, man nor beast, get down here without me knowin' it."

Zac pulled the Sharps out of his buckskin bag and loaded a

round. "Heard the sound. Sometimes you got to know what to listen for, before you can hear it. That rocky outcropping that lines the floor on the lip of the valley—gives off a sound when a horse moves across it. The echo carries it down here."

Jenny seemed relieved that someone had heard her.

"Don't you worry none, chile. We got us a free field of fire down here. With that harvest moon out there, we can empty a mess of saddles afore they even gets close."

The bells on the line rang and Zac and Hattie stuck their rifles out the gunports on both windows on either side of the door.

"Don't shoot!" a voice in the darkness rang out. "It's me, Emily Morgan."

"Come on ahead; walk your horse on in," Hattie screeched. She turned around. "It's the marshal's sister. Good woman. Cain't nobody count fer one's relatives, no way."

Zac and Jenny shot each other a glance.

Emily tied up her horse and dusted herself off before coming in. "Thank you. I didn't know if I'd find you up. I spoke to you at Tom's grave the other night, Mr. Cobb. The nightriders are at it again."

"Please, call me Zac."

"They're going to lynch that young Doctor Lewis tonight, unless you can stop them."

Zac was in the process of tying on his crossdraw holster before the woman had finished her sentence.

"Zac, that's Sarah Lewis's husband," Jenny said. She reached out and took hold of Zac's arm. "Sarah's the woman I was with on the stage. They've only been married little over a month."

He checked the loads on his Peacemaker, placed it back in the holster, and then pulled out and checked the action on his Shopkeeper Special. He planted the small one back in the holster on his right hip. Leaning the Sharps on the heavy table, he picked up the sawed-off shotgun. "You two can use the Sharps, if you need it. There's shells in my bag over there." He strapped on his spurs and shrugged on his buckskin jacket. "Let's go, show me where."

He turned at the door and, looking past Jenny's frightened face, spoke to Hat. "I'll need a fresh mount."

"Go 'head on, take the long-legged buckskin out there, he's got plenty a bottom to 'em."

Zac slapped and cinched the saddle onto the buckskin and clapped his spurs to the animal's ribs. Minutes after Emily's arrival, they were galloping out of the valley and down the long slope toward Sutter Creek. They heard the sound of the shotgun blasts long before they got to the creek bottom. Zac rode hard for the sound of the gunfire.

The cabin was surrounded by over a dozen masked gunmen who were pouring shots into its sides. Several men in front of the cabin were lighting torches and shouting. Zac drew rein and surveyed the scene from behind the trees.

"You want us to burn down your cabin, with that wife of yours in there with you? We'll do it, if that's what you want." Zac recognized the voice of Toby Summers.

"No, no! Don't do that! I'm coming out; leave my wife alone."

Zac could hear the sound of the woman crying inside the cabin. Emily had caught up with him now and he held his hand out, motioning her aside. He took out the sawed-off shotgun from the bag around his saddlehorn and handed it to her. "You watch my backside," he whispered. "Anybody tries to get around me, dust 'em with this. Somebody heads back your way, empty their saddle."

The men around the cabin had all heard Lewis offer his surrender and were walking toward the front of the cabin to await his exit. Zac moved the big buckskin forward and lowered the brim on his gray hat. Lewis creaked open the door to the cabin and, with his hands raised, moved out toward the men bunched around the torches in the front of the building. Zac could clearly see two ropes, not just one, in the hands of the mob. He edged the buckskin closer.

Three of the men ran forward and locked the man's arms behind him while another group of men ran into the cabin and brought out the screaming woman. "Don't touch her; don't hurt her," the doctor yelled at the men who were pulling his wife out of the cabin. "You said you wouldn't hurt her."

Zac moved the buckskin around the trees. He wanted to come in from behind the mob and take them unawares. The mob was preoccupied now and he moved closer, keeping an eye on what the men were doing.

"Here, you just sign this quick claim deed and we'll let the woman loose."

They produced a paper and pencil and allowed the captive man to free his arms from the men behind him, who had been holding them tightly. Other men in the group still held on to the struggling, screaming woman. They laughed at her, ignoring her screams.

Zac emerged from the trees behind the mob. The men who held the woman saw him first. They eased up on her and kept their eyes fastened on Zac, who was coldly looking on them from atop the tall buckskin. "Toby, we got ourselves some company." The deputy spun around and dropped the doctor's arm. He then backed away, cautiously. One by one, each of the mob turned to face the new menace.

"I see you boys haven't learned anything about other people's homes and property," Zac said. His deep voice resonated among the moonlit trees. "You best leave these people be and get back on your horses."

The deputy was silent. He looked up intently at Zac's face. Zac's brown eyes reflected the red glow of the flickering torches. His stature and presence on the horse gave him the almost haunting appearance of an avenging angel come in from the darkness, an avenging angel with fire in his eyes, a ghost sent by God to settle all scores.

One of the mob, a hothead with a black beard, showed his irritation. During their last encounter, Zac had sent a knife flying in the bearded man's direction. Determined not to let himself be buffaloed by the tall stranger again, the man edged toward the darkness from the outskirts of the mob. When he thought he had a clear field of fire, he slapped leather.

Zac had seen the man's movement just moments before and

had dropped his hand from his saddlehorn to a spot near the handle of his Peacemaker. He was not a gunslinger and had learned through the years that his cunning, daring nature, and the calm resolve to kill if need be, were the things that kept him alive— along with the fact that he was a dead shot. He jerked back on the reins and drew his .45 when he saw the man draw and shoot.

The airborne slug roared between Zac and the neck of the buckskin, and Zac lifted his revolver to fire. As his opponent sighted down on him for another shot Zac took careful aim. His Peacemaker barked, sending a stab of flame into the night air directly at his bearded foe. Zac's shot landed alongside the man's second shirt button and instantly buckled his legs, dropping him to the ground.

Zac spun around to face the mob, catching movement among several of the men in the front line. Spotting a revolver in one of the men's hands, Zac unleashed another round that sank into the man's midsection. Yelling and cursing and clutching his stomach, the wounded man crashed to the ground on his knees in pain as his revolver tumbled out of his hand.

Wild confusion prevailed. Zac knew the mentality of a mob. It seemed to have a life all its own. He knew that if he could cause doubt and confusion, the group would take itself out.

As Zac backed the buckskin into the darkness and continued to fire, the doctor scooped up his wife and ran for their cabin door. Several of Zac's well-placed shots were scoring hits. Men from the mob ran in all directions and began a scattering of wildfire shots in Zac's direction. The shots were misdirected, with none of the remaining mob taking the time to stop and take aim at the retreating dim figure on horseback.

Some men held their frightened horses' reins and continued to fire, while several of the members in the rear of the group left the mob and galloped off toward town. Zac heard the familiar blast of the Meteor ten-gauge and watched two terrified, riderless horses gallop back through the firelight toward the other side of the creek.

The sight of the riderless horses rushing past them panicked the remaining men. They turned toward the other side of the darkness and began to fire in the direction of the shotgun blasts. Zac was now totally engulfed by the darkness. He had thumbed fresh cartridges into his Peacemaker and now took deliberate aim at one of the wild shooters and fired several shots, at least one of which scored a hit on the man's arm and upper shoulder. The man screamed out in pain and dropped his weapon.

"Let's get outta here, Toby, we're surrounded!" someone yelled.

"We can't see 'em, Toby, let's go!" another screamed.

The men continued to fire as they scurried onto the backs of their horses. "Follow me," one yelled, and galloped after the riderless horses across the creek. A few followed as they kept firing into the dark, and the remainder stampeded for the opposite shore of the creek and up the rise. They were headed back to Volcano like the devil himself was on their trail and nothing was going to stop them.

Zac walked the buckskin back into the area of the cabin where the torches, now on the ground, were dimly burning. He rolled over the second man he had shot, and he screamed in pain.

"Gut shot, are you? Zac asked."

"Blast you, man. You done shot me in the belly. I'm hurtin' mighty bad."

Zac looked him in the eye. "Bad way to die. Lucky thing for you, you got a doctor here that can make your going a little easier on you." He called out to the cabin, "Doc, Doc Lewis, everything's okay now. You can come out and bring your medicine bag. There's a man hurt bad out here.

"I hope they paid you enough to do this," Zac said.

The man groaned and tightened his grip on his midsection. "They'll kill you for this," he groaned.

"Maybe," Zac said, "but you're dead already."

Zac watched the lights in the cabin begin to glow and looked up to see Emily leading her horse into the light, shotgun in hand. "Thanks for cuttin' loose when you did. Got 'em turned around and panicked 'em, it did."

"I did like you said. I emptied two saddles. I think I got one in such a way he won't be using an arm ever again, and the other one I plumb near scared to death."

"Good girl," he said.

C H A P T E R 17

+ + + + + + +

ROMAN EVERS HUNKERED DOWN on the hillside that led to Hattie's place. The moon would be high for a while yet, and he was hoping Zac would make short work of the night-riders while there was still plenty of moonlight. He didn't want to miss. It didn't sit quite right for him to wish Toby's bunch to fail, but he didn't have much confidence in Toby Summers' ability to lead. Toby's group did all the hanging. Evers smugly thought that anyone could lead a mob of no-count drifter drunks in a lynch party, especially one that was just going after tin-panners; that didn't take no sand at all. Summers could be relied on to do that, no doubt. But pitted up against someone who could shoot to kill, someone who had a determined look in his eye, someone like this Zac Cobb he had heard about, well, that was another matter.

He knew that the other members of the tight group Judge Harkness counted on all had their problems. Every one of them had things about them that made them unreliable. Summers could be buffaloed and Morgan was hot-headed to a fault. He saw the way Judge Harkness was. The man was cool, he saw everything. When the time was right, Evers knew the judge would have to turn to him to get the job done. Bringing back Zac Cobb, that would be quite a feather in his cap. To have that man out of the picture would give them all more time to take what they wanted to take.

Evers liked what people around town called him behind his back—"the chiller." He'd smile on the inside when he heard it.

140

They said he was cold-blooded like a snake and that he chilled people when he looked at them and when he shot them.

His look at people did have a chilling effect. That was because he didn't just look at people, he studied them. He explored them for shortcomings, for any motive, any habit, that might expose a weakness, that might give him an upper hand. His dark eyes were almost black, with a cold stillness in them that showed little life. He wasn't muscled like Breaker Morgan or even Toby Summers; his lanky look was deceptive, however. Like a racehorse, his muscles were long and well shaped and he carried himself in a tall, erect frame.

People never remembered much about him, except the scar on his cheek, a scar he'd gotten in a knife fight; his rather smallish feet, and the cold stare of his eyes—eyes that looked deeply into a person. He'd never seen this Zac Cobb up close, but his lone encounter with the man on this very hillside had taught him plenty. Cobb was a careful man, a man hunter. He watched his back trail. And he was a man who didn't miss, unless he wanted to. He knew Zac had fired past him on the hill only because he didn't know for sure who he was. *Perhaps*, Evers thought, *the man is too soft for his own good.*

Evers kept a mental book on everybody he knew, even people who he knew he'd never meet in a fight. They might tell him something by the way they acted that he'd need to know; Emily certainly had.

When he saw the marshal's sister leave his office earlier that night, Evers saw something in her eyes that at first puzzled him. This was a determined woman. She was always doing something that needed to be done, and the discovery that Toby had the nightriders at work tonight, and that Emily might have overheard the plans, made Evers' mind ask, what if? What if she had heard? Who would she go to? What would they do? His scheme began to take root.

To pull off his plan tonight, he had to depend on what he knew about Emily Morgan, that she would go to the only man she knew who could stop the lynching and whould go with her. Just by the look in her eye, he knew instinctively she was going to find this Zac Cobb. She'd find him and he'd go and scrap with the nightriders. When he finished embarrassing Toby Summers one more time, Evers knew he'd have to ride back to Hattie Woodruff's place over this same moonlit hillside. Only thing was, this time he was uphill; he was shooting down at the man. Cobb might be looking at his back trail, but he had to come this way.

He settled down behind some rocks he had piled up and positioned the needlegun. He heard the shots fired down by the creek diggings and knew it was only a matter of time now. He was a patient man. He only hoped that Zac had taken the woman who had been on the stage with him. The thought of having her for a time before he killed her was eating away at him. It stirred his longings. *That woman had backed him down*, he thought, *now he had to have her, she had to pay.*

He coolly rolled a smoke and lit it.

✦ ✦ ✦ ✦ ✦

Zac helped Doc Lewis carry the wounded man into the cabin. Every step they took resulted in yells and curses from the dying man. They positioned him on a vacant cot in the cabin, and while Sarah proceeded to boil water, Doc Lewis led Zac and Emily outside.

"We'll get him settled and you two can head on home. Me and the Mrs. will be all right here. I don't think those boys will come back here tonight. We'll have to clean this man up and then I'll operate, but I can tell you right now, I wouldn't give much for his chances."

He looked into Emily's eyes and put a hand on her shoulder. "Miss Emily, I should have listened to you right off. I might very well be out there now, necked up to a blackjack oak. People died tonight, all because of my pride. I thought it was up to me alone to defend my family." He paused and scratched his head. I guess I'm just like most men, we like to do things ourselves. We're too proud to take help from people and, it shames me to say it,"—he hung his head—"too goldarned bullheaded to take advice from a woman."

"Doc, this here group is out to get the whole valley," Zac said, "and they will too, one claim at a time. Your best bet is to try to organize the tin-panners along Sutter Creek. Until you've got more guns than they've got, none of you are safe. This is a hardbitten bunch, and they've got what passes for the law on their side."

The doctor shrugged his shoulders. "It's hard for me to bunch this group a folks together; they all come here to be left be and that's the way they intend it. They all want to strike it rich sose they can go somewheres else and be left alone. Besides, me being from Texas don't help none. I ain't hardly been able to drum up a medical practice 'cause of that."

Zac smiled. "I understand. I spent some years in Texas afore coming to California, and I can see where some folks is touchy about Texans. Don't let that worry you none, though, everybody wants to stay alive. Just put some of that Texas pride to work and convince 'em they need to be together on this, or they most assuredly will hang separately. This bunch is gonna come back soon and hit you with everything they can. Time is working against them. They know word is getting out. They got to get this creek and wash the gold out pronto, before the U.S. Marshal hears about what's going on or the governor's office finds out about it."

Doc Lewis put his hand up to his chin and rubbed it thoughtfully. "This Judge Harkness was appointed by President Grant. I hear he ran a Yankee prison camp during the war, so my guess is he's got some friends up there somewhere, but he's throwing a lot of voters off of their claims and I don't think that will set too well with the governor, no matter who Harkness's friends are.

"I'll come back and help you tomorrow," Emily said. "Maybe these folks will believe me. I'm the marshal's sister and after what I heard, they got to believe me."

The wind was picking up from the south, brightening the flames on the dying torches. The three of them looked overhead at the storm clouds rolling in over the Sierras. What had been bright moonlight only an hour ago was now pitch darkness.

"I should stay and try to help Sarah," Emily said.

"No, Sarah knows what she's doing," Lewis said. "You go on ahead. This storm's whipping up and you've got a ways to go yet."

"Emily, come back to Hat's with me," Zac said. "The woman's got plenty of room and I know Jenny would enjoy the company. Somehow, I think she's about had plenty of Hat. Besides, I don't like the thought of you on the road to Volcano tonight with that bunch we just chased off between here and there."

"Oh, all right, I'll stay with you. I can't say as I'd look forward to meeting any one of those nightriders on the road tonight."

They stepped into their stirrups and turned back for the hillside road and home in the valley beyond. Zac's buckskin horse recognized that they were on the return trip to hay, and his gait picked up. Zac didn't like riding other people's horses. He'd spent too much time in training his own, but getting to Doc Lewis's place in a hurry was a lot easier with a fresher horse. The long-legged buckskin had plenty of drive in him, and before very long they stood at the base of the hillside that led to Hat's place.

Roman Evers had long since given up on a distance shot with the rifle. It was his favorite way to kill, not because he was afraid to face anyone, but because he liked to make sure of a clean job, one without any hitches. Now, with the storm moving in and clouds cloaking the moonlight, he knew he had to do what he could closer in. He had positioned himself near the top of the hillside and now had his two Smith and Wessons ready for the kill. He'd come out from behind the boulder at the top of the hill and have done with the man right there. Killing him up close would be a matter of pride.

✦   ✦   ✦   ✦   ✦

Zac and Emily had ridden back without talking. The day had been a full one and both of them were too tired for small talk. Instead, his mind raced over what he had to do next. He had to have a hand in organizing the miners on the creek. He also had to wire the company and see about getting a new agent in charge of the office in Volcano, someone who could be counted on.

They had stopped at the base of the hillside, and Zac peered into the darkness along the road. The breeze was blowing down the rise, and the buckskin's ears were tilted forward. He seemed to be picking up something in the wind that didn't belong there and reaching out with his ears to make sense of it.

Zac was always one to pay attention to the animal he rode. He used his own senses to their fullest extent and saw the perceptions of the animals around him as other eyes and ears to be counted on. They told him a lot, only it was up to him to understand them, and to heed their signs. It was harder to do with a strange horse, one he hadn't ridden, one he didn't know.

He turned the buckskin down the road and, holding his hand up to Emily, trotted a few yards, stopping to listen. The fresh breeze blew the oak leaves in a frantic rustle and then in a steady rippling current to the north. In this area, like on the coast where Zac lived, rainstorms always seemed to come from the south. He raised himself in the saddle and seemed to sniff the rain in the air. It wasn't falling, but it was about to.

He lifted the thong from the hammer of his Peacemaker and moved a few more yards down the road. The hair on the back of his neck was bristling. He didn't like the way things felt. His sixth sense was telling him something was wrong. He was being watched; he just didn't know by who or where they were. If the nightriders were coming back, he didn't want to be on the hillside as a target when they rode by.

Zac turned back to Emily and moved back to the base of the hill. He lifted the thong on his holster back on top of the hammer of his revolver. Bouncing on a horse uphill would be just the thing it took to lose a gun, and he didn't want to do that. He swiveled around in the saddle, once more checking his back trail.

He didn't like it. Most of the time, he never followed the same trail twice. He'd been in this business long enough to know how dangerous it could be to lay down a pattern. He'd been this way twice already tonight and one of those times had been trailed, but Hattie had laid out her place just so. There just wasn't a second way in or out of her valley, at least not on horseback. Zac figured, if there wasn't any other way, he might as well make it quick.

"Well, let's get on up there," he said. "'Bout time we got to bed. This gelding ain't mine so I'm not sure what he's reacting to. Possibly he's spotted some critter. I learn to trust these things though."

They both slacked their reins and headed up the hill, at first on a slow walk, but then in a bounding canter. Zac drew rein at the top of the hill, with Emily right beside him. The clouds had covered the moon, and from the darkness around the rock Deputy Roman Evers stepped out, both guns drawn. He fired several shots from the hip and took aim with another. Both Zac's and Emily's horses spooked and scrambled on the hard shale beneath their hooves. Zac felt the sting of a slug across his upper rib cage. Instinctively, his hand grabbed for his revolver handle, but the thong on the hammer held it fast. Another searing round slammed into Zac's side. He jerked the horse's head around, veering the buckskin just as another slug was unleashed. It slammed into the head of the horse, killing the animal instantly. It dropped like a rock on top of Zac, pinning him underneath.

Hitting the ground, Zac's breath came out with a rush. He was also losing blood—from the feel of it, lots of blood.

Zac lay quietly on the ground in the driving rain. The sound of the cloudburst was helping to cover the tone of his labored breathing. He was pinned underneath the dead buckskin good and tight, probably broken up on the inside by the way he felt, and even if he hadn't been shot, he'd never have been able to move. He knew that. He lay still in the rain with sweat beading up on his forehead, sweat mixed with rainwater. He waited for whoever had fired the shots to come closer and put one more bullet into his head. He waited and prayed. He could sense the man, standing nearby, standing, watching him, and perhaps taking aim.

Emily's horse had bolted down the hill toward Hat's house,

and as the gunfire continued she had turned the animal and began to race back toward Zac. Everything inside her told her to keep running but she couldn't. The rain had started to fall, lightly for a few moments, and then in a heavy downpour.

She reached for the shotgun she was still carrying and cocked the hammers. The gunfire had stopped and she could see that Zac was down—down on the rocks with a man standing over him. Riding full tilt, she pointed the shotgun at the dark figure. She had only one shot left from her encounter near the doctor's cabin. She knew she had to make it count, and that whatever happened, she couldn't wait a moment more. The shotgun boomed and unleashed a load of shot toward the figure. She missed. The man froze in his tracks.

Zac lay still. He was barely conscious, drifting in and out. He knew that the dead weight that held him down was not letting him up, he was helpless. The rain continued to fall, beating on his exposed face and keeping him conscious. He had felt the man standing over him and then, hearing the loud report of his Meteor, he heard the boots of the man running away.

"Zac, Zac." Emily had scrambled off of her horse and knelt down beside him. She lifted his head in her hands. "Zac, can you hear me?"

There was a low moan. It was the first indication to Emily that he was alive. Mumbling, with a barely audible voice he said, "I'm hurt. I'm hurt bad. Get Doc Lewis."

The figure who had run away from Zac's side was now on horseback and rode down the hill toward the creekside road. Emily strained to see him. In the distant darkness the man pulled up and shouted back at her. "Better get that old woman's shovel and dig a hole for him."

Emily recognized the voice immediately. "Tell her she won't be needing that shovel anymore either." Evers' voice boomed out over the rain. "We know she has a mine there, and when we come back, we'll come in force. Tell that woman of his, too, that I'm a gonna come a courtin'." He laughed loudly. The man turned and galloped away on the ridge road toward town. He obviously thought he'd finished the job on Zac Cobb, and for all Emily or Zac knew, maybe he had.

CHAPTER 18

✦ ✦ ✦ ✦ ✦ ✦ ✦

ZAC'S MIND DRIFTED helplessly. He had heard the report of the shotgun and felt the rain on his face, but after that, he neither heard nor felt anything. Voices sounded like distant trains moving through a tunnel in his mind. He knew he had been moved. The pain had ripped through him when the buckskin had been dragged off. Now, though, all he could feel was a dry, parched throat that felt like a lance had been rammed down it by someone trying to find his toes. He ached all over from the inside out. And he was terribly thirsty.

He knew a dim light burned overhead because his eyelids could feel the heat of the light. He wanted to open his eyes to see where he was, but he couldn't. He felt a cool cloth on his forehead and now a cup held to his lips. *Thank God*, he thought, *water!*

"Here, Zac, drink a little."

The voice sounded for a moment like his mother. It soothed him. That and the cool water to his lips made him feel alive, though he doubted he was. *If it is mother*, he supposed, *then I am dead.*

"Zac, it's Jenny. Darling, drink a little more."

His eyes slowly opened. He saw her as if through a fuzzy glass. He'd never seen anyone or anything so beautiful. Behind her and above her shoulder, a lamp glowed in the darkness. He could see he was in a mine. It was cool and he could smell the dust. She pressed the cup to his lips and he drank. The cool water moved all the way down his insides.

She removed the cloth from his head and dipped it in a pan of water, squeezing it and then placing it back on his forehead. "Zachary, you need to rest. The doctor is going to operate soon."

Zac could hear the sound of people walking on the wooden floor above them. It came to him. He was under Hat's floor, in her mine. *Why here?* he wondered.

The trapdoor opened from above and he could see Hattie coming down the ladder. She was followed by Doc Lewis. Zac's eyes went back into his head and he closed them. The pain was throbbing.

"He's awake, Doctor," Jenny said.

"Zac . . ." The doctor removed the cold compress and placed his hand on Zac's head. He was listening to his chest through a tube. Zac's eyes fluttered open and he noticed the sheet and the fact that his clothes were missing. "Mr. Cobb," the doctor spoke again, "you've been broken up pretty bad, I'm afraid. Couple of ribs at least." He replaced the compress. "I wish I could say that was the worst of it. But you've taken a pretty serious gunshot wound. It appears to be lodged near your spine, and if I don't remove it, it could result in future paralysis. Besides, if we just leave it, infection could kill you."

"I ain't gonna give these people the satisfaction of killin' me," Zac croaked out.

"Well, I'll say one thing for you, partner, you got yourself plenty of fight left. That's a good sign in my book. Now, we've boiled the instruments, and I'm gonna have to probe for the bullet. If I cut you open to get it, I'd have to gut you like a fish, and I'd rather not do that down here."

"Why am I here?" Zac asked.

"Boy," Hattie spoke up, "we thought whoever did this might come back with some others to find ya if'n we didn't hide ya. So this here woman of yourn and my own self done toted you down here."

"I wouldn't have advised moving you so much," the doctor said. "But you're here, and by a miracle, you're still alive."

"Yeah, boy, we was plenty gentle wif you. Found out later that it didn't make no nevermind anyway; they know about the mine. I don't know how they found out about it, but they did."

Jenny leaned over Zac and spoke softly. "Emily is trying to organize the tin-panners."

"I gotta get outta here then," Zac said. "Where's my clothes? Who took my clothes?"

"You ain't goin' nowhere for a spell, pardner, not unless it's the cemetery lookin' down on Volcano. This here woman of yourn took your clothes and done cleaned you all up. She's a fine nurse, she is."

Zac closed his eyes.

Doc Lewis rattled his instruments, tumbling them out of the pan and onto one of Hattie's blue tin plates.

"Here, Doc, let's give him something to drink," Hattie said. "I got some stuff here that'll deaden the pain." She chuckled. "Quite considerable, I might add."

The doctor turned around to look at her. "Hat, the only way I'd let you give him some of that stuff is if I'd killed him already." Turning toward Zac, he took the probe. "Partner, this is gonna hurt like crazy."

✦   ✦   ✦   ✦   ✦

Emily had spent her day visiting the diggings on the creek, but she had little to show for her effort. The miners weren't all that fond of the new doctor, him being from Texas, and educated to boot. She didn't dare tell them about how hurt Zac was and that he might not live. She knew these men. Zac was the only one they'd ever seen stand up to her brother and his deputies. If he couldn't fight, she knew they wouldn't.

An old miner, Able Crane, spoke for a group of the men by the creek. "We all admired the way he got Toby and Breaker to dig them graves, we surely did now. But he's jes' one man, and where does that leave us?"

"You've got to help. If you let this opportunity pass by, you might as well all pack up and leave the place to the men with the water cannons."

The men by their sluice boxes all turned from her and went suddenly back to work. What they saw riding up the road scared them. Emily was puzzled until she turned to watch Breaker riding toward her on his big Morgan horse.

"What you doing here, baby sister? Trying to scare these men away from their work?"

"No, I'm trying to keep them alive. I might ask you why you're here. You're the town marshal. This is a bit out of your jurisdiction, isn't it?"

He dismounted and hitched up his belt. "It may be at that, but wherever you are is in my jurisdiction. I wanted to pass on to you a little message for that old woman who lives over the hill. You tell her she's got today only to clear out. She's to bury that nephew of hers and get gone before tomorrow. We're gonna be there with everything we got. Also,"—he craned his neck around looking at the miners who had now quit work and were watching—"I been getting some complaints that you're out pestering these here boys." He stepped closer to her. "I also heard you were thinking about going into the male entertainment business, so perhaps I'm mistaken, and you're just out here drumming up some business of your own."

She reached out and scorched her brother's cheek with a hard slap. It infuriated him. He hit her with a right and sent her sprawling to the ground. The men stopped their work and turned to watch. "Here now, there ain't no call for that." One of the younger men stepped forward toward Emily and stood beside her.

"You'd better stay out of this," Emily said. "He'll do a lot worse to you." She got to her feet. She was still intent on driving her message home, no matter what the cost. She raised her voice so that all the men could hear. "Just remember, whatever you see him do to me is nothing compared to what he'll do to all of you, and very soon."

Breaker swung his foot at her ankles, sweeping her feet out from under her. "There, that's just where you belong, in the dirt with the other women of the street."

The young miner stepped forward. "That there's far enough," he said.

Breaker reached out and grabbed the man by the shirt and,

pulling him forward, slammed a left into his midsection. He then came up with a knee to the man's face, breaking his nose and sending him to the ground, blood spurting in the dirt. "You better stay down. Count your lucky stars. Normally, anybody who tries to raise a hand to me dies in the effort." Breaker held up his ham-sized hands. "I kill him with my bare hands."

He walked over to the man lying on the ground and stomped on his hand, prompting a scream of pain. "There ya be. That's what you get for messing in business that don't concern you. See how you like mining with one hand." Drawing his revolver he stared at the group of miners, who were silently standing by their sluice boxes at the creek's edge. "Anybody else want a word with me? Anybody wanna question what I do to my own flesh and blood sister?"

The men turned back to their work one by one and began the business of ignoring anything else that might happen. The bloody man on the ground began to crawl back to his equipment, panting in agony.

"I guess it's just you and me, sis. Looks like I'm the only one round here that wants to help you, and it's up to me to save you from yourself."

Emily got to her feet and began to swat the dirt from her dress. "I've never prayed for a man to die, but in your case it would be a mercy."

He stepped toward her and she backed away.

"You ain't worth hitting no more," he said. "I'm about done with you. You may think you're Miss High-and-Mighty with all that book talk of yours, but when you're still scrubbing floors or working the cribs with no-account miners, I'll be eating oysters in San Francisco, and everybody will be stepping aside for me." He stepped into the stirrup. "You leave these miners be. If I hear any more talk of you trying to incite these people, I'll come back here and kill you myself, sister or no sister." He planted his spurs in the big mare's sides, and the animal galloped down the road toward town.

When Breaker was out of sight, Able Crane walked over to Emily. "Ma'am, ever'one of us admires you plenty for what you jes' done. You showed us something. Now don't get yer hopes up none, but we'll talk about it. That's all I can promise. I gotta warn you though, ma'am, unless you see us coming up the road, you'd better plan on going it alone.

* * * * *

Emily rode into Hat's place with a sober look all over her face. She walked into the cabin, where Hat was seated around the table with Doc Lewis and Sarah. "I'm sorry," she said, "but unless I'm mistaken, we're all there is."

Lewis scrambled to his feet. "What happened to your face, girl? Let me put something on it."

"My brother came riding up to where I was talking to some of the men down by the creek. I guess he didn't take too kindly to what I was saying." She shrugged. "Didn't like the slap I gave him either, I suppose. I brought it on myself; I guess I asked for it."

The doctor began to gently clean her face with a wet cloth. "No woman should be hit by any man," he said. "In Texas, we'd string a man up who did a thing like that."

"Too bad we're not in Texas," she said. Then smiling slightly, she added, "There's something I never thought I'd hear myself say."

Everybody laughed.

"How's Zac?" she asked. Her voice seemed tentative and quiet.

"He's alive," Hattie said. "Guess that's 'bout all that kin be said for him. Barely, but alive all the same."

"I did get the bullet with my probe, but I had to go pretty deep. I think I got right close up to the spine. I was mighty careful, but that's prayerful business in there."

"Oh, dag nab it, Doc, don't bring no prayer into it. Jes' don't."

"What's the matter?" Emily asked.

Sarah smiled. "Oh, it's just something Zac said when the doc was starting to operate on him. Hattie asked if there was anything she could do and Zac told her yes." Sarah paused and looked at Hattie. "Zac said she could do him a favor by going to church and getting herself straightened out."

The old woman walked to the corner of the room and mumbled something under her breath. Sarah lowered her voice. "I know a body can't trust that woman in business, but I think she meant it when she made him the promise."

Emily smiled. "I wish I could say I was as successful. I'm afraid the men in this town are all scared to death. They said they'd think it over, but I don't hold out much hope. One thing we can count on, though," she said, looking at Hattie, "Breaker is coming this way, and soon. He's gonna hit you with everything he's got."

"Well, I'd jes' like to see him try. I'll make me a lot a widows in this here town to keep company with me." Hattie had straightened herself up to all of her five feet. Maybe I kin kill a few a them fellers afore I . . . straighten myself out." She crossed her arms and squinted at the group.

"Where can we take Zac where he'll be safe?" Lewis asked.

"I ain't a goin' nowheres," Hattie growled. "I'm a stayin' right here and protectin' what's rightfully mine, me and my Spencer."

"I can understand your sentiments, Hattie. I said the same thing myself last night when this woman here warned me. If she and Cobb hadn't ridden up when they did, I'd a been cold in the ground today." He looked at Emily and then at Hat. "What you ladies do is your business. Sarah and I are new to the territory so I don't know where to go, but there has to be a place where we can take Zac and Jenny. A good hiding place."

Hattie's face brightened. "I don't knows if'n it'll work, but I know where I'd hide out if'n I had to." She stiffened. "'Course I don't, mind you, so I wouldn't do it myself. It's mighty dangerous, but nobody knows about it, nobody 'ceptin' dead injuns, long gone and buried."

"Where?" Emily asked. "I've been around here a long time myself."

The old woman giggled. "It's spooky, it is. Kinda gives off a sound like ghosts hauntin' in the night. Nobody in his right mind would go down there if'n he didn't have to. I found it back in '48 when I was a lookin' fer the mother lode. It's a large cave; a ways off. Take three er four hours by my wagon out there."

"Can it be entered easily?" Lewis asked.

"That there's the beauty of it." She scratched her head. "It'd be a problem fer my nephew right now. There's only one way in or out—straight down a hole in the ground with 'bout a hunnerd-an'-fifty-foot drop to the floor o' the place." She gulped a mite of her chaw. "A body hangs there like a spider with no foothold or nothin', till he hits the floor."

"I can see what you mean. That would be a problem for Zac."

"The place is beautiful—all them stone icicles hangin' from the ceilin' an' stone spikes along the floor, with little pools of water here an' there. That's what makes the moanin' noise. Fer some queer reason, the water bouncin' in them holes in the rocks gives off this spooky sound." She raised her hands and wiggled her fingers. "*Oooooh*, it goes, *oooooh*. Gives a body the heebie-jeebies, it does."

"Frankly, I'm not even sure Zac'd survive the wagon ride. He might not even make it through the night, lying down there on the cot." Lewis crossed his arms and thought. "But one thing for sure, we can't leave him to the mercy of Breaker Morgan. If we just leave him here and do nothing, he's sure to die."

"I'll pack up some grub and hitch up the team," Hattie said. "But mind you, I ain't stayin' in that place. I'm a comin' right back here. If'n I die, I'm a gonna take that no-account marshal wif me." She looked at Emily. "I'm sorry, I knows he's your brother and all." She spat a stream of tobacco juice into a can. "But he's a no-account all the same."

CHAPTER 19

+ + + + + + +

"I'M READY TO TAKE HIM if you can get him lowered down," Doc Lewis called out from the bottom of the hole. His voice echoed and had a tinny quality to it. They had rigged a block and tackle to the opening of the cavern, and the three women began to lower the stretcher with Zac strapped to it. His eyes were barely open when the cot went down into the yawning darkness.

Lewis had strategically placed several torches around the massive floor of the main room and the light flickered, creating shadows on the walls as it bounced over and around the frozen stone stalactites. Zac's stretcher spun slowly around and had begun to sway as the women lowered it. "Be careful," Lewis called up. "Don't get him swinging too much."

Zac had opened his eyes and watched as the light danced on the walls. Overhead, he could see the women straining at the ropes. He had weakly protested the trip to the cave and the notion that everyone seemed to be bent on saving his life, even if it meant killing him in the process. He had been perfectly willing to stay at Hat's, even if it involved his lying on his bed with a cocked pistol. He was willing to wait for the marshal to come with his group of nightriders. He'd heard that's how Jim Bowie died at the Alamo, and if he had to, he'd go out the same way, a body going to his death while taking his enemies with him. It seemed only right to him. The notion of dying in the face of the enemy fit every idea of a hero that he'd learned from his childhood books, but he could not remember one single knight in shining armor who'd met his Maker while falling into a cave.

Nobody could tell him that wasn't what Hat was going to do once she'd deposited him. They'd have to carry her out of that place of hers feet first. If he hadn't been so worried about what would happen to Jenny, that's just what he'd have done. He smiled slightly. Jenny was doing this to save him, and he was doing it to save her. The thought struck him as laughable.

Groundwater seeped almost constantly into the roof of the enclosed crater and fell to the floor below. The sound of the water landing on the floor gave the place the name Hat called it, "Moaning Cave." Several splashes landed on Zac's face, causing his eyes to blink rapidly. The water trickled down his forehead and cascaded off of his nose and down his cheek. It felt cool to his touch.

All around him, droplets of the water from above swooped through the pink and orange torchlit darkness and landed on the floor of the cave. The low moans of the backfiring water's echoes gave the place the eerie sound of a cemetery that had suddenly released all of the spirits in the belly of the earth, each one protesting its exposure to the pain of the world it thought it had left behind.

His side ached and his back seemed to blaze with fire. Inwardly, he took some comfort in the simple fact that he was feeling something, even if it was pain. His stretcher was in the middle of the vast room. To either side of his swinging cot lay sixty or seventy feet of air space.

He took in the expanse; it looked to be at least two hundred feet across, wall to wall. He shifted his head and could see what he believed to be the floor coming slowly up at him, but it was still a hundred feet or so beneath him.

The room's size was intimidating, and his heart began to pound so loudly that he seemed to hear it beat in the darkness. He blinked, straining his eyes to catch the details of the cavern. He'd been in a few and he knew every one of them was different, each had its own set of peculiarities. He focused his eyes to his left in disbelief. He could see a strange velvety covering on that wall—was it moving? A quivering mass of tiny vampire bats, each crawling for better position on the wall or on the sides of the protruding stalactites, stood the hair on the back of Zac's neck to attention. The creatures shook and straightened their wings, occasionally letting out a screeching noise that blended with the moans of the ghostly cave.

Zac closed his eyes and let his mind drift. He had never simply waited to die before. He'd waited to fight often enough. More times in his thirty years than he wanted to remember. And he had waited to kill; but he'd never waited to die. Now it seemed he was doing the unthinkable; he was hiding from an enemy and waiting to die. That thought, along with the squeaks of the blood-craving bats, made his insides crawl.

Death was inevitable for everyone, he knew that. He thought he'd made peace with the fact when he was fifteen years old, sleeping in his butternut uniform on the ground of northern Virginia.

He knew that if a person had done all he could and wasn't ashamed of his life, then to die was no shame either. He'd always said that when the time came to die, a body had better make sure that dying was all that was left to do.

He didn't feel that way now, though—not just yet. He had unfinished business. Hat needed him. To leave her now would be to expose her to the worst sort of thief and murderer. And then there was Jenny, he and Jenny. He didn't want to leave this world with nothing in it to show for his passing but his footprints. Yet he knew that was just what he'd be leaving. He'd done what he did with his life on purpose. His parents had left their world with him and his brothers still in it, and a lot of friends to boot. But for Zac, he could count his friends on one hand, and felt lucky to do that.

He was a fighter. The thought of abandoning people who needed him and the notion of a job assigned to him left undone made his stomach crawl. He wasn't going to die. He'd hang on a little longer.

As these thoughts raced through his mind, he knew the truth about what kept him going, about what gave him the will to live. He couldn't abide the thought of injustice. It existed—

everywhere—but when he saw it before him, he was determined never to allow it to exist within his reach. He'd been living with the notion of mending what he saw as crooked for fifteen years now, and he wasn't about to stop.

The blazing red-hot iron of working out the truth had branded its mark on his soul, and when he saw something wrong that needed to be made right, he had to try with everything that was in him to fix it. It was what kept him going when others would have quit; not thoughts about himself, or even others for that matter, but thoughts about what was right. He never administered the justice of the law, he never stooped to the motive of revenge, but he brought a reckoning with him wherever he went.

"Steady," the sound of Doc Lewis's voice jolted him out of a dreary, wakeful stare. "I got you now." He felt the doctor's hand steady the swaying stretcher. Doc raised his voice and called out to the women on top, "He's almost there. Go easy now. Lower him easylike." Gently, the cot rested itself on the slightly sloping floor. "That's it!" he yelled out. "I got him now."

The man began to untie the knots that secured Zac to the cot. "Now don't you worry none. We brought enough of a larder to keep you in vittles for a while and some medical supplies to boot. I'll be a checkin' on you from time to time." He shot Zac a glance and smiled. "You will be a powerful lot of trouble in getting to, but I got to tell you, those womenfolk up there are determined to keep you alive, so you best cooperate if you know what's good for you."

"My gun—you bring my gun?" Zac whispered.

"Sure. But we didn't fetch your rifle or that short shotgun of yours. Hattie sorta coveted to use those her own self, and I'd say she's gonna have opportunity to, long before you do."

The doctor peeked up at the hole and lowered his voice to keep those on top from overhearing him. "I don't think the old woman 'specks to get outta that place of hers alive, and by the way them boys came after me the other night, I'd say she might be right. She was mighty powerful worried 'bout you stayin' in that place of hers when those nightriders come a callin'. They're huntin' for you, you know. Say it's on account of those two men you shot in front a my place."

He shot a glance down at Zac. "We did bring your little belly gun though, and some extra shells. We got a large bundle of fire-wood, some coal oil, couple of pots, and enough vittles and soup-makings to last you a few weeks. That oughta be enough time to see you up and around, at least a little. Till then, you'll need to stay down here, outta sight—although, for the life of me, I can't see anyone daring to turn up here to look for you. I wouldn't go down this hole myself if I didn't have to. Too hard to get into and nigh unto impossible to get out of." He looked around the massive room. "Place kinda spooks me, too."

He peered up at the ceiling of the cavern. "That woman of yours is something special, though. I'd hang on to her if I was you. She's insisted on coming in and taking care of you in this hole. She's got salve and dressings for your wounds."

He turned back to the ropes. "I'll be coming back to check on you every few days, too. I'll call down, even if I don't come down." He wrinkled his eyebrows. "If you've passed on, I wouldn't want to leave that woman of yours down here."

"I appreciate that—" Zac croaked out.

The man cut him off. "You'd never catch my Sarah going into this hole. Wouldn't catch her, my saintly mother, or half the angels in God's own kingdom. You got yourself some woman up there."

Zac watched Lewis pull himself up the rope. The enormity of the cavern made it impossible to get a toehold on the sides of the walls, and the hole to the outside was directly above them.

The doctor was a young man and strong. Had he given his time to only medicine, he might have been softer, but the man dug in the ground and was no stranger to hard labor. Even so, Zac watched the strain on the doctor's face as he grabbed the rope hand over hand. *If anything happens to him and Jenny,* Zac pondered, *years from now, some kid'll find my bones down here or, more'n likely, some misguided prospector.*

What seemed like an hour passed before Zac watched the tired doctor reach the top and scramble out of the hole. Moments later he saw Jenny being lowered into the opening.

"Don't look down!" they shouted at her. "And try to hold yourself still."

Jenny held her head high, and Zac watched her descend from out of the flickering shadows. She wrestled against the ropes that were cutting under her arms and began to career back and forth. The wheeling movement of the litter startled her and made her feel all the more like a piece of bait being lowered into the belly of a whale. She calmed herself and tried to focus and concentrate on the instructions Doctor Lewis, Sarah, and Hattie were screaming out from above, being careful to keep her eyes fixed on the wall at a point above the level of her shoulders. The swaying motion, though, made it hard to fix her attention.

She pedalled her feet to try to counterbalance the unwanted motion. Even as she moved, she could visualize the rope being sawed on the coarse rocks at the lip of the hole above her. She lifted her head to try and see and then became even more frightened; directly in the path of her motion was the moving, pulsating carpet of bats clinging to the wall.

Several of the creatures screeched out a warning to the assembled flock, and a number of the black animals with their pink open mouths squeaked at Jenny and flew off toward her.

She screamed as the creatures came near her head, and she waved her arms to try to ward them off. "Bats!" she screamed. "Oh no!"

The motion of her arms made the swaying even more pronounced and brought her nearer the assembled bats that remained on the wall in front of her. As she swung helplessly toward them, they flew off in all directions and their screeching filled the cavern, jumbling with Jenny's screams and giving her the impression of Dante's Inferno, that she was entering an eye into the abyss of judgment.

From above they stopped the rope and yelled down, "We're gonna pull you back up. It's too dangerous. Hang on," Doc Lewis said, "we'll get you out."

Jenny's heart was racing and she continued to wave at the marauding bats, screaming at them with everything that was in her. She felt the rope start to pull her upward, and with the movement the rope's pendulum motion begin to stabilize. "Stop!" she screamed. "Stop!"

She was very frightened, more frightened than she'd ever been in her life, but she was also determined not to let her fears stop her from doing what she knew she had to do. "Stop. You lower me down, right now." She panted out the words, "If I don't go down there now, I never will, and nobody else will either. Do you hear me?" she yelled out at the top of her lungs. "Let . . . me . . . down!"

Zac watched her drop down on the rope. *That's some woman*, he thought. *No man deserves a woman like that.* He watched her move into the dark shadows and then back into the flickering torchlight.

When her feet touched the ground, she craned her neck up toward the opening and shouted out, "I'm down. I'll get untied, then you can lower those other supplies. Don't forget to send my purse down, too."

"The perfect lady to the end," Zac whispered through a smile.

She overheard the grating comment and, turning to his cot, gave him a feeble smile. She was still feeling wobbly from the descent into the cavern. "Don't . . . go thinking now that I'm interested in powdering . . . my face down here. My Pepperbox is in that bag." She paused and swallowed. Her throat was very dry. "It's . . . not very ladylike to be armed, but I suppose I . . . can't very well depend on you to protect me down here, so . . . I'll just have to protect myself."

"I suppose so," he breathed.

✦   ✦   ✦   ✦   ✦

Hattie scampered back to her place. For all she knew, the marshal and his men might already be there. She ran her red roan horse most of the way and left the wagon for Doc Lewis and Sarah. She was determined not to be forced out of her place.

It was hers. She'd built it herself after she'd struck the vein of gold that ran through the mountain. She had built the log cabin with little help from anyone, at least until she had the floors and frame up enough to hide the mine. How anyone had found out about it was anybody's guess. She'd never considered herself much of a detective. It wasn't that she trusted people too much to suspect them of wrongdoing, it was that she trusted no one.

She raised the horses and pigs for show—gold was her game and she had lots of it. Her needs weren't many, and what gold she did sell was to get supplies from town. She'd always sold a small amount through other people and never told them where it came from. She'd been plenty cagey, telling the middlemen who sold the gold for her that they'd be better off to say they got the stuff from their own claims. That bit of news would make their claims all the more valuable, and they could sell them off for a bigger profit if they had a mind to. It puzzled her how anyone could have known about her mine, but she'd be ready for them. She'd be ready and she'd take plenty of them out with her.

As she rode up to her house, she pulled out the sawed-off shotgun, the one she'd borrowed from Zac. She dismounted from the roan and let the reins drop to the ground. The winded horse made its way up to the outside trough and began to drink while Hattie walked softly to the door. She had raked the ground around it when she left, so the dirt was soft enough to show any footprints. And they were there all right, bold as brass, one set of prints going into the cabin and none coming out!

She cocked both barrels on the shotgun and stood to one side of the door. Pushing the short, business end of the weapon up against the door, she shoved it open with a nudge. She had always nursed creaks into her door hinges, never liking to be surprised, and now they came back to haunt her.

The door hinges let out a plaintive cry. *Reeeek. . . .* The sound echoed through the quiet cabin. "Dag nab it," she whispered under her breath. She poked her head through the door and spotted him sleeping on the cot in the corner. Tiptoeing toward the prone figure, she stood over him and pushed the cold edge of the gun barrels up next to his temple. His eyes popped open and his unshaven face blanched white as a sheet.

"Mouse Nichols, you mealy-mouthed, pasty-faced, no-account 'scuse for a man. What you doin' here in my cabin, sleepin'? I oughta scatter your brains, and I would, too, if'n I didn't hafta clean 'em up afterwards."

His lips tightened. Freezing his limbs tightly beside his body, he edged out the words. "Hat, don't you go and kill me now. I ain't done nuthin' to you."

She pressed the barrels deeper into his temple. "Boy, you better never let me ketch you sneakin' round here whilst I'm a gone. I don't ever wanna see you round my diggin's without me here in the place. I'd kill you quicker than I would a snake in my corral. I surely would."

"Please . . ." His voice shook slightly. "Back off, would ya? I'm a here to hep you. You is plenty hot in town right now, and you'll be needin' somebody to cash in some a thet there gold fer you and tote things back and forth."

She pulled the gun away from him and stepped back. "I reckon you is right," she said. "I do need some fresh supplies and lots of ammunition, enuf fer a war if I hafta."

He sat up and swung his feet over the side of the cot. He turned his head around. "You need anything else? Medical supplies, say?"

"Heard 'bout that, did ya? Well, he's gonna be all right. He's safe and sound now where nobody'll want to go 'n' look fer him."

"Done squirreled him away, did ya?" He knew Hattie Woodruff to be a suspicious woman and one not to trifle with, but he also knew that the knowledge about Zac's whereabouts could be his ticket to San Francisco. "I hope he's safe, Hat, them boys from the marshal's office ain't even lookin' fer him, though. They all done figured he's a here with you. I wouldn't want anythin' to happen to him myself. He saved me from the rope, ya know. I ain't gonna fergit that, not by a long shot."

"Well he's fine, but he ain't here." She looked him over and cocked her head. "I s'pose I could use yer help. I hate the thought a bein' away from this place, never can tell what no-count drifter'll show up.'' She looked him in the eye. ''Mebbe you can drive the wagon there and take the doc tomorra. He can show you the place.'' Her face turned stern. ''Mind now that yer not follered. Them same people that hung your pardners and tried to tie a noose on you would like it a lot if'n you led 'em up to him, like the brainless fool that you are.''

Mouse grinned on the inside, but kept his stunned appearance intact and dutifully nodded his head.

CHA20TER

+ + + + + + +

EMILY TRUDGED DOWN THE ROAD toward the diggings on the creek. The rain had dried and caked the yellowish mud into a hard pack of sharp, pointed rock-like frozen clay. Her shoes were worn, and all too frequently the sharpness of the rocks and the hard-packed clay sliced through them and into her feet. She stumbled forward and gritted her teeth.

She had nothing to gain by what she was doing, she knew that, nothing to gain and everything to lose. *Probably nobody will listen anyway*, she reasoned. She hadn't even gotten much help from the tin-panners the last time she had tried to warn them. They stood and watched Breaker beat her and watched him brutalize the one man who had tried to help her. She knew how alone she was. She hadn't even been able to borrow a horse at the livery this morning. The man had politely smiled and told her Breaker thought it was best that she stayed close to town.

If she couldn't get the men at the creek to listen to her, she knew what it would mean. Breaker and his band of nightriders would ride down the canyon and sweep them out of it. It might not be today, it might not be tomorrow, but she knew it had to be soon. There was just too much heat on the judge's hydraulic mining operation to allow them the luxury of time. They couldn't wait, she knew that. They had to have all of the creekside and have it now. And from what she had learned, they had to get hold of Hattie Woodruff's place even sooner.

She had stopped kidding herself about her real motives. Revenge was what she had in mind, not justice. She had made a promise to Tom to see his killers punished, no matter who they were. She didn't know for certain who had put the rope around his neck and pushed him off of that bridge, but she did know who was behind it—her brother and Judge Harkness.

She also knew what they were after, and she was bound and determined not to let them have it, not because it was the right thing to do, but because she wanted them to feel the pain of having their dreams crushed like hers had been. It was a pain that lasted a long time. With each step across the muddy road, with each sharp thrust of the hard ground, with each stab of pain, it was all she could think about.

It bothered her some. To a degree she was acting exactly like her brother. She wasn't using her fists or guns to get what she wanted, she was using other people. Stopping the gang of men who were supposed to be the law was for the tin-panners' welfare, but it was in her own interest to stop them, too, in a deeper way, a way that aroused her passions like gold never could. *Maybe it's more than Tom*, she thought. *Maybe it goes back a long ways.* Her head rambled around with the notion that maybe by hurting Breaker, she was getting back at her father, her father's whip, and getting back at Breaker's cruelty, a man who had become exactly like her father.

The wind ripped through the oak leaves overhead, and she clamored over the mound of tin cans that lined the diggings edge and wiped off her hands.

Her eyes caught sight of Eddy Jackson and she recognized him at once. He was standing on his gravel bar in the middle of the creek and working his rocker, spading in the gravel and washing it down with water from the creek. His boots and his crushed beaver top hat were black, but every other part of what he wore was a splash of wild color. His shirt was of orange-and-green-checked cloth with bright yellow suspenders peeking out from under his red-checkered vest.

He looked up at her with his soulful eyes set in something that could only be described as a smooth, pasty-white boyish face. His curly black hair erupted out from under his hat, and ringlets bounced down around his ears. The bushy mustache and large beard that covered only his chin still couldn't conceal the fact that Eddy was just a boy, a boy a long way from home. His eyes looked at Emily in a steady gaze that seemed rather pitiful to her.

"Eddy, I need to talk to you." She raised her voice to be heard over the water.

She watched him put down the bucket and slosh across the creek to the rocks that lined it. He took the red handkerchief from around his neck and dipped it into the stream. Taking off his hat, he wiped the dirty cloth across his pale face. Squeezing the cloth in his hands, he clumsily ambled up the rocks toward Emily.

"Hello, Miss Emily," he puffed, still wringing the handkerchief in his hands. "How are you?"

"Eddy, we don't have much time. My brother and his men are coming. Sometime soon they'll be coming down that road and will either try to take over Hattie Woodruff's place, or run you and the other placer miners out."

"I heard about what happened to you here the other day, and I'm real sorry."

"That's not important now, Eddy."

"I'm sorry it happened." He blinked his eyes and stared at her. "I'm glad to see it didn't disfigure you none, though."

"Thank you, Eddy, I'll be all right."

"I mean you're still real pretty, Miss Emily. What he did to you didn't hurt your looks none, and I'm real glad about that."

Emily knew Eddy was a sweet boy—simple, but sweet. She took hold of both of his shoulders and gripped them firmly. "Eddy, you got to go get your pistol. Go get it and follow me. It's important that we go now. Every minute we waste is one we won't get back."

He blinked his green eyes at her and wrinkled his small nose. "My pistol? Why do I need my pistol?"

Emily knew Eddy wouldn't be of much help, but he'd always shown great devotion to her when he visited the dining room at the hotel, and right now, she'd just be grateful for one more male body standing by offering at least some appearance of strength.

"Eddy, my brother will kill you and the other miners along the creek." She shook him. "We've got to do something now. He'll kill you or he'll drive you off of your claim and you'll never get any gold out of here; you'll never get back to Ohio or wherever it is you're from."

"Indiana, Miss Emily. I'm a Hoosier." He squirmed out of her grip.

"Well, if you're ever going to see your folks back there again, you better get that pistol and follow me."

"I already got some gold outta that gravel bar of mine. How can you say I'll never get any more gold out? I got some—got it in a glass jar on a shelf in my cabin over thar. You wanna see it?"

"No, not right now, Eddy, we don't have time. Please, Eddy, just get your pistol and follow me. We got to go down the road and get the other miners to turn out and stop these nightriders—stop them before they come for you."

He blinked and stared at her, letting what she was saying soak in. "Okay." He spun and started for the cabin. Twirling back toward her, he pushed his hat down on his head. "You wanna come in and see my gold? I'll show it to you."

"No, I'll wait right here for you. Just get your pistol."

He walked to the cabin and stopped at the door. "Should I take something for us to eat? Are you hungry?"

Emily stamped her foot on the ground and raised her voice. "Eddy, you're making me crazy. No, I'm not hungry, but if you don't get that pistol of yours and follow me, you and I may be dead."

He disappeared into the cabin and emerged moments later with a black powder Colt stuck into his pants, cramming cans into his pants pockets. Catching up with her, they strode down the road toward the main camp of the miners. "I got me some oysters in cans. You like oysters?"

Emily didn't respond, she just stepped up the pace down the road. She realized she probably should have just gone past Eddy Jackson's place and right to the main diggings, but she liked the man. What was not to like? He was a good man, a hard-working man, just a little simple, that was all.

They rounded the bend of the creek that flattened out and allowed the stream to fan out into numerous sand and gravel bars. The gold-panning action was strong here in this part of Sutter Creek.

The placer miners were using sluice boxes and long toms. The hillside was being washed out, one spadeful at a time. This same section of stream that was taking forty to fifty miners months and months to filter through, and providing them all with a living, and some of them with much more than just a living, Emily knew would take the hydraulic miners only a few weeks to finish, and only make one man rich—Judge Ruben J. Harkness. She knew what the place would look like, too, after Harkness was done with it. Nothing would remain but a muddy mess.

The miners watched her walk up the road and stood, leaning on their shovels. Emily knew that each one must have known why she was there. They stood staring, wondering what to make of the two of them. Emily was moving toward the stream when she saw their heads turn up the road and heard the horse's hooves. A man on horseback was riding from town, riding deliberately, though not in a big hurry. As the man got closer she could see that it was Toby, Deputy Toby Summers.

Looking surprised to see her, he drew back on the reins to bring his horse to a stop beside Emily and Eddy. "Emily Morgan, what in blazes are you doing here?"

"I think you know why I'm here." She planted her hands on her hips and stepped toward the man.

The miners in the stream were putting down their shovels and walking up from the creek.

"You're just here to start trouble. I'd a thought you'd learned your lesson."

"Appears to me that the man who should have learned a lesson is you, Toby Summers." She swung her head around and saw the miners coming closer.

Eddy Jackson stepped nearer to her. "You want I should do anything, Miss Emily?"

She ignored him and looked back up at the deputy. "After that man shot down some of that lynch mob of yours, I'd a thought you'd stay in town and not come riding out here."

Summers' horse was growing a little skittish at the approaching group of men. It turned him around and he jerked the reins on the animal, popping the horse's head back toward Emily and the men.

"I'm headed up to that old woman Woodruff's place."

"Then you better be going with an army," Emily said. "She'll shoot you on sight."

"I'm just gonna look around, I ain't gonna take the old woman on." His face grew flush, realizing he'd said way too much to the wrong person.

"You better get up behind this horse with me. If Breaker catches you here, he'll use a bullwhip on you for sure." He reached his hand down to her and she stepped back.

"I've had a taste of his bullwhip before," she said, "and his father's before him." She shot him a stern look. "I ain't going with you, and he ain't ever going to lay another hand on me again. I'll shoot him down like a dog first. You tell him that. You tell him it came out of my own mouth, too, you hear?"

"Here, Miss Emily, I got myself a pistol you can use." Eddy straightened his pants and reached into his pocket for one of the cans that were bulging his britches. "I got me some nice oysters here, too, for you and the deputy, if'n you wants some."

Instinctively, the deputy drew his .45 and fired a shot into Eddy's narrow midsection. The impact of the shot jolted the man backward, and while he still held on to the can of oysters, he lowered his head and watched blood spread across his checkered shirt. He looked up at the deputy on horseback. "Why'd you wanna go and do that? I ain't never done nothing to you."

Summers swung his horse around and cocked his revolver. He lifted his eyes to the men who were now gathered around. "You men all saw that. He drew first. I thought he was drawing down on an officer of the law and I had to defend myself. You all saw it."

Eddy dropped to his knees in front of Emily and looked up at her. He put his free hand over the wound and then withdrew it, gawking at the bright red blood. "He done gutshot me, Miss Emily. I'm kilt. Why'd he wanna go and do that to me? I ain't never done nothing to him."

Two bearded miners knelt beside him and put their arms around his shoulders.

The other miners gathered around, and one of them took the can out of Eddy's hand. Another miner withdrew the pistol from his belt and looked it over. "It ain't even loaded," he said. "No balls and no caps." He looked up at the mounted lawman. "Summers, this man wasn't drawing down on you, he couldn't hurt a fly."

The miner looked down at the dying man on his knees and then back up at the deputy. "He stayed to his own self, down on a played-out part of the stream, so's he wouldn't get in anybody's way."

"I don't care what you say," Summers said. "The man was heeled and tried to shuck it out on me, anybody could see that. He was armed and I defended myself. It's as simple as that, and that's my word on the matter." With that, the deputy clapped his spurs to the horse's side and bolted back down the road toward Volcano, leaving the group of men and Emily pressing around the dying Eddy Jackson.

✦ ✦ ✦ ✦ ✦

Breaker and the men he had rounded up and deputized galloped down the creek road several hours later. They were heavily armed, and Breaker was leading the way on the big stud that he always rode. The horse had great spirit and stamina and was hardly breathing when they rode past the empty cabins along Sutter Creek.

Breaker had left Toby Summers in town. He didn't want to risk riling up the tin-panners after hearing the story of Eddy Jackson. As he rode past the empty cabins and the abandoned sluices and rockers on the stream, though, he wondered where everybody was. *Probably at a funeral*, he thought, *or maybe they just decided to hide out.* He had slowed down while they rode by the diggings, but seeing there was nobody to oppose him, he put his spurs to the big animal and bolted forward, trailed by his twenty-some-odd new deputies.

He reined up at the foot of the hill leading to Hattie's place. "Okay, boys, check your loads before we go up there. Put a sixth shell under the hammer and get yourselves ready. That old woman shoots a Spencer carbine and she's good, mighty good, from what I hear. Probably got good sighting distance spots all around that valley of hers. We'll get as close as we dare and then rush her."

Several of the men glanced at each other. They knew that following Breaker's plan was going to get somebody killed, it was just a question of who. The best targets were gonna pay. They loaded their remaining rounds in silence, and Roman Evers began to slip around the side of the group and head up the hill.

"Hey, where you think you're going?" Breaker's voice was quiet, but caustic. "Stay right where you are."

Breaker moved his horse up the hill to the side of where Evers now stood. "What do you think you're doing?"

Evers had remained stationary, not looking back at the marshal as he approached. Now he craned his neck and spoke in a low tone. "I didn't want to say anything in front of those men, but this here is as foolhardy a plan as ever I saw. Summers didn't scout this place out like he should have. You might be riding into a trap. That woman might have sharpshooters all over the sides of these hills."

Breaker was seething—he didn't like his wisdom or his authority questioned, ever. "That's just one old woman up there. You scared of one old woman?"

"No." Evers looked him straight in the eye. "I'm more scared of you and what you haven't planned for. You take those men down there, and she's got some help, you'll get us all killed." He leaned over closer to the marshal. "Even if she's by

173

herself, if she drops more than two or three of those men, the rest of 'em will light outta here like a bevy of quail. You just sit tight for a few minutes and let me look things over."

He slapped the scabbard on the side of his saddle. "Besides, I got my needlegun here. If that old lady sticks her neck out of that window of hers, I'll drill her dead flat."

Without waiting for a response, the deputy squeezed his knees on his horse and climbed the hill, skirting off to the hill-sides on the south slope. Breaker's face shone bright red. He swallowed his pride and turned back to the waiting posse.

"Where's he going?" one of the men asked.

"He thinks he can get off a good shot with that can plunker of his and save us some trouble."

"We gonna give him a try?"

"Nah!" Breaker exclaimed. "We ain't got time to wait. He could be creepin' around all day. There's only two types of peo-ple in this world, them that does and them that gets it done to 'em." He jerked his thumb up toward his chest. "I'm the type that *does*. Let's move out."

The men fanned out and started up the hill, arriving at the lip of the valley in several minutes. Breaker moved them for-ward over the shale rocks as quickly as possible. He didn't want them sculpted too long. The men could hear the noise the horses made over the rocks. It seemed to echo everywhere. It was loud, it made them nervous, but it couldn't be helped.

"That be far enough, mister marshal man!" The old wom-an's voice echoed through the valley. "I got you in my sights." There was a pause while the sound of the echo carried. "You're so big, Breaker Morgan, you'd be hard to miss."

Breaker turned to the posse. Small beads of sweat appeared on his forehead. He stuck out his chin. "When I give the word, dismount and we'll work our way to her on foot. We'll use those boulders for cover."

He squinted toward the south wall, looking to spot where the deputy had lighted himself and hoping by chance Evers might be able to see the old woman good enough for a shot. He suspected, however, that Evers would be just content to let the old woman kill him, before he did anything. Seeing nothing, he turned back to the posse. "Now, get off them ponies and make a run for cover. We'll wear her down."

Breaker dismounted, putting the horse between him and the cabin. "Now, get to them rocks." He waited until the men had begun to run and Hattie had fired her first shot before he bolted for a nearby group of rocks. Hat's first round scored a hit. The old woman had taken her time and squeezed off a shot like a good bird hunter would at a bevy of flushed quail. She had sighted in on one of the running figures and squeezed the carbine's trigger. The man lay on the ground gripping his thigh, blood spurting, when Breaker raced by him, barely paying him any mind.

Hattie's laughter boomed through the valley, followed by a sinister ripple of cackles. She showed no fear, but right now had put the members of the marshal's posse in great panic. They crouched behind the rocks, returning fire and listening to the man's moans on the ground behind them.

"Oh, boys, help me, boys . . . she's done gone and shot me . . . you gotta help me . . . I'm bleedin' to death."

Hattie threw open the shutters of one of the cabin windows and yelled out. "Okay, boys, they're all yours. Tear into 'em, rip 'em up."

From the rim of the canyon, rifle fire began to explode. The initial burst of gunfire sent three of the posse to the ground, one of them killed outright. All around, the surprised thugs took shelter from the descending slugs. Shards of rock flew in the air as the bullets glanced off them. Dirt danced on the ground as the slugs pockmarked the area where the men were scooting close together for shelter.

Breaker grimaced as he pressed himself close into the rock. *I can see that deputy of mine didn't exactly find a spot to shoot that woman from. He didn't give us no warning, neither.* He began levering his Winchester and returning fire in the direction of the smoke from the rim of the canyon. Now he knew where the miners from the creek had gone. Toby Summers' mistake had cost them dearly. They were all dead, and he knew it.

"Cease fire, cease fire!" The posse all turned their heads behind them and saw a man dressed in a black suit and riding a buttermilk-colored horse. He held a rifle in his hand with a white handkerchief tied to the barrel, waving it back and forth so everybody could see. "Cease fire! I'm United States Marshal Sam Frazier, and I'm here to place these men under arrest. Stop your shooting."

CHAPTER 21

+ + + + + + +

PEOPLE LINED BOTH SIDES of the street as the beaten posse rode back into town. Marshal Frazier carried their weapons in a sack tied to one of the empty horses. Two men lay across their saddles and all of the men were disarmed, facts not lost to the onlookers. The captives swung down from their saddles in front of the marshal's office and filed into the room.

Behind the desk sat a somber Judge Harkness, and stood an obviously shaken Toby Summers. The sight of Breaker Morgan, unarmed and at the mercy of another peace officer, was enough to unhinge the knees of any man. Marshal Frazier dropped the sack of guns onto the floor. Frazier's brown eyes looked down on the salt-and-pepper-bearded man. "You Judge Harkness?"

"That's right, sir. I'm the federal judge in this district, appointed by President Grant."

"I've heard of you." He paused, not extending his hand. "I'm Sam Frazier, United States Marshal. I guess I'm gonna have to remand these men to your custody." He looked back at them, focusing on Morgan in particular. "If I hadn't showed up when I did, they'd all be laying out there on top of their saddles." He turned back to the judge. "You got yourself a war out there."

Harkness bit off the end of a cigar and struck a match. "We do, Marshal, but we have leads that the marshal here was following up on it."

"You think that old woman out there is the one that's been robbing stagecoaches and stealing bullion?"

"No, we don't, but she's hiding someone who has tried to aggravate our investigation."

"Well, Judge," Frazier said firmly, pushing his flat brim hat back, "I won't argue with you on how to interpret the law, but I am familiar with how to enforce it."

He jerked his thumb, pointing to the crowd of men behind him. "These men have no jurisdiction whatsoever outside of your own township here. Whoever it is that's robbing those coaches is somebody I'm after. I've got authority to do that. Wells Fargo sends out their own folks to deal with the problem too, and they've got some good ones. The county sheriff in Plymouth has authority to chase these people, but this city marshal here, he's got no more business than the man in the moon does trying to work on this situation."

Morgan had heard enough. He moved to the pile of guns on the floor and picked his sidearm and holster out of the pile. Strapping it on, he said, "Maybe what you say is true, but if somebody in my town is behind all this, then it becomes my business. I'll find out about it, too, and I'll whip 'em like a dog."

"Well, whoever it is, it isn't that old lady, and it isn't any ragtag group of miners either," Frazier said. "I came into town on the last stage that got held up, the one that was blown to smithereens. I can tell you for a fact that the man leading that group was no miner. I saw his face pretty good and watched him shoot. He was a cold-blooded killer, that one was, looked like he enjoyed it, too. He was no tin-pan sluicer."

Harkness lit his cigar and blew a cloud of smoke into the air. "Well, Marshal Frazier, we do appreciate your help, and the fact that you're here on the job will make us sleep a little easier at night." The man's eyes twinkled. "I know the marshal here appreciates the fact that you got him and his posse out of that ambush, too." He cast a glance in Breaker's direction. "He's a very capable man when he's not outnumbered and outgunned."

"I can see that," Frazier replied. "Let's just make sure he doesn't get out of town either, shall we?"

Breaker's face was turning beet red. He was like a powder charge, ready to explode at any moment. Harkness could see it.

"If you're finished, Marshal," Harkness said, "then we'll let you get to solving these robberies. I know Wells Fargo must be plenty tired of losing all this money. You need to know, though, that we're on to the group that's been doing it and we've been hanging whoever we catch."

Frazier let out a sly smile. "Judge Harkness, I'm sure you're quite close to the group that's been behind these things, and with your help, who knows what could happen. Now, I'll leave you and your men to try to do what's best. If you can't find me at the St. George, then I'll be riding around, doing my own investigation."

He pulled his hat down flat on his forehead and, brushing past the men in the crowded room, strode out into the street. Harkness watched him walk away and puffed on his cigar. In a soft but gritty voice, he spoke out of the side of his mouth. "Clear these people outta here, Morgan. You, me, and these deputies of yours have got to talk."

+ + + + +

Jenny sliced pieces of firewood with the big Arkansas toothpick knife that Zac always carried. Smaller pieces of wood flamed up hotter and gave off more light, and right now she craved bright light.

The bundle of supplies that had been left for them contained a number of candles and now she had half of them positioned on the floor. They were flickering, but didn't supply enough light to suit her. Normally it would have been plenty, but with the moaning sound of the water dripping in the cavern, the shadows of the stalactites, and the occasional screeching of the bats on the ceiling, she was feeling frightened, alone, and even a little queasy.

She'd never considered herself a worrier, but that was changing. *Perhaps it's the bats*, she thought. Zac was no help at all. The descent into the cavern had worn him out, and now all he did was sleep. She sifted through the firewood stack and separated out the wood she thought would be easier to slice.

"Uhhh." The moan from Zac snapped her head around and sent her scampering over to him.

"What's wrong?" she asked.

"Uh . . . aaah." He moved his lips, but couldn't form the words.

Jenny felt his forehead and knew at once that he had a fever raging through him. Squeezing out the cloth, she dipped it into cooler water and replaced it over his forehead. "Wait," she said. "I'll go get you some cold water."

She felt foolish telling him anything, much less telling him to wait. He wasn't going anywhere for a while, maybe never again. He probably couldn't even hear her.

She took the tin cup and slung a canteen over her shoulder. She had heard the water dripping all over the cavern and knew if she looked, she would find some clean, cold water.

Taking a piece of firewood, she tore off a strip of her petticoat and wrapped it around the tip, then doused coal oil onto the cloth and stuck it to the small fire on the floor. It erupted with a blazing light. Holding it high, she inched into the darkness.

Scattered over the floor, she could see the reflection of hundreds of small puddles, which emitted the moaning echoes of splashing water. The shadows of her torch danced on the surface of the strange stone structures and sent small swells of dread through Jenny. She inched forward cautiously, carefully avoiding the flat pools of stagnant rain that pockmarked the floor. They would only get her feet wet.

The floor of the cavern was rippled with velvety bumps that appeared like solid waves of smooth stone under her feet. She climbed a group of rocks that rose from the floor, clumsily hanging on to the cup and torch with one hand while gaining a handhold with the other. Halfway up, she knew she'd never be able to get down with a cup of water and avoid spilling the thing, but at least she could fill the canteen, if she found anything.

The ledge flattened out and produced yet another rising mass of rock that led up higher. She was hesitant to move much farther, but still felt compelled to go up at least one more level. A slight breeze crossed her face from above. The torch flickered, motivating her to try the next level. If she could find one more way out of the cavern, then maybe, just maybe, they could avoid going back up through the hole in the main room. She'd pay whatever price to avoid the bats.

She could very easily have begun to doubt the wisdom of her coming to the gold country after Zac in the first place, but she didn't. It had made him mad, she knew that. And now, to be down in this hole with him, when he was so sick and she was so frightened, made her mind race.

Her mother had always told her that it wasn't proper for girls to chase boys. Well, she wasn't chasing him . . . she was fighting for him, fighting for all she was worth! She had always been someone who knew what she wanted. She'd never let anything stop her before, and she wasn't about to now.

She didn't want to leave Zac by himself for too long, climbing around up here. Even though he was helpless right now, it was a comfort to her just to have him near. To see him close, to see him still alive, gave her courage to go on. She wasn't about to let him die. She'd grab on to him and pull him back from the very edge of eternity itself if she had to. He was her man. He didn't know it yet, or didn't want to admit it, but he was hers all the same.

She crawled out on a flat upper chamber and could feel the breeze more strongly now. The flame from the burning torch quivered. *There has to be fresh air coming from above, there has to be*, she thought. She slashed through the darkness with the flickering light and stepped onto the floor of a smaller room. It stretched out before her, then dipped away into a darkened hole at the farthest corner.

From there she could see what appeared to be rubble and then a wall, but she knew there had to be more, there had to be an opening. The flame on the end of her makeshift torch leaned toward her. There had to be an opening on the far wall.

She moved forward and saw a large pool of crystal clear water at her feet. Here she could fill the canteen. The water was cold and it looked clean. She unscrewed the lid and pushed the wooded cask beneath the surface. The gurgling sound was pleasant to her ears—something besides the moaning of the dripping in the room below.

Plugging the cask tightly, she stood up and walked around the darkened edge of the water pool. She swung the torch to her left and was surprised at what appeared. What she thought had been a wall was a shelf of rock that ended abruptly at the height of her stomach.

Stooping down, she held out the torch. There beneath her was another pool of water. Dozens of white fish swam silently beneath the surface. Bending down and carefully placing her foot under the shelf, she stepped along the pool. There was something very strange about these fish. She waved the torch over the surface of the water. They didn't respond to it. They had no eyes! *How curious*, she thought, *they're living in the darkness but they don't know it*. The water was deep and seemed to stretch away—perhaps to an underground river or lake.

The roof of this shelf came up to her chest, and, bending beneath it, she crawled forward. She could see that there indeed was another chamber ahead of her, an alcove filled with water that stretched beyond the view of her light. She straightened herself back up. She wouldn't go in there, not yet. She had to get back to Zac; her torch was beginning to dim. But first she had to see where the upper room led to, had to find the outside passageway, from where the breeze came.

She carefully skirted the upper crystal pool and came to the far wall. Here, rising up from her feet, was an elongated passageway. It rose at a forty-five-degree angle and seemed to twist and turn through the rock, but it had to end on the outside; the breeze was too strong for it not to. Her torch flickered. She could see and feel with her hands that the hard rock of the cavern had given way to disturbed topsoil. Straining her neck and shoving her head into the passageway, she thought she could see the faintest glimmer of sunlight from above!

She had to leave it. As much as she wanted to find another way out, a way without bats and dizzying heights, she knew she mustn't stay away from Zac any longer. Her torch was growing dimmer and she knew that she had to act fast.

As she turned around, her foot slipped on the smooth rock.

She caught herself on a root, digging her fingers into the tangle to steady herself, and kicked a rock with her foot into the shallow hole beside where she was standing.

A loud buzzing noise came up from the dark hole. She swept the light over the void. It moved, or something on the bottom of it moved. The buzzing sound intensified. She held the flickering and dimming light lower to get a better look.

Snakes! Diamondback rattlesnakes! Dozens of them! They slithered and moved over one another, rattling away at the warmth of the torch and coiling themselves to strike. Several of them were training themselves on the light of the torch and tasting the faintly lit air with their darting tongues.

Jenny suddenly jerked back, pressing her back to the wall. The hasty movement of her body snuffed out the last of the flaming torch. She froze with fear. Sweat formed on her body in the coolness of the cave, and a trickle began to make its way down her spine. Her eyes were puddling up with silent tears as she clung to the darkened wall. Why had she waited so long? Her mind raced. The snakes had been quiet until she kicked the rock onto them, now she could still hear their rattles, the buzzing echoing through the room. They had to have a way into the hole they had been sleeping in. They had to have a way in, and a way out! She knew she had to move, had to move quickly, before one of them decided to take the way out, wherever that was. She couldn't just stand there and wait.

She tossed the smoldering stick to the side and heard it splash in the crystal pool where she had filled the canteen. She didn't know how deep the water was. She didn't think it was very deep, but she didn't know for sure. She tried to remember the way back to the ledge. The path had been narrow and the floor slick with groundwater. There was little room for a mistake.

Shifting her feet toward the side, she clung to the wall and moved ever so slightly. Her foot had already slipped once, and only the root had stopped her fall into the snake pit. Extreme caution was needed now in the pitch black darkness. She moved her feet from side to side, careful not to pick them up. She'd wanted a better way out when the time came to leave the moaning cavern. She didn't want to go back out the way they'd come in, but now her better way was nothing but a trap, a death trap. Her mission had left her in a smaller room above the main room where Zac was, away from him and away from the flickering light that surrounded him.

She couldn't see her hand in front of her face, but she kept shifting her feet back and forth along the wall. Her heart was pounding wildly and her breathing came in jerks. She wanted to scream, she wanted to cry, but she couldn't. Just at that moment the thought occurred to her that she didn't know what else was down here in this cave with the two of them. She had seen the bats, she had seen the snakes, now what? And if there was something else down here, could it see her in the darkness? Could it hear her? Could it smell her?

She heard a gentle splash in front of her, across from the pool and near the far, low slung wall. *What could it be?* she wondered. Maybe it was one of the blind fish, and then again, maybe it was something else? She kept moving her feet, never stopping, always moving.

The walls of the cave seemed to be as sweaty as she was. The ground water and the coolness of the cavern itself had produced a clammy surface, fluid to the touch—smooth, damp, and cool. Her fingers slid along the side of the wall. Normally, she had a good sense of direction, but below the surface of the earth and in total darkness, her bearings were way off .

She squinted, trying to make out something faint. A flickering glow had appeared in the distant gloom. Nothing should be there, but there it was. She inched closer.

+ + + + +

Deputy Roman Evers stepped out into the office. He had been in the holding cell area listening to the federal marshal's report and watching. Breaker's response had surprised him the most. He fully expected the big man to explode. From what little he had seen, he thought the humiliation the marshal wore on his face had come close to pushing him over the edge.

Breaker was a man to bust into a situation where care and caution would eventually have gotten him what he wanted. Breaker relied on his strength, whereas Evers depended on his cunning.

"Oh, Evers, come on over here." The judge had caught his movement in the back of the room and summoned him.

Breaker swung his massive head around, reached out and grabbed Evers with his beefy hand, and pulled him closer. "Yeah, Deputy, where were you when the shootin' started?"

Evers slid his knife out of the scabbard he carried behind his back. He flashed it in Breaker's face and spoke softly. "Loosen your grip. There was nothing I could do. You should have waited for me like I told you to."

Judge Harkness leaned back in his chair and blew cigar smoke into the air. "You three are a fine kettle of fish. We got Evers here, who can't show his face in town on account of a woman who jerked his mask down"—he puffed on his cigar—"and then backed him down. 'Course shooting a passenger with a United States Marshal standing there didn't help either. Summers, here," he nodded his head toward the silent deputy, "decides to get the miners all heated up by killing some fool who couldn't shoot a muskrat." He turned to look at the huge man. "And, Breaker, you can't control your own sister."

Behind the three men who were being singled out, Mouse Nichols slipped through the door. He quietly seated himself on a bench. Harkness saw him, but said nothing.

"Now listen here," Harkness went on, "we need to get that marshal out of town. We can't kill him. You don't do that to a U.S. Marshal and expect to stay out of the newspapers. We can, however, draw him out of town."

He paused and blew another column of smoke. "I think it's time for another of those daring holdups of these road agents. This time it probably wouldn't hurt to have casualties. That would be sure to send the good Marshal Frazier scurrying."

Breaker turned to see Mouse sitting on the bench. He reached over and grabbed him, pulling him to his feet. "You see this thing sitting there?" he asked. "I don't want any of my business known to him."

Mouse was squirming. He sputtered. "I . . . I gots somethin' you might want to know."

Breaker shook him. "What is it?"

"Let me down first, I got to tell what I know to the judge."

"It's all right, Breaker. Let the gentleman go."

Breaker loosened his grip on the man, who straightened his clothes and rebuttoned his shirt. "I know where you can find this Zac Cobb, him and that woman who came in on the stage after him."

Evers rose to his feet from the chair he had taken a seat in.

"Only thing is, Judge," Nichols went on, "I need some assurances and something else from you to see me on my way."

The judge leaned back in his chair and put his feet on the desk. He flicked the ash from his cigar and reached into his pocket, removing a leather poke. He bounced it in his hands. The sound of the coins made Nichols' eyes widen. "You tell us what we want to hear and this is yours, Nichols. This, and a head start."

CHA 22 PTER

+ + + + + + +

EMILY STOOD ALONE in the cemetery. The last of the miners had walked away. She heard them moving down the hill and toward Volcano. They didn't leave quietly. They'd been sad at the burying, but now they all seemed anxious to get to some serious drinking in town.

She hadn't remembered much about the service, just what Pastor Young had read from the Psalms. "The Lord is my shepherd. . . ." A tear came rolling down her cheek. She knew what the Bible said about the "valley of the shadow of death" was true about Volcano. No, she didn't fear the evil in this place, she hated it—hated it with all that was in her. She hadn't known Eddy very well. He'd looked at her when she passed by his place on her way to visit Tom. She knew he'd admired her. Still, Eddy was a like the lamb the parson had read about—someone lost, someone needing protection. He didn't really belong here, and he didn't deserve to be shot down like a dog.

Watching her from afar, Pastor Young had stood silently, allowing her to have her moment of private grief. He'd learned over and over that grieving was a personal matter. He could help the person, but he couldn't do it for them. She hadn't noticed him still there, but suddenly he walked up to her and wrapped his arm around her shoulders. "I'm sorry about Eddy, I truly am. I heard what happened, and I'm sorry you have to go through this."

She dropped her head and stood there, silently.

"I know you must be blaming yourself for what happened to

Eddy, but you shouldn't. You didn't pull the trigger. You were only doing what you had to do to try to stop the violence. I admire you for that. You were doing the Lord's work down by the creek that day. You were trying to protect the miners, trying to do for them what nobody did for your Tom."

The mention of Tom's name sent another dagger into Emily's heart. The pain was readable on her face, and Pastor Young knew he had unintentionally made her grief even worse.

"I might as well have pulled the trigger myself," she said. Her guilt prodded her into pouring blame on herself. "I kept telling him, 'Eddy get your pistol; get your pistol, get your gun.' " She paused and then shook her head. "I shouldn't have even stopped at his place. He couldn't have helped; he was harmless. All he ever did was pan a few nuggets to send money back home to his mother."

She looked up at the preacher. "And you're wrong about me trying to protect the miners. I wasn't thinking about them at all." A hardness came over her face. She squinted at him and the corners of her mouth turned down. "I was just doing whatever it took to stop that brother of mine." Her lips quivered. "I hate him. I hate him for what he did to Tom. And I hate him for what he's doing to me."

She pulled down the shoulder of her dress, exposing faint pink scars, painted on her back some time before by a whip. Looking up into the man's eyes, she explained, "This is the work of my father, and some of it comes from Breaker. Tom didn't see these scars. He looked at them, but he never saw them. He loved me for what I was on the inside." She thumped on her chest with a clinched fist. "He loved the real me, not the Emily Morgan that was the leavings of my brother's and father's whippings. The real me. Do you understand that?"

"Emily, you've got deeper scars—scars only God's love can heal. I'm not going to preach at you, not here and not now, but there's Someone else who knows and loves the real you. Someone your brother and his men can never take away from you. This person knows you and loves you, just as you are."

The bell on the church steeple rang out. He turned his head

to see the people who were already arriving. "Sunday service is about to start, Emily. I'd be right pleased if you'd join us."

Her head hung down and she nodded.

The organ blared out "When the Roll Is Called Up Yonder," and the people in the small whitewashed church sang at the top of their lungs. Emily had seated herself in the back row and looked nervous and out of place as the music started. She was offered a hymnal by one of the women, and held it with a shaking hand, trying to follow what was happening. She cast an occasional glance at the family that sat beside her. She wanted to make sure she was in the right place, doing the right thing.

Pastor Young had his eyes turned heavenward as he stood at the front. He always faced the congregation and called out the hymns, and then as his wife hit the first few notes, he would open his mouth and burst out the opening words, whether the people were ready or not.

The door to the church cracked open. It caught his attention because whoever had opened it was choosing not to come inside. He continued to sing, but watched the back of the church. There was enough of a gap in the door for whoever it was to listen carefully and perhaps see the people in the back pews. It made the pastor curious, but he continued to sing.

Let us labor for the Master from the dawn to setting sun. He began the next verse, but kept watching the door. It opened a bit more. *Let us talk of all His wondrous . . . works and deeds.*

It opened farther and he could see something very strange. *Then when all of life is over and our work on earth is done. . . .* Outside the church, he could see what appeared to be a rack of hams tied to a pole, leaning against the railing that led up the short stairs to the entrance of the church.

He gulped as the chorus started. *When the roll is called up yonder. . . .* The door opened widely, and standing at the back of the church was Hattie Woodruff.

She stepped back outside to the stairs and leaned over the rail to take a last spit. With a puff and a blow, she hurled the entire plug onto the ground and turned to wipe her mouth. Rubbing her hands on her tattered, dirty dress, she stepped back inside.

Her beaten black hat was pulled down to her ears, which stuck out of her scraggly gray-streaked hair. Her old brown dress was worn and dirty, and behind her wide black belt was a brace of six-guns. She wore heavy, hobnailed boots and walked slowly down the aisle, carrying a package made up of a dirty, knotted handkerchief. Each row she passed stopped singing at the sight of her, and by the time she arrived at the front of the church, the music had stopped altogether and the entire congregation stood in stone silence.

She looked around at the people who were closest to the front, surveying their astonished expressions. "Whatsa matter?" she asked. "Ain't ya never seen an old lady come ta church b'fore?"

Pastor Young spoke up. "Yes, Mrs. Woodruff, they have. I just don't think they ever saw one come in quite this way. You are welcome though, very welcome." He lifted his eyes to the congregation. "This isn't our place, it's God's."

"Well, I'm almighty sorry to bust up yer yowlin' an' singin' an' such, but I cain't stay. I gots to get back to my place afore the lawmen an' their lynch mob in this town burn me out." She cast a glance at the people in the front row and squinted.

Turning back to the parson, she went on. "I jes' wanted to drop off some hams and bacon fer you and yer missus. I took 'em outta a sow o' mine. That boar and his smell tweren't fit fer nothin' but sausage, and I brung that too. I also wanted to give you back yer money." Her voice rose and the words came out more rapidly. "Not 'cause I've a need to, mind you, but jes 'cause I decided to—my own self."

She placed the bundle of coins on the table in front of the pulpit. "This here squares me—squares me enough to ask ya to pray fer my nephew. He's stove up pretty bad." She turned her head toward the people sitting in the front row. Their mouths were open in stunned silence. "I know you folks is s'pose to pray, an' if anybody ever needed it, my nephew does right now."

She looked back up at Pastor Young. "I ain't here fer me now, figure I'm beyond any help there is. I'm here fer him. He asked me to come and get myself squared away, and I'm a woman who meets her obligations. I'm a woman o' my word; my pledge is my bond."

She glanced around at the congregation again, then returned her gaze to Pastor Young and lifted her chin. "If'n the law in this town does to me what they hanker to do, then I guess you'll be buryin' this old gal to boot, and I don't wanna owe nobody nothin'. Figure this money,"—she paused and spat out the next words—"which I don't owe you,"—she straightened her back and finished—"will cover my buryin'."

Upon delivering her explanation, she turned around and straightened her dress in front of the whole gathering. She hefted her belt, adjusted the heavy revolvers, and squared her shoulders. She was a proud woman, self-sufficient and self-respecting. She needed no man, she needed no one. She took care of herself and anybody who was hers. She was beholden to no one. She marched down the aisle and out the door. Stunned silence followed her.

Hattie swung herself onto the wagon and creaked it up the road and out of town. She picked up Mouse Nichols at the edge and told him to get under the tarp in the back of the wagon.

"Stay down back there. Too many people goin' in and outta this place. Some'un might spy you wif me, and I don't want thet. We'ze gonna get the good doctor and you can drive him to the place I tell you. When you gets there, you gots to hold on to the rope while he goes down." She slapped the reins to the horses' backs, putting them into a trot. "I'd go my own self, but if'n I don't get back, one of them weasels is likely to come onto my place without me there."

+   +   +   +   +

Jenny moved toward the light. Even in the distance, the small glow seemed to warm her, if only her thoughts. Only moments before it had been pitch black, and now the faint flickering glimmer in the distance sent a few rays of light through the darkness, not enough to help her see where she was going, but enough to give her a direction to move toward. Minutes seemed to creep by like hours, and at a distance she could see the faint light glance off the surface of the crystal pool she had drawn water from.

She moved her feet over the surface of the smooth, wet floor. The floor had small, rippling bumps that showed a flow of water had moved over its surface at some point in the past. Now, groundwater trickled down from above and seeped onto the sides of the cave, flowing down to the floor and over its slick surface. A small drop moved down the frozen rock icicle above her and fell, landing on the back of Jenny's neck. It meandered down her spine and brought a shiver.

She moved closer. The huge blackness in front of her showed that she was nearing the wall she had scrambled down to get to the lower pool. Putting her hand out and touching the surface, she searched for a handhold, then climbed up toward the light. Her foot slipped, but she held on and scrambled up the stone lattice.

Peering over the top, she could see the flickering candle. The lone flame was wedged into a crease in the rock. She lifted herself up and looked down the wall. She could see Zac slumped to the floor of the cave. Her heart pounding, she lifted herself over the top, scrambled to the floor beside him, and wrapped her arms around him. He fluttered his eyes and looked at her. Holding him, she cried.

She lay there with him on the floor for some time, stroking his hair and weeping. She'd never been known as an emotional type. She had cried at her mother's funeral, and she had cried privately when she got the letter of her fiancé's death, but she wasn't like the ladies of the sewing circle who dabbed their eyes when they read Tennyson. She had too much to do with her life to sit around and be fragile. But now she sat beside Zac and wept.

"I'm sorry." She wiped her tears with her sleeve. "I'm feeling a little too feeble, I guess." She let out a little nervous laugh and then more tears fell.

Zac opened his eyes and looked up at her. She had rested his head on her lap. Unable to move for the time being, she just wanted to recapture some feeling of composure.

"Jenny, this is what it's like, what it's like to be with a man in harm's way."

She blinked back the tears and looked down at him. She didn't want to say anything. Everything inside of her head knew that Zac had been right all along about their relationship. It was dangerous for him, and it was dangerous for her. She loved the man, but she didn't know if she could take it, and she knew enough about him to know that she didn't want to change him. He had to want to change himself; she couldn't do it for him.

"I been shot at too many times to talk about. This is about the worst, but it's all I know to do."

Her lips quivered. "Why? Why is it all you can do?" Tears began to flow. She knew now what he'd been trying to tell her for two years. She knew why he'd been trying to keep his distance. She felt deeply frustrated, frightened, and angry. "You can do anything you want to do, be anything you want to be."

He started to respond, but his voice cracked. He gulped. Jenny could see the pain in his face and held the canteen to his lips, allowing him to drink slowly. He looked up at her with his dark eyes and then closed them. Opening them again widely, he saw the tears running down Jenny's cheeks.

He spoke softly, in whispered croaks. "When I was a boy, my mother would read Sir Walter Scott." A slight smile crossed his face. "I always saw myself as a knight of the round table, someone who would find the Holy Grail, someone who would overcome evil. Pretty silly stuff, I s'pose."

She shook her head, but continued to cry.

"I guess I've never gotten that image of myself outta my head. I'm a man now, but inside me is still the boy of my dreams." He sputtered and coughed. "I can't see evil things and just walk away and plow a field somewheres. What I am won't let me do that, no matter how hard I try and no matter who it hurts."

Zac was a southern romantic; Jenny'd always known that. He was an idealist who many times quoted Washington, Jefferson, Tennyson, and the Bible to her, a self-taught man of letters. There were no colleges in his background, no private tutors on the front porch of a plantation. There were only parents who knew how to pray and who knew how to read, a mother who played the violin, and a father who practiced the golden rule. It was what had made him the kind of man that she could love. Without what he was on the inside, he wouldn't be worth having.

"You're only one man, Zachary Taylor Cobb. You can't change the evil in the world all by yourself."

"I don't have to change the evil in the world. I just have to do my job. And right now, I got to stop those robberies." He blinked and his eyes moistened. "I got to stop those lynchings of innocent miners 'cause some employee of the company is selling information to the snakes that run that town."

She looked into his eyes and wiped her cheeks. She was silent for a few moments, thinking. Her heartbeat had returned to normal, and she felt calm again after her encounter with the snake pit and the darkness after her torch went out. She wasn't a woman to panic or make decisions out of fear.

"Thank you for putting that candle up there for me. How you thought to do it, I don't know, but it must have been painful for you. I hope you haven't opened your wound." She stroked his forehead. "I'll be here till you get back on your feet. I just can't say what I'll do after that. I'll stay here to get you up and around, but I won't stay around to watch you die."

CHAPTER 23

✦ ✦ ✦ ✦ ✦ ✦ ✦

SEVERAL DAYS HAD PASSED since Doctor Lewis's last visit into the cavern. Jenny couldn't be sure of the time, but it seemed that long. The doctor had looked over Zac's wounds and had had to suture some of the ones that had opened during his crawl with the candle for Jenny. At least his fever had broken. He was talking more lucidly now. Jenny stayed away from the subject of his job and their life together because she hadn't made up her mind what to do and didn't know what to say.

Doctor Lewis had brought more firewood and supplies, and now she stirred a pot of potatoes. She was overcooking them and breaking them up. They'd be easier for Zac to swallow, she figured. He watched her stir the boiling water. She knew what he was thinking, maybe not the exact words but the thoughts, nonetheless.

She watched him through the steam. He was handsome. She'd seen other women look at him and fairly fawn all over him. They obviously liked what they saw in him, and she liked what she saw too. Of course she knew the man behind the dark eyes and large mustache. She liked that too—liked it a lot. But she also knew the pain and heartache that came with caring for Zac Cobb, and she didn't know if that was a life she wanted. She wanted to be a wife. She wanted to be a mother. What she didn't know was, did she want to be Zac's wife and the mother of his children?

She didn't want to be constantly left behind, not knowing if he was coming back, or if he'd return to her a cripple. It hurt her to see him so helpless. He had always prided himself on needing nothing and nobody, and now he needed her help just to eat.

She looked at him again. She sighed quietly. She did want to be his admirer—she and almost every woman she knew.

"You're not saying much," he said.

She stirred the potatoes. "There's not much to say, leastways not much we haven't said before. I hope you like these things. I have some chicken soup here, too, that Sarah fixed up for you."

"The potatoes will be wonderful. I'm lookin' forward to something solid for a change."

"Can't say as they'll be too solid when I'm done with them. Got to break your stomach in gentlelike."

Jenny sat beside him and served the potatoes and some bread on a tin plate. Zac ate them heartily, and she had to remind him to slow down. "Go lightly on that now, you hear?"

He smiled. "You're a mighty fine cook, even camping in a cave."

"This stuff is nothing. A child could put together what I've done."

"Maybe so, but they couldn't make it so agreeable like I feel when I look up at you."

She got up without saying a word and walked away from him. He said things that made her feel like a woman and she loved him for it. Just now, though, she didn't want to feel such things. She didn't want to think about her and Zac together.

"Here, let me get you a cup of this hot soup. The broth has some chicken in it. It'll help you heal up."

They both heard a faint sound from the opening above them. They looked up to the ceiling of the cavern and saw a man coming down the rope.

"Is that you, Doctor?" Jenny asked.

The man was sliding down the rope rapidly, and through the shadows it was hard to make out his identity. It was troubling, to say the least. Doc Lewis would have called out, and nobody else that they knew would be foolhardy enough to come down into the hole. Jenny had a sinking feeling. Maybe something had happened. Maybe Hattie was dead or some other catastrophe had befallen the doctor or the miners. Doc Lewis had told them about the U.S. Marshal in town—maybe it was him.

The man was closer to the ground and Zac didn't like it. "Get me my revolver," he said quietly.

The man's feet hit the ground and he spun around. "That won't be necessary," he said. It was Deputy Roman Evers, grinning from ear to ear.

"That's him," Jenny said. "The man I told you about." She scooted back away from the firelight and spoke softly. "I know what he wants. He wants me, not you."

"Go, girl!" Zac said. "Leave him to me."

Jenny grabbed some matches and a candle with her handbag, and moved quickly into the shadows. As the man pressed forward, she scurried behind some boulders.

"That'll do you no good, Missy. I'm here for you." He smiled, craning his neck around the room. "You got nowhere to go down here."

Jenny moved around the rock face and climbed up the sloping formation behind their camp. If she could, she'd get back to the crystal pool, to the underground river. *There's got to be another way out*, she thought.

Scrambling up the formation, she kept herself low. She could see down to where Zac lay with that evil man standing over him, his gun drawn. She tried to hear what he was saying, over her pounding heart.

"Mr. Cobb, you've given a lot a people I know a great deal of worriation. They're real scared a you. 'Course, nobody knew you'd crawl off into a hole to die." He chuckled, then lifted his head to survey the room. "This is quite a hole, too." Smiling, he looked down at the wounded man. " 'Course you got yourself that pretty little nurse to comfort you. Bet she's quite a comfort, too."

"You leave her out of this," Zac said. "I'm the one you got to worry about. I could whip you on my worst day."

The man was casting his eyes about the room, trying to spot where Jenny had gone. "Yeah, I bet she'd be quite a comfort, that one." He looked down at Zac. "I plan to take her my own self before I leave here." He smiled. "You ain't gonna be much to her for a while anyhow."

Zac rose up on his elbows, but the man stomped him back down on his cot with the heel of his boot. "You got yourself some spunk for a man that's dying." Leaning over Zac, he spoke in a soft, guttural voice. "I'm the one who shot you."

Jenny flattened out on her stomach. *He shot Zac,* she thought. She glared at him from above. *He was looking for me, but he found Zac.* She watched the man and remembered what Zac had said about evil. If ever a man was evil, Roman Evers was. *He should die,* she thought. *He toys with people like he's playing a chess game.*

She could see the deputy with his drawn gun. She didn't want to witness this. She'd told Zac that she refused to watch him die, and now that was just what she was going to do if she didn't do something quick. Getting to her feet, she called out. "I'm up here!"

Both Zac's and Deputy Evers' heads spun around. They saw her standing on top of the rock formation.

"Come up here, Evers; just leave him alone."

Zac's hand shot out and he grabbed the man's ankle. As weak as he was, his grip was strong and he managed to pull the deputy's leg, sending him sprawling to the ground. Evers' revolver spun away from his hand. Zac attempted to get up, but intense pain shot through his back. Sweat beads formed on his forehead and he collapsed onto the cot.

Evers scrambled to his feet and quickly recovered his revolver. "You are a strong and quick man, Cobb. I can see why you worry people."

Zac's breathing was labored and he held his side, the pain tearing him up.

"When I finish with her, I'm gonna have to come back and finish you." He looked down at Zac. "And then I get to watch you die."

"If you think that's gonna happen, you don't know me, and you durn sure don't know her."

The man's teeth shone brightly as he smiled. "Maybe not," he said. "But I soon will."

Evers took a candle and began to climb up the rocks toward Jenny. She moved down the backside of the formation and, lighting her own candle, pushed farther back into the darkness. The crystal pool stood before her, and the tiny light she held flickered over its surface. She cupped her hand over the flame. Briefly, she thought about going down under the wall and into the dark water below, the place where the blind fish swam.

Maybe I can hide, she thought. *He might not look there.* She turned, and then stopped. *No, I won't do it. I got to see he doesn't get out of here. I can't let him go back to Zac whether he finds me or not.*

She moved back down, toward the far wall that gave off the breeze, toward the pit of sleeping snakes. She hoped for once that what she feared most—the snakes—were waiting for her when she got to the other end of the room.

Zac had begun to slowly crawl away from his cot. His hands worked on the smooth floor to get a grip on it and pull him forward. Each motion of his lean body brought a sharp pain over the length of his back. It felt like the bullet was still there, and on fire.

He reached the pile of supplies and stirred them with his hands, searching for the gun. He had to find the gun.

Jenny's candle showed the water running off the glistening sides of the cavern. It continued from the wall in a slow trickle and gathered in the crystal pool. She shook her shoes loose from her feet and felt her way into the darkness. Her bare feet would give her a firmer grip, and she knew she might need to stay nimble.

Behind her, she heard Evers climbing over the rocky formation. As she turned her head, she saw the glow of his candle appear first and then his head peek over the distant dark wall.

"It's me, gal, I've come a courtin' you, sweet darlin'."

She reached her hand into her handbag and took out her pepperbox revolver. Firmly gripping it in her hand, she dropped the bag and stumbled backward. She grasped the wall and steadied herself. She had to watch it, the snake pit was close-by.

"What you doing way back there?" he asked. "You gonna make me come and get you?"

Her heart pounding, she clamped her chattering teeth together and did not answer.

"Back there it's dark, little darlin'. You don't want that, do you? All alone in the dark, far from that big man of yours?"

Zac grasped the wooden handle of his .45. He gripped it tightly and crawled forward. He had to get to his feet, had to get to Jenny. He reached the rocky formation. Normally, he could have climbed it in a matter of seconds, but now he wasn't sure he could even stand up. He wobbled to his feet.

Zac placed his hand on the rocky outcropping and leaned against it. The pain was unendurable. His head began to swim, and he caught himself on the rocks to keep steady.

His hand squeezed the gun and locked it up tight in his grasp. *I can't drop this*, he thought. *If I do, I'll never be able to pick it up again.* He reached for the first handhold and pulled himself to it. The pain sliced through him, but he kept moving. He had to get there. He'd never be able to forgive himself if anything happened to Jenny.

Jenny moved farther backward, in the direction of the far wall. She was shaking. The temperature was constant in the cave, but suddenly she was cold and goose bumps formed on her arms.

"Hey now," the man's voice was ecstatic. He bent down in the distance. "Took your shoes off, did you now?"

She saw him moving forward in the dark. She had killed varmints before, along with the mountain lion whose pelt hung beside her fireplace at home, but the thought of taking a man's life wrenched her insides. *Oh, God, please!* she cried out inside. She didn't know if she could do it. It was one thing to threaten him on the road in broad daylight, when she was angry, but this was different. Here it was just the two of them.

She moved still farther backward. Her candle flickered in the breeze. She cupped her hand over the flame. *Oh, Lord*, she thought, *I can't let it go out. I don't want to be in the dark again, not with him.*

She looked to the wall and, finding a protected spot along its side, wedged the stub of the candle into it. It burned steadily. The light gave out a soft glow, and from where she had placed the candle, it blazed on the ceiling and kept the floor in the shadows.

Zac had reached the first small ledge. The floor was only four or five feet below him, but it felt like a hundred. Everything in his body ached. His head was spinning. He blinked to clear his vision, but the rocks were spinning around his head in a circle. He reached for another handhold and pulled. Every muscle was straining and suddenly it happened—the pain ripped through him and he froze on the wall, like a fly suspended in honey. And then he fell.

Jenny could see the man more clearly now, moving closer along the sides of the pool. "Little lady!" he called out. "You can't go much farther. You best stop where you are."

Standing beside the pit of snakes, she knew she had to be careful. She didn't want to accidentally kick a rock down and disturb them. If they made any noise, everything was finished for her. Jenny stepped forward into the soft candlelight. *I can't let him see the snakes*, she thought. *I've got to think of some way to take his mind off where he's stepping, something to distract him just enough.* The gun shook in her hand.

"There you are." He was at the edge of the candlelight now, and she could see the gleam in his eye. "I must say, you're a real beauty, too, well worth waiting for."

His voice sent shivers up her back. She took her free hand and pushed her hair back. *I've got to keep his eyes on me*, she thought. She lifted her skirt slightly, showing her ankles and calves.

A tear rolled down her cheek. Her hands were shaking, and she held them and the gun in the folds of her dress. She had to hide the gun until she couldn't miss, and she had to hide her fear.

He smiled and his face beamed. "I can see you're not going

to put up much of a fight. That's too bad. I like a woman with some wrestle in her."

"What good," she sighed, "would it do me?"

"None at all." He moved forward, his eyes glued on her white ankles.

As he moved closer to her, she could see he had a knife in his hand. "You won't need the knife," she said, her voice shaking.

"I figured to cut you loose of some of them things you're wearing."

"Please don't do that," she said. "You won't have to do that." Her hands were shaking even more and she lifted the dress higher. He smiled broadly and put the knife away.

She watched him hold the candle up. *I can't let him notice the snake pit*, she thought. *It's my only protection—if I can't shoot him. I've got to keep him looking at me.* "Put your candle down so—so your hands are free," she said. Perspiration was beading up along her back, and still she shivered from the cold she was feeling inside her body. The look of the man chilled her to the bone.

His dark eyes flashed at her. "Yeah, that's a fine idea." He stooped to the ground and, making a puddle of hot wax, pushed the end of the candle into it. The light on the floor did just what Jenny hoped it would; it kept the silent pit of snakes in the shadow of her dress. The breeze made the flame flicker. He kept his eyes fixed on her legs, refusing to notice anything but her. He stood up and moved slowly toward her.

She dropped her skirt and used both hands to point the Pepperbox straight at him. Her hands shook as she held the gun. "Stop where you are," she said. "Don't take another step."

"There you are," he grinned. "I just *knew* there was some of that wrestle left in you." His voice was deep and smooth as he stepped forward. "You don't go giving yourself away without a fight, not you." He moved closer. "You got yourself church bells and baby cribs rattling around in your head, you do. I knew that about you first time I saw you. I knows women." He inched ahead. "Now you just put that thing down."

She held the gun out. "I'd sooner die than let you touch me."

"That won't be necessary, little girl." He proceeded forward and then paused. "Although when I'm done, you may want to, I 'speck."

"I don't have any notion of dying here." The gun trembled in her hand, but she tried to sound brave. "My intention is for you to die here."

"You can't kill me," he laughed. He began once more to advance toward her, his eyes looking into hers. "You're a good girl. You ain't gonna shoot nobody." He inched closer. "You might a killed a mountain lion and some snakes and such, but I just don't believe you could pull the trigger on a man who's looking right at you."

Her hands quivered and she tried to steady the revolver.

"You see," he said, "to kill a man, you got to look him right in the eye and pull the trigger. You got to have no conscience at all about watching a man die. That's what makes that man of yours back there so good. He'd as soon kill a man as he would squash a bug. I respect that in a man with a gun. I'm like that too, but you, you're a good girl."

"He's not like that at all." Jenny was trying to work up an anger. *God, please help me do what I have to do*, she thought. *I can't let him go back and kill Zac, I just can't.*

He reared back slightly and then moved closer to her. "I like your spunk, good girl, it's gonna make this even more stirring to the blood." He was now only an arm's length away and Jenny's hands shook.

His hand shot out and he grabbed the gun. The palm of his hand covered the hammer so that try as she might, it wouldn't go back. Wrenching it free, he grinned at her. "See, you couldn't kill me, you just ain't got it in you. You're a good girl."

He set the revolver down and pushed it aside. "There now, we wouldn't want it going off accidental like." He took a step toward her.

Jenny backed up slightly, then he lunged at her. Stepping aside, the snake pit was now in front of her. He grabbed for her, but she wrenched her hands out of his grasp. Wobbling on the edge of the pit, he teetered for a moment and swung his arms to keep his balance. Several stones fell into the shallow hole, and the first buzz of the snakes caused the man's eyes to widen. "What the. . . ?"

His boots slipped and he grabbed for the edge of the cave wall, but the ground on the edge of the pit gave way and he slid into it feet first.

The snakes coiled and swirled around their prey and Jenny backed up, pressing herself against the side of the wall with her arms stiff at her sides. A look of panic swept over Evers' face as he felt the first strike. "There's snakes down here! Get me outta here, fast!" He clung to the side of the pit, taking several more strikes. "You knew this," he gasped. "You did this. You brought me here! You little wretch."

"You came here yourself." She spat out the words.

His eyes fastened on to hers, blanching with each strike. "You done killed me after all, girl." Each strike produced another plea. "Oh, God, I don't want to die with these snakes! Throw me that gun of yours. Or shoot me yourself; don't leave me like this!"

CHAPTER 24

+ + + + + + +

MOUSE HAD WAITED BESIDE the opening of the cave. Several times he'd stuck his head into the cavern's entrance and saw only the flickering candles and the glow of the fire below. Everything was silent. He didn't want to make the mistake of leaving Evers in the cave, but he didn't want to call out. His voice would be recognized. He waited for what seemed like hours until he heard the woman crying.

He could hear the sobs when he held his head down into the opening. They were not the sounds of a woman in danger, but the sound of a sustained, tearful mourning. When her weeping rose above the moaning of the cavern, Mouse pulled back from the opening.

Hopping toward the fire, he squatted down beside the coffeepot that was resting on several flat rocks along the edge of the blaze. He reached for his handkerchief, but it wasn't in his pocket. Picking up the pot with an old rag, he poured a cup of the steaming liquid.

He squinted at the sun going down across the brown hills. He'd wait for Evers until it went down, but after that he'd head out. He patted his pocket to see if the claim was still there. It was. After dark, if Evers didn't show, he'd go on to Hat's place. He didn't want to risk going back into town, but maybe he could get some traveling money from Hat, at least enough to get him to Sacramento. He sipped his coffee and watched the sunset.

+ + + + +

It was pitch dark when he pulled the wagon up to the top of

the valley. He smelled woodsmoke. He tried to put the fact that Evers hadn't shown up out of his mind. He knew he'd have to face it sometime, though, and the thought of it with Breaker Morgan's hands around his throat frightened him plenty. He had to get some money as soon as possible. Then he had to light a shuck outta this place to somewhere he wasn't known.

Below, Mouse could see the lights through Hattie's windows. The shutters were tight, but a faint light seeped through the cracks of wood. Only the wind broke the silence in the valley. He slapped the reins on the backs of the mules and rolled the wheels of the wagon across the shale outcropping and down the rocky slope. The wheels made the usual loud noise over the rocks and echoed to the valley below.

"Thet be far enough fer ya." The old woman had thrown open one of the shutters and placed the barrel of her Spencer on the sill.

"It's me, Hat, Mouse Nichols. I got your mules and your wagon too. I been keeping 'em safe for you ever since I took Doc Lewis to the cave."

"You keep that thar trap of yourn shut 'bout that. Somebody might hear ya yellin' and all. Been wonderin' whuts kept ya. Knowin' your sorry hide, I figured you done gone and stole them mules and my wagon to boot." She squinted at him in the distance. "You all by your lonesome, Mouse Nichols? You ain't got nobody else wif you now, do ya?"

"No, I ain't, Hat. It's jest me. I need a place to hold up for a spell."

"Awright then, slap them mules and get on down here. Get 'em in the corral and fetch 'em some hay. When ya got 'em rubbed down, ya can come on in your own self."

When Nichols entered the house, Hat was stirring a pot on the stove. The steam was rising. "Set yerself down," she said. "I done fixed up some hoppin' john for my own self and I can feed ya a little, if you've a mind."

Swinging his leg over an empty oak barrel, he hunched down at the table and picked up a spoon. "I'd eat anything you fix, Miss Hattie."

She walked to the table with the pot of steaming rice and black-eyed peas and scowled. "Only time anybody calls me 'Miss' is when I is givin' out grub—or gold! Hope all yore 'spectin' is grub."

He watched her pile the hot food onto his plate, and taking a lump of old bread, he tore it in two. He picked up a knife, sliced off a piece of lard, and smeared it on the bread. "Well, actually I did have a business proposition for you, Hat." He spooned in the rice and beans, wiping his beard with the back of his sleeve and cramming a swatch of lard-caked bread into his mouth. "I need myself some travelin' money," he mumbled, "or I'd never consider parting with it."

"Partin' wif it? Must be your dear, long-departed daddy's watch that won't work, I'm a figured." She walked over to the stove and started to shovel the remainder of the food onto her plate. "He left it to ya when ya was jes' a boy; it's solid gold and very valuable. 'Course it won't work, but 'cause you're so fond a me, I'm the only one you'd consider sellin' it to, and it breaks your heart to do thet."

She put down the plate and crossed her arms. "I heard plenty o' them sob stories in my day." A smile crossed her lips. "Used a few, too."

"No, ma'am, ain't no such thing." He spooned the hot food into his mouth. "You'll know how valuable it is when I tell you." He looked up at her. "Normally, I would never think of selling it. It's got blood all over it, and it makes my heart hurt just to think of leavin' it."

"It does sound like a watch that don't work."

He fixed his eyes on his plate and continued to eat, occasionally peeking up at her as she stood by the stove eating. "You got some whiskey I can wash this down with?" he asked.

"You kin drink from thet water jug on the table there. I'll loosen your innards with some a my 'who-hit-john' later."

He hoisted the jug and held it to his lips. Setting it down again hard on the table, he said, "Hat, I need to get outta this country fer a spell. All this shootin' is making me nervous. My skin is all I got in the world and I intend to keep it."

"You always did place sech a high stock in your own self, for the low-down, slimy critter thet you is." She pulled out a plug of tobacco, cut a slice of it off, and popped it into her mouth.

"Now, Hattie, that ain't nice."

"I ain't nice!" she shot back, chewing with vigor. "I'm jes' all-fired honest and truthful."

He held his tongue. *Honest and truthful ain't anything anybody who's ever swapped horses with you would say*, he thought.

"I know you always tried to do right by me," he said. "That's why I come to you first with this." There was a long pause while he broke off some hard bread, wiped his plate with it, then crammed it past his wet beard and into his mouth.

"It's my claim, Hat. I wanna sell you my claim. You know yourself that it's gettin' good color, and since Tom and old Joe is dead, I guess that makes it all mine to sell and you can have it for ten cents on the dollar."

"That ain't yourn to sell no more. You think I don't know how them nightriders work? I done heard. That there claim you wanna sell me in all likelihood belongs to Judge Ruben J. Harkness and his Whitewater minin' thieves."

Mouse reached into his pocket and produced the claim deed. Wiping his mouth with the back of his hand, he laid it on the table. "There it be, all legal and signed away. It's all mine, and for a little travel money it can be yours."

She walked over to the table and picked up the paper, casting a careful glance at the deed first, and then at him. "Where'd you come by this, Mouse Nichols?"

He folded his arms and stroked his beard. "What you see there, Hat, would make that whole gang all filled with furiation, if'n they knowed you had it." His eyes twinkled. "I knows you to be a woman that sets plenty a store in furiatin' her enemies, so I brung it to you first."

"I can see Tom's sign-writin' on it and make out old Joe's mark. Them boys signed this thing afore they got hoisted up, but how'd you get a hold on it?"

"I gots my own way a gettin' things. All our names is on the claim, and it ain't no good without mine on there too. Now, what do you say, you want to buy me out? It'll make you a rich woman."

"I already got more money'n I'll ever spend. You know thet." She chewed the plug and spit a stream of juice into a can on the table. It gave a tinny ring. "You seen my vein down below here. Why would I want that scruffy little claim of yourn?"

Mouse's eyes danced. He swished another piece of bread on the plate and then looked back up at her. "You'd want it 'cause of what it would do to the judge for you to have it. If you got this here claim, then he can't very well wash that valley away without you. You'd have him like a twist a barbed wire round the neck of a newborn calf."

He could see her eyes brighten at the notion, and then slowly watched them harden. Her lip curled. She spit another spray of the juice into the can.

"I'm gonna have to think on it a spell. Till I do, you kin stay here, if you've a mind to, and work the claim some."

She sliced off another piece of tobacco and held it on the edge of her sharp blade. "I don't rightly know how you came by thet there piece a paper, but if I find you been in cahoots with the judge and his people, I'll shoot you dead as a stone my own self. I done killed Yankee scavengers and some horse thieves in my day, and I wouldn't blink an eye if it came to making wolf meat outta you."

+ + + + +

The wagon ride was somber. The sky was dark and a light rain was falling. Zac had been on his feet for several days now, but even though he was up and around, the sharp pains revisited him, first in the form of a jab in his side and back, and now a passive dagger that would stab near his spine when Zac least expected it. When it did that he would freeze stone still or double over with the pain.

The location of their hiding place was known and they had to move on. Evers' body lay covered in the back of the wagon. Jenny wasn't able to let him die by snakebite. She had thrown him her Pepperbox revolver and hid in the darkness while he fired the gun on himself. Now the body was emitting an odor, but neither commented on it. The entire subject of their narrow escape was something that both Zac and Jenny had agreed not to talk about.

"Your aunt will be glad to see you, for a number of reasons." Doc Lewis had the reins and was trying to make small talk during the ride. The fact that neither Zac nor Jenny was being very talkative was apparent as soon as the doctor dropped into the hole to get them out. They had both greeted him with weapons and little else.

"See, she's been worried about you." Lewis looked over at Jenny. "The both of you." He chuckled a little, trying to soften their hard expressions. "Folks in town are still talking about last Sunday. Old Hat went to church, just like she promised she would. Brought some ham and bacon, and all the preacher's money back to boot. Yessir, was a plumb puzzlement to people, way she done that."

"Drop Jenny off at the edge of town." Zac spoke matter-of-factly. "When we take this mess to Olson to bury, I'll have to pay a visit to the judge. I'd like to find this U.S Marshal, too."

They drove silently to the edge of town and Jenny got down off the wagon. The streets were quiet and she stood there beside the heavy rig without uttering a word. Lewis pointed to a small cabin behind the hotel. "Now, Miss Jenny, that's Emily's place right there. She'll be wanting to see you, and we'll pick you up when we get finished."

The drizzle dripped off his gray hat as Zac stared straight ahead into the street. Jenny continued to stand silently beside the wagon. There was something going on between them that Lewis could feel. He could hear it shouting at him, even though neither one of them was saying a word.

Lewis turned to Zac. "You want I should move on?"

Zac lowered his head and then eyed Jenny. "I got enough to get you back to San Luis."

She spoke softly. "I'm not going just yet."

He just looked at her and the moments passed. "I figured as

much. Suit yourself. We'll pick you up on our way out of town. This place isn't safe for you, but then I'm not sure any place is around here. If you don't see us before morning, you hightail it out of here. You understand?''

She quietly nodded her head.

Zac looked straight ahead and motioned forward with his chin. Doctor Lewis slapped the reins and moved on down the street toward Olson's barbershop and undertaker parlor, leaving Jenny in the rain watching them drive off.

Minutes later Zac found himself walking past the noisy saloons toward the judge's office. He stood outside and stared at the light for several minutes in the upstairs office. Occasionally, he could see the man's shadow at his desk, saw that he was alone.

He walked up the stairs and carefully down the hallway until he stood at the judge's door. Slowly twisting the knob, he opened the door and edged himself inside.

Harkness raised his head from behind the glowing lamp and seemed startled. His hand moved.

"I wouldn't," Zac said.

Slowly, the judge got to his feet. "Mr. Cobb, I wouldn't think of drawing a gun on you. I haven't lived this long by being ignorant of other people's capabilities." He motioned his hand to the settee. "Please have a seat. You look a little worse for wear."

"No, thank you. I prefer to stand."

The older man moved from around the desk and stood by the red leather couch. He reached for the cut glass decanter and poured the amber liquid into a crystal glass. "May I offer you a drink, then? It's the finest available anywhere."

"No."

"You really should consider it, Mr. Cobb. You don't look so good, if you don't mind my saying so."

"Harkness, you can sit and you can drink, if you've a mind to. I'm just here to talk and I want you to listen."

The judge sat on the couch, crossing his legs, and began to sip the whiskey. "I'm all ears, Mr. Cobb."

"You must know, Judge, that Wells Fargo isn't as interested

in what happens to you as it is in the ongoing robberies being committed in this area. What you do or don't do with your mining operation is between you and the U.S. Marshal's office. It doesn't involve Wells Fargo. What they send me to do is put a stop to robbery, and they never are very picky about how I choose to do my job, just so it gets done."

"Well then, you and I can declare a peace, Mr. Cobb. I can end the robberies and you can leave and go somewhere else to dish out Wells Fargo lead."

"I'm afraid it's not quite that simple, Judge. I said Wells Fargo just wants the stage robberies to stop, I didn't say anything about me personally." He took a step toward the judge. "You see, when you decided to go after my aunt, and one of your hired killers made the mistake of trying to hunt down a lady friend of mine, you made this personal."

Harkness sipped the whiskey. "You Cobb boys take things mighty personal. You know, I had two of your brothers in the prison camp I ran during the war. It was on the Great Lakes and men froze in their bunks, but I never saw either of them boys even shiver, least not in front of me."

Zac's face had a look of surprise that was hard to disguise, and Judge Ruben Harkness was enough of a poker player to know just how to read the slightest expression on a man's face. "You didn't know they were alive, did you."

"No, I didn't. I won't deny that."

"Well, they are. One of 'em was a kid with reddish hair. Looked to be nineteen or so when I had him, 'course the war and the prison made men turn old overnight."

"Joseph."

"Yes, that was his name. Joseph Cobb from Georgia." He lifted the glass. "Innocent-looking young feller. The other one, though . . ." He paused as if reminiscing. "Jet black hair and green eyes, or should I say eye. He lost one, and his left arm, I believe, at Gettysburg. Rebs left him on the field when they pulled out, and his brother wouldn't leave him there alone. Well, that one was a man to deal with, as cold a man as I ever saw."

"That would be my oldest brother, Julian."

"Right, Captain Julian Webster Cobb. A dickens of a man to work with, too. He led three escape attempts. We caught him all three times and whipped him within an inch of his life each time. Still he kept trying."

Harkness chuckled. "Never flinched during the whippings, wouldn't give us the satisfaction, I suppose." He sipped the whiskey and looked at Zac. "You remind me of him quite a bit. It's the look in your eye."

"Then you'll take what I'm telling you seriously. You'll call your dogs off and clear out of here, because if you don't, I will kill you. I'll shoot you down without warning . . ." Zac paused as a searing pain shot through his spine, but he froze and didn't react to it. He continued, ". . . and never lose a wink of sleep."

The judge watched him carefully and swished the liquid around in his glass. "Let me give you some advice, Mr. Cobb. You are at the end of what you can do here. I'm not sure you have the strength anymore. Now, I suggest you go back to those miner friends of yours and tell them that I'm willing to pay them two hundred dollars for each of their claims, and I believe I'm being more than generous. And your aunt . . . I may be a fool, but you can tell her that I am willing to pay her a thousand dollars for her place."

He raised his glass and took a swallow. "You see, Cobb, like you said, Wells Fargo would be easy to please, and that makes you the only thing we have to worry about." He smiled.

"With what you claim to have seen about the Cobbs, you haven't remembered much. I got all the strength I need to take you down. I just dropped off that buscadero bushwhacker of yours at the barbershop. He's starting to stink, so you'll have to pay your respects to him in a hurry."

"I kinda figured when I saw you that I wouldn't be seeing Evers."

"Well, you figured right there. My only regret is that I didn't kill him myself. That is something I plan to remedy, though, when it comes to you and those other two lawmen of yours."

The pain had eased in Zac's back and he turned and walked

toward the door. The judge had placed the glass down on the table and moved his hand into his coat. Zac swung around in time to see it.

Zac's look froze him. "On your best day and my worst, I'd have four bullets in you before you drew out that little .32."

The judge's hand shook.

"Harkness, you have four days to close down your affairs here and move out. You sell everything you own, pack up what's left, and take one of those Wells Fargo concords out of here. You'll be safe from being robbed. I can practically guarantee it."

CHAPTER 25

✦ ✦ ✦ ✦ ✦ ✦ ✦

THE WAGON HEAVED OUT of town while the rain continued to fall. Its box was heavy, but empty. It rattled. Both of the women came out the door when it rolled up to Emily's place. The lights were quickly doused and Emily carried a bundle over her shoulder.

"Zac, Emily's got to go with us. It's not safe for her here," Jenny said.

"Absolutely. Climb in."

He rearranged some of the loose items the wagon still had in it, and Emily climbed aboard and squatted down. "I sure appreciate this. I hope it'll be all right with your aunt," she said.

As Jenny climbed in the back of the wagon to sit with Emily, Doc Lewis chuckled. "How could she refuse? She's got religion now. She's a church-goin' woman." With that, he loosened a small whip and snapped it to the rumps of the horses. They lurched the wagon forward.

He turned his head to Zac, who was sitting quietly beside him. "You were feverish and more'n likely outta your head, but how you got her to make that promise beat all I ever saw. I never would have bet on that happening in a million years. That there aunt of yours is the orneriest cuss of a woman I ever did see."

"People never do anything they don't want to do," Zac said. "Hattie just found an excuse to do something that's been gnawing away inside her soul for a long time."

"How you figure that?"

"Well, sometimes people are aching to do the right thing, it's

215

just that all the years of doing the wrong thing piles up on them and it takes a kind of predicament to bring it out."

Jenny listened carefully. Even with Emily in the back with her, what Zac had said caught her ear. He was the kind of man who weighed what he said, and she knew he always meant each and every word.

"Zac," she spoke in a low but deliberate voice, "I'm wondering, what's the right thing you've been aching years to do?"

Zac continued to face forward, gazing through the rain at the road ahead. His look was stern, yet thoughtful.

"What is it, Zac? What do you want?" She was fearful of what he might say and didn't want to arouse his anger or make him feel cornered, but she had to know. She had to know now.

He turned his head to look at her. A softness came over him. There was no smile, no twinkle of the eye, but a soft look, nonetheless. She knew he wasn't about to joke with her. She knew he recognized exactly what was being asked.

"Peace, I guess. I want peace."

He turned his head and faced the front of the wagon, staring down the long creekside road. Jenny nudged up closer to him. She held on to the seat with her hands. There was no time for privacy, but she knew she had to hear more.

"What kind of peace do you want, Zac?" She gulped. "I don't mean to crowd you, I just need to know, that's all."

She spoke to the back of his head, not knowing what he would do, but he turned back again to look at her. The others were quiet. Even though they were all in the wagon together, they knew this time belonged to Jenny and Zac.

"I want peace in my own mind, I guess. I've been at war for the past fifteen years. I change enemies, but it's the same war."

"Is the war inside you, Zac?"

"Yes, I suppose it is. I guess it's a war between what I need to have as a man and what I want to do with my life. I've never been feared of dying. My only fear is in never having lived to do what my father did."

"What's that? What did your father do, Zac?"

"He loved his God. He loved my mother. He loved his own

216

children, and he built his own home. That's what he wanted most in life and that's what he did best." He paused and dropped his eyes, as if remembering back over the years. Then he added, "He did it all without any thought about himself."

"Why can't you do that too?" she asked tentatively.

"I guess I can't do that now because of what I do. I hunt people down and put them away. That's what I do, and a man can't just give up what he does best in order to have what he wants."

Jenny looked into his eyes and knew that what he really wanted most in life was her. He didn't have to say it, she knew it. His eyes were alive with fire now, as he gazed into hers. She could see the desire in them, a longing to tell her how he felt about her and a need to be loved as a man.

She closed her eyes, however, and settled back into the wagon beside Emily. Lifting her head back up, she saw him continuing to examine her with his eyes. The wagon proceeded down the road and the rain continued to fall.

The entire group was silent as the wagon covered the distance to the bottom of the hill outside Hattie's valley. Doc Lewis drew rein. "Okay, you're all going to have to walk a ways now. With the slippery slope, I got to put the whip to these horses to get 'em up there."

The party climbed down, and the doctor lashed at the hindquarters of the horses. The wheels spun slightly, and then with the horses pulling hard, the wagon rolled up the hill.

"Here, Zac, put your arm over my shoulder," Jenny said. Emily walked ahead and Zac complied and draped his arm over Jenny.

"Thank you for telling me what you did back there," she said. They walked slowly up the steep incline. "I think I understand. There's some things I'll never understand about men, but I know they all like to do work they can take pride in and feel good about."

He quietly nodded his head.

"The only problem," she said, "is that what you take pride in as a man means putting yourself in great danger and doing so on a regular basis."

He turned his head as they walked and looked at her, then he looked back down to the path.

"We haven't been talking about this, we've been skirting around it like you'd circle a rattlesnake," she said.

The pain knifed into Zac's back as he stepped forward. It froze him in his tracks and Jenny could see him wince. "It hurts?" she asked.

"Like the devil!" he said.

"Can you go on?" she asked.

He pulled her closer with his arm and faced her. "I can go on up this hill; what I don't think I can do is go on hurting you. You're in pain just like I am, and I feel like I'm the cause of it all."

"I'm just going through what I asked for when I followed you on this trip. I don't blame you."

"Jenny, you're a wonderful woman. I've never known one like you since my mother. You've been through hell here."

"Zac, you know it's easy for a woman to do that—when it's for somebody she really cares about."

They started up the hill again. Zac leaned on her and spoke. "You know how I talked about somebody who wants to do the right thing but keeps doing the wrong thing till some predicament makes 'em stop?"

"Yes." She looked up into his eyes.

"Well, I might be getting to that point myself. Honestly speaking, I don't know if I have the strength to keep on doing what I'm doing, and it's got me scared. This deep wound I took might put me on the shelf. The funny thing is, I been shot in so many places in my life, I done lost track."

"I know, I saw some of those old wounds."

"I guess I'm feared that by the time I'm ready to quit, I'll be so crippled up there won't be much left to give you. That's the way it was with my daddy."

"I didn't know that."

"Well, it's true. He went off to the Mexican war and came back with only one leg. He got around on it pretty good, but still, I think when he saw us and all the work we had to do to make up for what he couldn't do, and especially everything my momma had to do, it hurt him."

When they reached the top of the valley, the wagon was waiting. Down below, they could see Hattie's place, the windows barred and the smoke curling out of the chimney. Jenny took Zac's arm off of her shoulder, but held on to his hand.

She looked up into his eyes. "Zachary Taylor Cobb, I think you know I'd love you with no legs. I just don't want it to come to that. You and I both have got to make up our minds about what's important. You've got to decide if a family is more important than the manly pride you take in what you do, and I guess I've got to decide to let you be what God made you to be."

They walked down toward the waiting wagon. He stopped and straightened up to hear her better, to listen to her with his eyes.

"You're a man of courage who can't abide injustice, and I want you to know that I'm proud of you. If you never change, I'm proud to know you and I'm proud to love you."

Jenny's words were followed by silence. Zac looked steadily into her eyes and took her chin in his left hand. With the fingers of his right hand he brushed her hair aside and stroked her cheek with his thumb. He leaned down and gently kissed her.

The sound of the empty wagon rolling over the shale brought Hat to the window. "Who's out there? I kin see like an owl in the dark, and I'll kill ya too quick to talk about."

"I'm not as sure of Hat's eyesight as she seems to be," Doc Lewis said, turning his head toward Zac and speaking in a low tone, "but she's got this place so well figured, I bet she could shoot us blindfolded, just by hearing the sound of our voices." He looked straight ahead and raised his voice. "It's me, Hat, Merriweather Lewis. I brung you some company. Hope you got some coffee a fixin' on the stove."

The woman yelled out, "You bet I do. Come on down." There was a pause before her voice croaked out, "And my eyesight's better on my worst day than all of yourn combined. You can be durn sure a thet." With that, she slammed the shutters closed.

219

The doctor turned to Zac, smiled, and shrugged. "See, it's like I said, there ain't nothing wrong with her hearing." He moved the wagon toward the house. "I might say, there ain't much changed with her attitude since that church visit of hers, neither," he added.

They walked into the huge room of the low, log structure and wiped the mud off their boots.

"That ain't 'zackly necessary," the old woman shouted. "Fact is, this place is so dirty, ofttimes folks has to wipe off their boots afore they go out into the clean out-a-doors." She twisted her belt to the front and repositioned the black powder revolver she carried.

Zac walked to the stove and poured a cup of coffee. "Well, Hat, what you lack as a housekeeper, you make up for as a cook." He handed the cup to Emily. "Here, ma'am, you're looking a mite chilled; this'll warm you up." Turning back to the stove, he poured another cup and handed it to Jenny.

"Why're you all back here?" the old woman asked. "I'd a thought you were safer in that there cave till you got yourself all healed up. Not that I ain't all-fired glad to see you, boy. You standin' there is shore an answer to my prayers."

"Prayers?" Zac pulled the cup from his lips.

He could tell from the wicked look she shot him that it would be best to go no further on the subject. "Somehow," Zac said, "the marshal and his men found out where we were. One of his gunny deputies, that Roman Evers fella, came slithering down to pay us a visit a few days ago." He poured another cup of coffee and sipped the steaming black liquid. "Besides," he said, "I'm all healed up and I figured you might need an extra gun."

Hearing this, Doctor Lewis spit out a spray of coffee and Jenny pulled her cup away from her mouth. Zac swung his head from side to side, gaining eye contact with each of them. "Well, I'm coming along, I'd say." He looked at Jenny. "I've had some pretty good nursing."

Hattie tossed him his buckskin tobacco pouch and Zac, reaching for it, missed it, allowing it to fall to the floor.

Emily bent over and retrieved it. "Here, let me get it for you."

Hattie smiled at him and handed him his pipe and matches. "You left this stuff here, boy. Cain't say as them reflexes of yourn is somethin' I'd like to rely on."

Hattie cast her eyes on Emily. There was a hint of suspicion in the look. She had grown very fond of Jenny and was feeling a mite protective. "Maybe you got yourself too all-fired used to womenfolk scraping fer ya."

"Maybe I have at that," he agreed.

"I'm sorry," Emily said. "I can see you're pretty crowded here." She had begun to feel out of place and awkward.

Jenny reached over and put her arm around her. "Aunt Hattie, it's too dangerous in town for Miss Morgan to stay there. She's the one that got the miners to take her brother's threats seriously."

"Well then, gal, you're more'n welcome ta my place." Hattie gave her a hard slap on the back. "Them miners pulled my bacon outta the fire. If'n it hadn't been for that U.S. Marshal, they'd a buried that mob out there in the valley."

Zac was cleaning out his pipe and his head jerked up. "What's the marshal's name?" he asked.

"Seems to me they said it was Frazier," Hattie said. "Sam Frazier."

"He's a good man," Zac said. "Doesn't have the privilege of working around the law like I do, but he's a good man anyway. Guess he'd protect anyone within the law, no matter who they were." He packed his pipe with tobacco and thumbed the mixture down tight into the bowl. Striking a match to the stove, he raked the flame across the mixture.

Hattie sliced off a piece of chewing tobacco she carried in her apron and politely offered it to Emily. "Here, chile, you want to wrap your gums around some a this stuff? It'll settle you down a mite."

"No, thank you," Emily said.

"Suit yourself." She rolled the slice on her blade over her thumb and placed it in her mouth. "Anyhow,"—she began to chew—"how'd anybody find out about thet there cavern? You let 'em follow ya, Doc?"

"No, ma'am, I was pretty careful."

The door that went through the floor to the mine below was open, and a ladder extended through it and into the room. It began to shake, and soon Mouse Nichols emerged, protruding above the portal.

"Come on up here, Nichols, we got ourselves some company."

Puffing on his pipe, Zac watched the man climb up the remainder of the ladder. Much of what had happened to him on this trip had been due to saving Nichols' life from the mob of nightriders that had hounded him, and now Zac wasn't so sure it had been a good idea.

Mouse dusted himself off and turned back to the trapdoor, pulling up a bucket. "You got yourself a mighty fine vein down there, Hat; rich stuff, rose quartz laced with pure gold." He picked out a couple of samples and proudly walked toward Hat to show them off. Zac noticed that he avoided eye contact with him and that when he spotted Emily, his eyebrows arched and his mouth bent.

Hat looked over the samples and spit into a can. "You was followed when you went to the cave wif supplies, Mouse?" She eyed him carefully.

"Why, no, ma'am, I weren't. I snuck in there pretty good."

Emily, who had stayed by the stove, moved closer to the two of them. She interrupted them and offered a comment. "The information about where Zac and Jenny were would have been worth a pretty penny, I think."

Mouse looked back at her and straightened himself upright. He nervously fingered the knife he carried behind his belt.

Hattie looked directly at him. "Yeah, that's what I'm a thinkin'."

"What're we talkin' about?" Mouse asked.

"Somebody told Morgan where those two children of mine were hiding." She switched the chaw to the other side of her cheek and continued to chew. "That there deputy of his, the Evers feller, he came down that hole to kill 'em. Nobody knew about it but me, Doc Lewis here, and you.''

''Well, w-why would I a told anybody?'' he sputtered. ''Those people almost hanged me.'' His face was beginning to perspire. Beads of sweat mixed with dirt started to roll off his forehead.

''Mebbe you were tryin' to figure out a way to get that claim deed back,'' Hattie replied. She turned from him and walked to the stove to refill her cup. ''Begosh, Nichols,'' she said over her shoulder, ''you'd sell out your own mother fer enough gold, and you know it. You just ain't no durn good.''

He swung around and faced the room. ''You ain't bein' fair to me, Hat. I ain't done nothing. Nobody can accuse me of anything.'' He wiped the sweat off of his forehead with the back of his hand.

Emily stepped closer to him. ''You look like you could use a handkerchief.'' She held out the bright yellow cloth that he knew.

''Where'd you get that?'' he asked.

''You remember, I showed it to you at the jailhouse. I did see you there, talking to Judge Harkness.''

''I was just trying to post my own bail, that's all.''

Emily's voice was calm and cool. ''I found it''—she stepped closer to him, her voice rising—''stuffed into Maggie Cowart's mouth, where you left it after you stabbed her. I already told you that, but maybe these people need to know what kind of a man you really are.''

Emily had everyone's complete attention. The smoke rose upward as Zac puffed on his pipe from across the room and watched Mouse carefully. Hat spun around from the stove. She stopped her chewing and dropped her hands to her side.

''Give me that.'' He snatched the handkerchief out of Emily's hand. ''You're a liar. I don't know no Maggie Cowart.''

''Oh, you knew her all right. You knew her and you told her about all your gold. You used to brag to her about how rich you were gonna be. When those nightriders hung my Tom and old Joe, you figured it was her doing, and you wanted to make sure nobody knew that it was you who bragged about how rich that claim was."

"I don't know what you're talking about."

Jenny and Doc Lewis had backed away from the two of them, and Hattie stood stone still by the stove. She knew she shared the responsibility in what had happened; it was her gold that Mouse had been peddling in town. It was her gold, but the story behind it belonged to Mouse Nichols alone. She had used him though, and she knew it.

"You know exactly what I'm talking about, Mouse Nichols," Emily went on. "You turned on your own partners for profit, and you killed my friend Maggie to cover it up. And anybody who'd do what you did would certainly pass on these people's hiding place."

He reached out and grabbed her, extracting the knife out of his belt at the same time. Spinning her around, he held the knife to her throat. "Don't move!" He looked at Zac from across the room. "You move for that gun and I'll slice her good."

Emily stood there stoically. "He's good with a knife," she said. "I've already seen what he can do."

As he moved her to the door, Hattie slowly reached behind her belt and pulled out her black powder revolver.

"I mean what I say, Hattie. Put that gun away. I'm just gonna walk out that door and disappear from here."

"You ain't goin' nowheres," Hattie said. "You ain't 'bout to take my food, take money from me, betray my own kin, and then walk out my door standin' upright."

He pressed the knife into Emily's throat as Hattie cocked and lifted the gun. "You shoot that old horse pistol from that distance," he said, "and you'll kill her, if I don't." He held his head close to Emily and edged toward the door.

Hattie stood across the room by the stove and looked down the barrel of the gun. Its octagon steel stood out ramrod straight, never flinching. It followed them as Mouse pushed Emily farther toward the door. Hattie squinted and her finger tightened around the trigger.

The pistol roared and belched out flame and lead from across the room, its solid ball burying itself into Mouse Nichols' forehead and dropping him to the floor. The acrid smoke filled the room.

Everyone had frozen in place—everyone, that is, except for Hattie Woodruff. She stepped toward the man, never taking her eyes off of his now still corpse. "You're a fool, Mouse Nichols. I've killed cockroaches across a room with this thing, and you're no different."

Zac walked across the room and rolled Nichols over. He reached into the man's pockets and turned back toward Hattie. He held up the contents with both hands. "He's carrying gold from your mine and a hundred dollars in shiny new twenty-dollar gold pieces. I'd wager they came from Harkness."

Emily began to cry.

CHAPTER 26

✦ ✦ ✦ ✦ ✦ ✦ ✦

THE MORNING FOG HUNG in the valley. Ground fog was quite common, but that morning it was especially thick. The sun barely peeked through it, and everyone lay on their cots around the room. It was as if they didn't want to face the day, didn't want to admit what had happened the night before. Doc Lewis had left for home, but Hattie, Zac, Jenny, and Emily lay awake, none of them wanting to be the first one to move. The darkness of the fog helped them to deny the morning's existence.

The sound of horses' hooves brought Hat immediately off of her cot. *More than one horse*, she thought. She grabbed the Spencer rifle from over the door, and Zac slowly rolled off of his cot and reached for the sawed-off ten-gauge.

She threw open the shutters and propped the Spencer on the ledge. "That be far enough, whoever you are."

"It's me, Hattie, Judge Ruben Harkness, and I've brought the law with me."

Zac edged toward another window and opened one of the shutters.

"You are the most unwanted person I've trained my sights on in a long time, Judge, and thet's a sayin' somethin'."

"We're not here to see you, Hattie, we're here to arrest someone else."

"This is Breaker Morgan. Don't go buckin' the law. We're here to arrest a Miss Jenny Hays."

"On what charge?" Zac shouted.

226

"Murder!" Morgan barked. "The murder of my deputy."

Emily was now up to the window. She yelled out. "You coward! Always trying to use a woman to get what you want."

" 'Zat you, baby sister? Might a known I'd find you in this nest of murderers."

"Morgan," Zac said, "you got no jurisdiction out here."

Harkness spoke up. "Somehow we thought you'd say that, Mr. Cobb. That's why we brought the United States Marshal with us. The murder of a peace officer falls in his area of accountability."

"I'm afraid so, Cobb. Sam Frazier here."

"Sam, you're a fair man," Zac said, "surely you're not goin' to let them trump up these charges."

"Sorry, Zac. I know you and I wouldn't want to cross you for the world, but the marshal here has some evidence. You brought Evers in last night, and when we examined the body, it appeared he'd been shot with an Allen Pepperbox. I understand that's the gun that your Miss Hays carries."

"That don't prove nothing, Sam. Lots of people carry those things."

"That's true, but it does give us sufficient cause to make an arrest."

"Besides," Morgan broke in, "Evers was on an investigation to find her as a material witness to that stagecoach holdup that she'd been in, and you're the one that brought back the body."

Jenny had joined Zac at the window. She nervously wadded his shirtsleeve in her hand. "I should have left him to the rattlers."

Hattie had turned her head and watched Jenny cling to Zac. She turned back to the window and yelled, "I done killed the mangy cur my own self. He tried to molest me and I shot him down."

Hattie turned back toward Zac and whispered, "Where'd I shoot him?"

Zac was silent and Hattie again turned her head out the window. "I shot him and I shot another one of your employees last night—Mouse Nichols, a common thief in my own home. I shot him and I'm a gonna do the same thing to you if'n you don't clear out. Morgan, I'm gonna put an extry window in your thick head."

It was Zac's turn. "Sam, give us a few minutes. Stay right where you are, though. I can't vouch for my aunt's lack of respect for the law, but I can testify to her aim."

"All right," he said. "You got ten minutes to talk it over and get Miss Hays' things packed. I'll warrant for her safety, Cobb. I'll personally guarantee it."

"Thanks, Sam."

They turned back from the windows and gathered by the stove. "I don't like it," Zac said. "Harkness has got something up his sleeve."

"There's only one thing we can do," Hattie said. She glared at them. "The thing we're gonna do is allow me to go to trial for thet. I'll claim self-defense."

"Hat, that's a lie. There's no justification in lying."

"I don't rightly care, boy. I told plenty o' lies in my time, but this would be the only one I done told to help somebody else and not my own self."

"Hat, it pains me like you'll never know to say this, but lying for the right reason is the same as lying for the wrong reason. You know who taught me that?" He stepped toward her. "Will and Evelina Cobb, that's who, and I ain't never forgot it."

"That's exactly why I'm a doin' this," she said. "I ain't never done no unselfish thing in all my life and you ain't takin' my chance away just now." Hattie picked up the tempo in her voice. "You're as weak as a sick pup." She shook her finger at Jenny. "Thet woman over there has been through enough grief for a man who can't make up his mind if he loves her enough, and that rebel gray pride of yourn ain't 'bout to stop me from doing this. I'll swallow my wrong lying and live with it later, jes' like you have to swallow your killin' to do what you think is right."

Jenny stood by and was silent. Zac could see the fear in her eyes, could see her nervousness. The thought of going with those lawmen frightened her. She was a woman of great courage, but her encounter with Evers had shaken her, he could see that. "Hattie, what you're suggesting puts me in a bind, and I'm not even sure that Frazier out there will buy it."

"Well, dag nab it, y'all will never know till ya try, now will ya?"

"No, I guess we won't."

Jenny could contain herself any longer. "Hattie, it's me they came after. It's me they want. And it's all my fault, too. If I hadn't thrown that man my revolver and turned away, the snakes would have killed him. I should have just let it happen."

"Gal," Hattie said, "whose fault it is don't make no never-mind to me. Other people been payin' for my faults since I was born."

She stomped to the door, turned back to Zac, and put her hands on her hips. "Nephew, this is somethin' I'm doin'. I'm a gonna give it a try, at least. They don't want her anyhow. They want this place of mine, or better still, they want this place and you dead. Now you remember how you said that when you died you wanted it to be for somebody you loved?"

"I remember," he said.

"Well, this here is my chance to do just that, and I ain't lettin' the highmindedness of either of you two stop me, neither. 'Course, I don't have no intention of dying. I'm a gonna face them cowards down and spit in their eyes."

She looked toward the table. "Speakin' a that, I'm a gonna need a goodly supply a my chaw. Gets mighty unstimulatin' in jail, and I knows right well."

"All right," he said. "You pack up some things. I'll see if the marshal will buy your story. I won't lie for you, though. Besides, I'm sure that's something you do much better than anybody I know."

"Yore durn tootin' on that score," she said. "Naw, you stay in here with that Spencer trained down on 'em. I'll go talk to 'em my own self." She leaned forward into his face. "Boy, you get yourself so highfalutin 'bout this lyin' business, I'm a feared you'd give my story away."

"All right, Hat, all right. There's no give with you."

"You got that right, Zachary Cobb."

Jenny moved close to her and touched her arm. "Thank you, Hattie, for what you're doing for me. But I'll go if it doesn't work." She looked at Zac. "I don't want any more shooting. Do you understand? I'll go. I just don't want anybody shot on account of me. I don't think I could live with that."

Hattie took her by both shoulders and looked her in the eye. "Don't you worry 'bout it, lamb. My lyin' is legendary hereabouts. You ain't goin' nowheres but to a weddin' wif that boy my sister birthed." She shook her and grinned. "The only thanks I want is fer ya to bear him lotsa pretty babies"—she paused—"and name the first girl Hattie."

Jenny blushed and Zac handed Hattie the bundle and watched her move out the heavy door. He took the Spencer and held it out the open window. "My aunt's coming out to speak to you. She's got a confession to make."

He watched her stomp toward the three men on horseback, with the bundle thrown over her shoulder. She shot wicked looks at Breaker and Judge Harkness and then pointed toward the covered corpse of Mouse Nichols. They all watched at the window while she began her explanation. Her arms were gesturing and waving like a farmer caught in a swarm of bees, and curse words that made Jenny and Emily blush flew out of her mouth.

" . . . And that's the way it wuz. Durn fool. I guess I was a pretty attractive gal in my day, and that deputy of yourn musta thought he could molest me with . . . im . . . punity. Well, he couldn't. I ain't no woman of easy virtue."

Marshal Frazier had a broad smile across his lips and even Judge Harkness had to smile a little. Morgan, however, was unmoved. "You 'spect us to believe that cockamamie story? What do you take us for, preachers who never bought a boar hog before?"

"I don't care what you think. You ain't got no what they call jury . . . diction out here. I'm 'splainin' my story to this here nice United States Marshal here. What y'all other boys believe or not believe ain't my concern."

Morgan leaned down from his horse and his anger flared. "How do you account for all those snakebites on him, then? You ain't said nothing about that."

"Well, you knows I breed pigs among other things. I must have some hundred odd sucklin' piglets back there wif their mommas." She looked up at Frazier. "You should see them all feed, Marshal, it sure is a sight." She put her hands on her hips and swayed from side to side. "Well, from what I seen of that there deputy of yours, I'd say all them piglets figured that man to be their momma and just suckled him to death."

Harkness smiled, Marshal Frazier let out a roaring laugh that echoed throughout the valley, and Breaker turned beet red.

"I ain't about to swallow that story," Morgan said. He turned to Harkness, "Let's send this old crane on her way and take the girl, like we came to do."

"Oh, let's take Mrs. Woodruff. Besides, she'll make wonderful company in the jail while she's awaiting trial." Morgan started to protest, but Harkness raised his hand. "Hattie, you saddle up whatever you're riding and another pack animal for Mouse's body over there. We'll go to town and you can tell your story to a jury in my court."

The woman wasted no time. She hurried to the corral and began to saddle up a mule and tie a halter onto a second mule. Harkness raised his voice to speak to the house. "Cobb, Marshal Frazier will take your aunt in to stand trial, but before Marshal Morgan and I go, we'd like a word with you."

As Frazier and Hattie rode off, leading the mule with Mouse Nichols strapped to it, Zac walked out the door with the sawed-off shotgun in his hand.

"Mr. Cobb," Harkness said. "Marshal Morgan and I have a proposition for you. Now I know you don't want to see that aunt of yours come to harm, and I can guarantee her release." He looked at Morgan and the two of them exchanged faint smiles. "All we require is your participation in a sporting event."

Zac stood silently while Morgan stood up in his stirrups. The big man was beaming with anticipation. "You know," the judge said, "on your first appearance to our fair city, you made the marshal here do something that was very demeaning."

"No more than he deserved to do," Zac said.

"Be that as it may, I believe the marshal feels he has a score to settle, and I think it's something he wants to happen in public."

"You got that!" Breaker shot out.

"So this is our proposal to you. You come to town and fight a no-holds-barred competitive fight with the marshal, and we'll release your aunt." He turned his head and watched the U.S. Marshal and Hat riding up the valley. "I'd sure hate to see her hung or locked up a long time. She's along in years." Looking back to Zac, he smiled. "Well, what do you say, Mr. Cobb? Have we got a deal?"

"You got this all figured out, don't you?"

"We do have the cards in this hand, Cobb. You see, this aunt of yours suits our purposes just fine, maybe even better than that pretty girl of yours. See, if Hattie goes to jail, or is hung, then all this property of hers," he waved his hand in a sweeping motion, "will revert to the court."

"You know, Harkness, I've seen evil in my day. I come across it for a living, but you are very near the top of the list."

"Why, thank you, Cobb. I'll take that as a compliment. You see, I'm a thinking man, and a patient man. Things come my way in life if I think about it and wait for it." He motioned toward the marshal. "Morgan here has never lost a fight or a scrap, and what he goes by, 'Breaker,' is a name well earned."

"I'm sure it is," Zac said. "All right, here's my word on the matter. You can plan your fight for seven days from now. You can also plan the trial for that day, but before the fight begins."

"There'll be no need for a trial if you come, Cobb," Harkness said.

"Oh, yes there will. I don't want these charges brought up again. Hattie will plead guilty, but in self-defense. You will then instruct the jury to find her innocent. Those are my terms."

"You have a fine legal mind, Cobb. Perhaps you've missed your calling."

"Harkness, I'm not sure I'd want to be a part of anything

where someone like you would be considered a—what do they call it—a colleague?"

Harkness's face dropped and he pulled on his reins, backing up his horse. Morgan looked down at Zac and grinned. "If you have got a legal mind, Cobb, I'd suggest you use it in drawing up a last will and testament, because I intend to kill you." He turned his horse's head and slapped spurs to the animal's sides, galloping to catch up to the judge.

CHAPTER 27

+ + + + + + +

THE EVENING FIRE CRACKLED in the fireplace and Emily busied herself with cooking. She and Jenny had hunted around the house to locate the needed pots and other staple items that went into preparing a meal. Zac sat beside the fire in a chair, smoking his pipe.

Jenny carried a cup of coffee to him. "Thank you for chopping that wood and building the fire. I must admit, though, you swinging that ax with those stitches still in you made me nervous."

Zac took the cup of coffee and stared straight into the fire. He sipped the hot black liquid and then placed the pipe back into his mouth.

She looked around the room. "That fire makes the place here seem kind of homey." Jenny held a broom in her hand. She had been busying herself with cleaning the large room and now stopped to admire her work. "I guess I've spent so much time in the restaurant and in that little place of mine that I forgot what a home was supposed to be like."

She looked down at Zac. "I don't know how she did it, but that aunt of yours built herself a fine home."

Zac puffed on his pipe and then held it in his hand. "Hattie never built this place to be a home. She built it to be a fort, a fort built over her mine. She's not given to such things."

"Oh, I disagree." She leaned on her broom. "She's a woman, same as any other, though I admit she doesn't show it much." She reached out and touched the mantel over the fireplace and then took down a photograph of a couple framed in ornate brass. "See, just like a woman, a picture of her parents on the mantel." She picked up the lace doily the frame had rested on and held it up to Zac. "It's just like you'd see in any woman's place."

"That's not Hattie's parents," Zac said. Jenny looked surprised and set the lace back on the mantel, then replaced the framed photograph.

"Those are my folks." He stood and, setting his cup on the mantel, picked up the photograph. "My mother and Hattie were sisters, although about as different as two women could be."

"I can see that."

"Hattie adored my mother, though. Anyone who knew her loved her."

"I can see that you do favor your father, Zac."

"Yes, I suppose I do. I favor him on the outside, but I 'speck I'll have to go a ways before I favor him on the inside."

"Hattie must have been very attached to them."

"I suppose you could say that. I just found out on this trip why she still is." Zac replaced the picture above the fireplace and walked to the red trunk in the corner of the room.

Jenny saw the distant look in his eyes, and when he opened the trunk and removed the violin and bow, there was something about the way he held it that made her feel like she was intruding on his privacy.

He didn't return to his seat beside the fire, the place where Jenny stood. Instead, he walked out the door carrying the instrument. Jenny followed to watch him. He placed the violin under his chin and began to run the bow over the strings. A sweet melody meandered across the valley floor, a tune she had never heard before. Like the haunting of a spirit, its beautiful notes seemed to surround the entire valley all at once.

Emily walked to where Jenny was standing and the two women stood there, frozen in disbelief. "I'd never have guessed," Emily whispered.

"Nor I," said Jenny.

"How odd," Emily said. "A man like that, playing so beautifully."

"I've never known that man," said Jenny. "All the time I've spent with him, and sometimes the closer I get the farther away I feel."

The women looked at each other and had the same sense of awkwardness. They turned from the door and went back to their chores. They listened to the music through the open door for over an hour before Zac came back into the house. He walked back in and replaced the violin, never saying a word about it, and they never asked.

Zac spent some time cleaning his guns and smoking his pipe and now was stretching himself to do light exercise. He had stripped off his shirt, and Jenny took note of the many healed wounds on his body. The surtured incision, however, still appeared to be red and angry.

"Zac," Jenny interrupted his stretching, "don't you think you should wait for Doc Lewis to take those stitches out?"

He swung his arms around his head and flinched with pain. "I got to do whatever I can to get ready for this encounter with Breaker."

"How can you do it?" she asked. "That man is an enormous brute. He looks like he could tear somebody in half."

Emily had begun to slice dried vegetables for stew. She put down the knife and wiped her hands on her apron. Turning from the stove, she walked over to Jenny and Zac. "I've seen my brother fight over the years . . . too many times to talk about. He uses his fists and when he gets the opportunity to hit somebody hard, they seldom get up again. I've seen him break a man's back. That's where he got his name; his given name is Turner."

"Turner," Zac smiled. "That's helpful to know."

"He hates it," Emily said.

"I can see why." Zac continued to stretch his arms and grimace in pain.

"How can you hope to best him?" Jenny asked. "Especially in your condition."

"My brother will do everything in his power to kill you, Mr. Cobb. You shamed him in front of the whole town that night, and he won't forget it till his dying day. He snaps at people on the streets that he thinks have been talking about him. I swear, he'll kill you, if he can."

Zac stopped stretching and grabbed his shirt. "Ladies, I appreciate your concern, believe me. I'm concerned myself." He turned to Emily. "I know your brother is a scrapper, but I'll be willing to warrant that his only fights have been with drunks these past years."

He put on his shirt. "He is large." Zac gave a broad smile. "In fact, he's huge. Of course, all that size is going to hurt him, too."

"How is that?" Jenny asked.

"Much of his bulk comes from too much dining at that hotel you work at, Emily, and from too little time spent chopping wood. Although I don't consider myself much of a farmer, working around the ranch keeps me from getting too soft." He buttoned his shirt. "I'm going to try to keep moving for as long as I can, and keep him as far away from me as possible. One thing's for sure, though, I'm not going to take him lightly."

"That's wise, Mr. Cobb. Like I say, I've seen my brother in more than a few fights. He isn't stunned easily. His head is like a lead brick."

"That's the other thing I'm countin' on, his head. Your brother is a hothead. He doesn't think about what he's doing. I'm countin' on that." He tucked his shirt into his pants. "I suppose I'm thinkin' about Morgan, because it takes my mind off of what's wrong with me. My back's got lots a pain in it still, and all this lying around has got me feelin' a little puny."

Just then the pain caught him in midmovement. His face twisted and he gritted his teeth.

He saw the look of shock in the women's eyes. "Don't waste your worry on me. I'll be all right. It comes and goes."

+   +   +   +   +

After the men in the jail had taken their supper, Harkness spread out a map. "We need at least one more daring robbery, something that will draw this Marshal Frazier out of town. You two are going to have to get a handful of the men that Roman was dealin' with and have them do another shipment."

"That ain't gonna be no problem," Breaker said.

They moved the lamp over closer to the map.

"How about there?" Morgan put his chubby finger down on the map. "Along the road from Plymouth to Placerville. That'd be perfect. That coach carries a lot of gold on it."

Harkness leaned over and looked at the lines that marked the county jurisdictions. "No, I don't think so. The sheriff at Placerville would take out after them boys, and our Marshal Frazier here might not get a chance to leave town. No, I think the stage from Plymouth through Fiddletown would be best. Word would get back here quick, and if those men head east afterwards, then they'll have to assume they're heading out of the state. That's got to involve the United States Marshal."

Harkness smiled at Morgan. "And you will be a material witness in our trial. We can't send you out leading no posse."

He crossed his arms. "No, our very conscientious Marshal Frazier will get the job of leading that long chase. Otherwise he'll stay right here and look over our shoulder until the whole operation dries up, if we're not careful."

Summers scratched his chin. "Judge, you want I should just keep on going till we get to Virginia City?"

"That's exactly what I want the men to do. I want fresh horses for the men north of the river, and then when they change horses during the chase, they'll go a long ways fast." He looked into the deputy's eyes. "But, Summers, I want you here. I want you lying low, till I need you."

"I don't get to go to Virginia City with the boys?"

"No, but if everything happens like I plan, you can spend the rest of your life in Virginia City if you want. No, I'm depending on you at the fight, just in case. We've got to make sure that Mr. Zachary Cobb doesn't survive Saturday's fight."

Morgan leaned on the map and stuck his face close to the judge. "That's a problem you ain't gonna have, Judge. I'm gonna kill that man, not just beat him up. He ain't gonna survive."

"Believe me, Marshal, using Summers is the next to the last thing that I want." He leaned back in the chair and, taking out a cigar from his inside pocket, bit off the end. "The last thing I want, however, is for that man to walk out of that ring still standing." He placed the end of the cigar in his mouth and rolled it around, then ran his tongue over its length to firm it up.

"Summers, I want you in a room at the St. George with a rifle." Striking a match on the arm of the chair, he raked the flame across the end of the cigar and puffed a glowing flame on its end. He looked up at the lanky deputy. "If our good marshal here doesn't bring an end to the man from Wells Fargo, then I want you to, understood?"

"When you boys gonna bring that old lady her supper?" Hattie's voice screeched out from the back room of the jail.

"Shut yer trap, ya old hag." Morgan was angry, it was plain to see.

"Now, Marshal," Harkness said. "I trust you're not going to take your wounded pride out on an old lady. I wouldn't want to see any harm come to her, at least not yet. When we dispose of her nephew, and with the marshal out of town, that would be an appropriate time. I don't think I'd like to see Mrs. Woodruff make it back to her place with that rifle she keeps."

He leaned back once more and puffed on his cigar. "No, I think once the woman is found not guilty and is released from our custody, that would be the time. When the fight's over, you can escort her to the livery stable. The rafters there would make nice gallows, don't you agree?" He smiled. "You can hoist her up in there. Be easy to say that the good people of this town were incensed that she murdered our brave deputy and then got off scot-free. They just won't be able to control their righteous indignation, that's all."

CHAPTER 28

✦ ✦ ✦ ✦ ✦ ✦ ✦

ZAC RODE TOWARD TOWN early Saturday morning
with Jenny and Emily. The ground fog had been waiting for
them when they saddled their horses. Its curtain hung over the
valley and made seeing beyond the ears of the horses difficult.
They skirted out of the valley and then turned west, in the opposite direction of Volcano. "Why are we going this way?" Emily asked.

"Being too predictable in your habits ain't healthy. I figured
we'd ride around toward the west and then circle back into town
by way of the Fiddletown road. They won't be expecting us to
come in that way."

"No, I reckon not."

They hit the creekside road and could only tell for sure
where they were by the look of the ground beneath them and
the sound of the tumbling water. It sounded fresh and clean,
surging and playing around the rocks and boulders, and yet it
remained unseen. This ground wasn't Zac's backyard, so he
paused to look at his watch. He'd time their ride on the road
before turning to cross the creek and circle back. They'd me-
ander through a cut and find the road from Plymouth and Fiddletown on the other side. It was a well-traveled road, unlike
this one, a stage road.

The women both knew that being this close to the valley's
entrance demanded silence. An ambush was likely. The judge
and his men were desperate enough to try anything, so they rode
on through the fog without making a sound.

Zac spent his thinking time not going over what needed to be done before the fight, or even the fight itself, but tracing where his life had been so far. He always teetered over how much was enough. He knew there might not be much in the way of reward for this job. More than likely the money taken off the coaches had been spent. What this bunch was interested in most was the mineral rights of the people they'd been hanging for the robberies and driving off of their claims. That was something Wells Fargo had little to do with. Still, everything he made went to the Cambria spread. It wasn't large, but it was his. The company had put out a bounty, and that would be enough.

He glanced at his watch and drew rein. "That ought to be far enough." He pointed toward the creek. "I figure we can cross here. We'll look it over careful first and pick our spot. Then we'll skirt the ridge till we find a cut." He smiled at the women. "I don't reckon you'll have to swim."

They walked the horses to the edge of Sutter Creek and looked at the water. The fog was lifted there and moved over its surface like a ghost over a large slithering serpent. The airy ooze floated down the valley while underneath it the creek's surface shone and ran on ahead.

"It's moving pretty shallow here, this'll do," Zac said. They moved out into the creek, and the women held their feet out away from the horses, trying to keep them dry. Zac looked back, amused. He thought Jenny and Emily looked like sea gulls drifting in the breeze with their legs standing out from the stirrups. The women shifted themselves in the saddle, trying to keep their balance without the benefit of their legs clinging to the horses' sides.

The horses plunged into the water and down a hole that allowed the current to lick the animals' bellies. The women straightened their legs out, lifting them even higher, managing to keep their heels above the stream only with great effort.

The horses lunged up the bank and Zac let the mare begin to pick her way through the trees. He turned her with his knees ever so slightly and headed up the hill. Their visibility was not good, but they were moving in the right direction. Twisted oaks loomed out of the mist and their rough, hard limbs seemed to reach out for the group, trying to grab for their faces and eyes.

They rode on uphill in silence, their horses straining and jumping. The three of them rode in silence, lost in their own thoughts about what the day would hold. Everything depended on this day, and they all knew it. There was no tomorrow.

More sobering was the fact that Judge Harkness, Breaker Morgan, and Toby Summers were thinking the same thoughts. Today meant all the difference for the Whitewater mine thieves and for any of the nightriders who had ridden with them. They might never know who they all were, but one thing was certain, they would be well sprinkled throughout the crowd today.

The three climbed the hill that reached above the fog, and the sunshine was filtering through a gray overcast sky.

"Well, down there somewhere is the Fiddletown-Plymouth road," Zac said. "We ought to deadhead right into it. When we do, we'll head back to Volcano."

He swiveled back in the saddle and looked at the women. "Before the fight starts, I got to make sure Hattie has been found not guilty and that new charges can't be brought. I'm also going to get both of you a ticket out of here to Jackson and then on to Placerville and Sacramento. The only thing they're interested in is the fight. If Breaker wins, then more'n likely, what happens to you two won't make much difference. They'll have what they want and have some time too. 'Course, you need to be on that stage and gone. There's one that comes in from Plymouth and Fiddletown this morning. You'll need to be on it, making for Jackson when it leaves."

They hit the well-traveled Fiddletown road about an hour later, and Zac pulled out his watch and checked the time. A quarter past ten. *The trial should be underway*, he thought.

They hadn't been on the road for Volcano for more than twenty minutes when they heard the sound of the stagecoach. Right away Zac knew something was wrong. The noise of the six-horse team and the chain traces showed that it was a vehicle in a hurry, not a runaway, just in a hurry.

Careening around a curve in the road, Zac could see that it

was taking the bend on two wheels. He shooed the two women back and fired his gun in the air. Several shots and his raised hand started the coach into a skidding stop. The driver had been swinging his whip but had put it down into the box and was pulling on the reins with all his might.

"Hooooold . . . Hold up there. Whoa, you carn sarn things. Whoooooa."

Zac pulled his Wells Fargo Special Agent badge out of his pocket and held it above his head. He saw the shotgun messenger on the box, holding his arm. "What's the big hurry?" he asked.

"Just got held up back there. There was five of 'em, not six miles back. They shot Jimmy here in the shoulder. Mighta killed us. They got my strongbox and we lit outta there."

"You bleedin' bad?"

"Nah, I think I got it stopped. We'ze just trying to get there and get a posse out after them fellas fast-like."

"Six miles back?" Zac asked.

"Yeah," the shotgun messenger volunteered. "They wuz sittin' by the side of the road and openin' the box like they had all day when we lit out."

The driver pushed his sloppy hat off his head and left the chin strap taut around his red neck. "They's there all right, but I wouldn't go back there all by yourself. They look to be pretty desperate men."

"Got any passengers?"

"Naw, we were empty," the driver said, " 'cept for the strongbox and the mail. They didn't take the mail."

"Well, if you got Jimmy's bleedin' stopped, then I'd like you to set right still here till I get back. Right now, I'm a pretty desperate man, too."

He turned to the women. "Ladies, if you'd like to look after Jimmy's arm, I won't be long."

"No," Jenny said. "I'm not letting you out of my sight, not until all this is finished. Emily, you can mind the man here." She reached out to Zac's bedroll and pulled the ten-gauge out of its moorings. "I'm going to ride along with you. I'm tired of watching everything happen to me. I'm going to make something happen myself for a change."

Zac didn't say a word. He'd seen that look in her eyes before. He touched his spurs to the mare and sent the animal tearing down the road with Jenny slapping her horse's withers with her reins. They both cut through the settling dust and sent the sparks flying from their horses' hooves.

Minutes later, Zac put out his hand and drew her to a halt beside him. "We go slow from here," he said. "I'm circling around and staying to the north side of the road. I'd like you in the trees to the south. When you hear me call out, fire one shot in the air and come out of the trees prepared to use the other. Understand?"

She nodded in the affirmative, and he pulled on the mare's reins and disappeared behind the brush on the far side of Fiddletown road. Within a matter of fifteen minutes, Zac heard the men talking alongside the road. He moved the horse quietly through the trees and dismounted. Looping the reins near the base of an oak, he drew his Peacemaker and filled his other hand with the little Shopkeeper special.

"Looky that! You ever see such a sight?" One of the men had ripped open a bag of freshly minted gold coins and was spilling it onto a blanket on the ground.

Zac moved through the brush quietly. He counted them. *One . . . two . . . three . . . four . . .* Peering his head around he saw another standing on the road keeping watch. *Five.* He moved silently to his left. He knew he had to be able to put his sights on all of them at the same time.

"Hurry up!" The man on the road was getting a little impatient. He walked back to the main group surrounding the blanket. "Split that up into five piles and let's get. We don't know who's coming up this road."

"Ah, shut yer trap!" one of the men on his knees with his back toward Zac roared back. "We ain't got nuthin' to worry about. Yer like an old lady. Summers done told us they'd take a while to get a posse together. 'Sides, we got to split this stuff up in order to carry it, and we got some fresh horses waitin' for us other side of the crossin'."

Zac cocked the hammers back on both guns. "That's far enough!" he shouted. "Special agent for Wells Fargo. Don't scratch, don't move, or I'll kill you where you stand."

The men froze and the man who had been keeping watch on the road dropped the cigarette butt out of his mouth. "Cobb," he said. "It's that Zac Cobb feller."

Zac yelled out. "Posse! Posse!" His cries were followed by a single blast from across the road. "Now," Zac said, "unbuckle those gun belts and let 'em drop, and you'll get to see another sunrise. Otherwise, breathe your last."

The men quickly complied. They rose up tall and allowed the guns to drop to the ground.

"Stand away from them," Zac said. "Put those hands up and back up there on the road."

The men backed away from him and stood with their hands raised. Several swiveled their heads and showed surprise when Jenny rode her horse through the trees.

"She's got one more load in that thing, and, gentlemen, the lady is feelin' so ornery today, I can guarantee you she'd use it."

✦ ✦ ✦ ✦ ✦

Zac pulled up outside the Jug and Rose and tied the bay to the hitching rail. He looked down the street a few yards and saw barrels that had been placed in a square. Ropes were strung between them, and straw had been scattered around the makeshift prizefighting ring. He saw that the ring was located directly under the judge's balcony and near the corner of the St. George. He checked his watch. It was 1:25. Pushing aside the batwing doors, he stepped inside.

The place was jammed. People stood everywhere, and the bar was filled with people who were sitting on top of it and riveting their eyes toward the far end of the room. There, placed on an elevated riser that usually served as a stage for Delia and the other dancing girls, sat Judge Ruben Harkness. He quickly spotted Zac.

"Well, well, well, if it isn't our illustrious challenger," he called out.

Every head spun in Zac's direction.

"Zachary Taylor Cobb," Hattie squawked out, "you're a durn fool fer a relative. I don't need yer help no ways."

"You see, Marshal," the judge looked over at the big man seated next to the witness box, "our man isn't one to go back on a wager. He's here for our fight. First, however, we'll have to dispense with this trial."

"Excuse me, your honor," Zac said. "There's been some trouble on the Fiddletown road."

Both the judge and Marshal Morgan cast looks at each other. Zac could see the surprise in their eyes even before he announced the reason for his news.

"The stage has been held up and people have been hurt," he said.

Harkness and Morgan seemed unsure of themselves, but the judge broke the silence. "How'd you hear this, Cobb?"

"I saw the stage on the road before I came riding into town."

"Well, we'll have to get a posse after them boys," he said, shooting a look at Morgan. "Whoever they are."

Standing up, he addressed the crowd. "Now, men, we need your help. You'll have to furnish your own guns and horses, but the marshal here will be glad to give out ammunition and give your animals a good feed when you get back. You will do that, won't you, Marshal Morgan?"

"Yeah, sure I will."

There followed a mumbling in the crowd and a great deal of talking back and forth among the men in the room.

Harkness looked at Marshal Frazier. "Marshal, I'm afraid you'll have to lead this expedition. Morgan here is the town marshal, and as you've said to me repeatedly, he has no jurisdictional authority outside of the city limits. Besides, he's a material witness in this pending trial, and I need him right here."

Frazier got up and shot a glance back at Zac, one which was returned by a smile.

Harkness went on. "Marshal Frazier, I'm sure the county

sheriff would be glad to assist you should you require it, but I'm afraid that the trail might be cold when you return with him from Jackson."

One of the men in the crowd rose to his feet. "Judge, the boys here ain't got no hankering atall to run off on some wild goose horse ride. We all showed up to see this here fight we been a hearing about."

"Yeah, yeah! Yer durn tootin'!" There was general agreement among the men in the room.

Frazier walked to the back of the room and stood next to Zac. "I'll be leaving in five minutes. Any man who wishes to join me can meet me in the street." He turned to Zac and spoke in a low voice. "I hope you know what you're doing, son." The noise of the crowded room and the resulting general conversation that had broken out successfully masked the words that passed from Marshal Frazier to Zac.

Zac turned to him and spoke in a murmur. "Marshal, this promises to be one of the best days of your professional career, believe me."

Frazier had a puzzled look across his face.

Zac went on. "Just one thing," he dropped his voice even lower. "Whatever happens, get yourself back into town as soon as you can. I can't say how long I'll be able to hold this boy off."

The lawman's face still seemed bewildered when he turned and walked out the door. The judge pounded on the table with his gavel. "Order!" he shouted. "This is still a court of law. I want order so we can get on with the matter at hand."

The men rearranged the chairs and got back in their seats when the judge turned to Hattie. "Now, Mrs. Woodruff, it's your allegation that Deputy Evers tried to molest you, and you shot the man in self-defense."

There were snickers in the crowd and Hattie got to her feet. "That's right, your lordship." Hattie was in her glory now. All eyes were on her, and she turned back to sneak a glance at the crowd. "Bein' a fine figger of a woman, which is all-fired rare in these parts . . ." She swiveled her hips and a ripple of laughter went through the room. Hattie raised her voice. "He com-

menced to force his affections upon me and I up and shot him."
The laughter grew and Hattie raised her voice still louder. "Because, no matter what else I is, I is—a virtuous woman."

Men began to loudly roar and others howled and slapped
their knees. The judge banged his gavel on the table and, losing
all hope of gathering order, picked up a pistol and fired two deliberate shots into the ceiling.

"That's enough, by golly, that's enough."

Men were still shaking with laughter in their chairs, and the
ones who had quit laughing out loud were now wiping the tears
out of their eyes or holding their sides. The judge now stood facing Hattie with both hands outstretched on the table.

"Hattie Woodruff," he said, "in view of your testimony"—
he craned his neck around the room—"and in view of the ab-
sence of contradictory witnesses, I am forced to declare you not
guilty, by reason of self-defense."

Shouts erupted from the room and laughter once again
roared through the building.

Hattie turned to the group of men sniggering at the bar. "You
boys buy me a drink and we'll toast to Deputy Evers' ill health."

The judge shouted for all to hear. "Don't forget, folks, we
have a fight. It will commence in the street in ten minutes."

"That'll be plenty a time to get drunk," one man shouted.

CHAPTER 29

+ + + + + + +

ZAC WALKED OUT of the Jug and Rose barely ahead of the crowd that surged through the door. A few men had already found choice seats around the ropes and seated themselves on the wooden sidewalks. Stepping aside, he witnessed the mad scramble for position. He looked up the street and watched Marshal Frazier ride out of town, accompanied by two men, both craning their necks around and looking somewhat regretful of the spectacle they were about to miss.

Several members of one of the town's debating societies had begun to argue the merits of "human fisticuffs" as a means of settling arguments. They had erected a banner near the Wells Fargo office across the street and were standing beneath it, going "cheek by jowl" over the merits of their arguments.

The people clapped their hands vigorously when the shorter, bareheaded man defended the manly sport. When the more somber-looking man in the dark suit and top hat rose to attack the prizefight, calling it a "prime exhibit to the demise of civilization," loud hisses and boos accompanied him. He paid no mind to the sentiment of the growing crowd. He only hitched his pants up higher and continued to decry the "animalistic influence of boxing and the scandalous reporting on the subject by the *Police Gazette*."

Breaker Morgan soon joined him on the sidewalk. He loosened his shirt and grinned. "Surprised you showed up, Cobb. I thought I was going to have to hunt you down."

Zac smiled. "That's funny, Turner. That's just what I was

gonna say to you." He watched the marshal blanch at the sound of his given name and then turn red. Zac left him there, angry and speechless, and walked across the street in the direction of the Wells Fargo office. Just then he saw Jenny and Emily ride into town. They looked worried.

Zac walked toward the other side of the ring and pulled off his shirt. He watched the women tie their horses and join the gathering mob. They both filtered their way through the people and stepped onto the sidewalk behind Zac. Several men weaved their way throughout the crowd, giving odds on the fight and feverishly taking bets from the bystanders.

Emily stood beside Jenny and put her arm around her. "It's going to be all right, honey, I know it will." She looked up at the balcony and saw Judge Harkness take his seat on the rocking chair and take out a cigar to light. He caught her eye and tipped his hat.

It was when she lowered her eyes that she saw Toby Summers. He made his way from the back of the Jug and Rose, where the judge's office was located, and was scurrying toward the back of the St. George with a rifle in his hand. *Why isn't he staying for the fight?* she wondered.

"Excuse me," she said to Jenny. "I got to see about something. You stay right here and I'll be back. These things don't start until the last dollar is bet."

Emily worked her way through the crowd and, passing beneath the judge's balcony, cut through the passageway toward the back door of the St. George. She opened it and stepped into the kitchen. Pots were steaming on the stove, but the entire place seemed to be deserted. She thought that natural, what with the fight about to take place in the street.

Every able-bodied man and most of the women in town were watching. She knew there was no love lost between the town and her brother. Most of the people in Volcano hated Breaker, and that included her. He had bullied his way into their lives with that star of his, and Zac had been the first man who'd stood up to him. Deep down she knew that almost every man who had placed a bet outside on Breaker wanted Zac to win. That way, no matter what happened, they'd be the better for it.

She walked around the empty dining room tables. Empty, that was, except for old Mr. Massey, who sat cutting a steak into little pieces in the corner. He loved steak, even though he had no teeth. Many times she had watched him take the tiny slivers of meat and gum them for what seemed like hours before swallowing. He never even raised his head from his plate when she walked by.

She had rounded the corner that led into the lobby of the hotel when a hand reached out and grabbed her, spinning her around. It was Delia Odum. "Well, well, if it isn't little miss holy drawers. Now what mission of mercy are you on today? Got yourself a man you're here to service?"

"Delia, I've got no time for you now. Let me go."

The woman only dug her claws in harder. "Not till you answer me, I won't. You came to me with those doe eyes and all those speeches of yours about gaining power over men." She tossed her black hair. "You had me going. You really put one over on Delia. But I guess that's to be expected. I know men and their lies. I guess I'm just finding out about formerly righteous women."

Emily jerked her arm free. "I got no time for this."

Delia smiled. "You looking for Toby Summers?"

Emily gawked at her and swallowed.

"Well, if you are, I know where he went."

"Where?"

"Oh, now you want more information from me. Will that make you nice to me? Can I just be one of the ladies of Volcano to you, or do I have to stay one of the daughters of joy?"

"Delia, this is important. I know that man's going to do something. I know it just as sure as I'm standing here."

"You can be sure of that," Delia said. "If that Cobb fella wins the fight, he won't last long. Not that I mind that. I know where my cream comes from, and it doesn't come from you or any of that righteous goody-goody bunch you set such store by."

Emily took Delia with both hands. "Don't you know that everything you've been passing on to Harkness and my brother, they've been using to hang innocent men?"

Delia shook Emily's hands off of her shoulders. "There are no innocent men. There are only men with and men without money. I prefer the men with money, that's all."

"How you can let that old judge put his hands on you is something I'll never understand."

Delia held her hand up and rubbed her fingers together. "Money, girl, that's what it's all about, money. What I don't understand is how you can turn against your own brother, your own flesh and blood."

Emily jerked down the shoulder and sleeve of her dress and showed Delia a portion of her scarred back. "See this? This is my brother—my brother and my father. My flesh and blood did this to me."

"I've seen lots worse than that," Delia said. "Wanna know where?"

Emily gawked at her and pushed her sleeve back on top of her shoulder.

"Your brother's back, that's where. He carries scars on his back like nothing I've ever seen before."

"My father," Emily said.

"Well, missy, a mule can only pull with the harness he's in. He's like he is, same as you. You may think you're so different, but inside you're both the same. You're hard, spiteful, and mean, same as him. Only thing is, he's more honest about it. He hates a person out in the open."

Emily stepped back. What Delia had said startled her. She pushed her hair back and tried to look composed, but the truth of the statement ripped into her soul. "Even if you're right," she said, "it doesn't make what's going to happen out there any easier to abide."

"You don't care what's going to happen out there," Delia said. "You just want Breaker to lose, you don't really care who wins."

"Where is Toby Summers?"

Delia put her fingers back up in Emily's face and rubbed them together. "Money, girl, it takes money. See, I don't care who wins, either, I just want the money."

Emily poked her hand into her apron pocket and pulled out a wad of bills. "Here, take that. Fifty dollars. It's my traveling money. Now where is he?"

Delia counted the money slowly and smiled. "Okay." She pushed the bills into her blouse and looked up the stairs." Toby's up there, in 219. It's the corner room where he can get a good shot if he needs to."

Emily ran to the counter of the hotel and went behind the desk.

"Although, personally, I don't think he'll need to," Delia added. "That Mr. Cobb is good with guns, but Breaker will kill him with his hands."

Emily picked up the Greener twelve-gauge shotgun from behind the desk and fumbled in the cigar box behind the counter for some shells. Breaking the weapon open, she dropped two loads into the chambers and snapped the gun shut.

She rounded the counter and, going to the bottom of the stairs, looked back at Delia.

"Don't worry 'bout me, miss holy drawers. I'm just going to saunter around outside and see if there's any more money to be made. What with the men out there all getting their blood boiled up, I'm sure I'll turn a sweet little profit somewhere." She laughed. "I love sportin' men, I declare, I surely do."

+ + + + +

Summers had moved the bed from the middle of the room over to the corner window. He removed his hat and laid it on top of the bedspread. He watched the betting take place below with some amusement and thought about how good it would feel to be able to put Cobb away. Morgan wouldn't like it, he knew that. But he'd only shoot if it was necessary. He'd shoot and then just stroll down the hall and look for the killer, like any lawman should do. It would be the easiest shot he ever made, and the most satisfying.

Several times he glanced out the side window at Harkness, smoking a cigar in his rocking chair. The man was cool, he had to hand him that. No matter what happened, he'd win. He'd get the whole creekside valley, with Cobb out of the way, and the old lady's mine to boot.

He flattened out a paper for his tobacco and sprinkled a little of it on top. Rolling it, he licked the paper and stuck the sides together, pinching off the ends. He raked a match on the floor and poked it to the edge of the mixture, igniting it. He checked his chamber and sighted down the barrel at the arena below him. He could see it all.

Laying the rifle on the bed, he inhaled deeply. When it was over, he'd take the old lady to the livery and take care of her there. He knew she'd put up a fuss and more'n likely go to her Maker kicking at the air, but when it was over, she'd be dead all the same. She'd be dead, and he'd be a lot richer. Maybe then he'd join the boys in Virginia City after all. He'd hit the town and see the elephant.

He heard the doorknob turn and started to bawl out whoever had come in, when he saw the muzzle of the shotgun. Even from across the room, it looked huge. The cigarette dropped from his mouth and onto the carpeted floor.

"Get up," she said. "Get up and stamp that thing out. We don't want no fires in here."

"Miss Emily, what you doing here?" He scrambled to his feet and began patting out the smoldering cigarette.

"I'm here to see that you don't interfere with that fight down there. Now step aside from that bed and shuck that six-gun of yours."

He slowly moved aside and reached for the buckle on his holster. "Miss Emily, don't be doing what you're doing. Some people are going to be powerful mad with you, and I don't think you being Breaker's sister and all will do you much good."

She cocked the heavy hammers on the gun, which she had forgotten to do earlier. Its sound made a definite impression on the deputy.

"Here now, what you gonna do with that?"

"Toby Summers, I'm gonna do to you what you did to Tom."

"Now wait, see here." He raised his hands high. "I'll cooperate; I'll do what you want me to do."

"Come on out here in this hall, and you come real slow and easy-like."

Summers moved slowly out into the hall and Emily backed up, keeping the shotgun trained on him. "Having you framed in this narrow hallway," she said, "I ain't about to miss."

Sweat beads began to form around the edges of the deputy's mouth. He licked his lips. "Just you watch yourself with that thing, ya hear?" He moved backward, keeping his eyes on her and the gun.

"One thing, Toby," she said. "Did my brother order you to hang Tom Whipple? Did he know you were going to do that?"

He grimaced, the corners of his eyes narrowing, and he once again licked his upper lip. "Now, Miss Emily, afore I say anything about that business, would you do something for me?"

"What?"

"Just take your finger off the trigger there. Me telling you might make you nervous or hot tempered and them little fingers of yours might accidentally tighten up or something. I wouldn't want that to happen." He gulped. "You can keep your finger around the trigger guard and I won't move a muscle. I'd just prefer they weren't touchin' the trigger, that's all."

She loosened her grip and pulled her finger out of the trigger guard. "So help me, Toby, if you move or if I don't think I'm hearing the truth, then I'll kill you right where you stand. I got nothing to lose, I don't care anymore. You understand that?"

"Yes, ma'am, I understand. I know you mean what you say, too. I've always respected you for that, Miss Emily."

"Go on then," she said.

"Well, ma'am, to answer your question honest-like, I don't think your brother knew a thing till afterward. I got my orders directly from Judge Harkness. In fact the judge, he told me directly not to say anything to your brother, you being engaged to Whipple and all. Personally, I don't think the judge trusts your brother all the way."

Emily's eyes dropped. "That's the truth?" Her voice quivered slightly.

"Yes, ma'am, that's the gospel sure 'nuf. I did leave one thing out, though, about that night."

"What's that?" she asked.

"Well, it's kinda shameful, I guess, but I think you ought to hear it." He paused and hung his head. "Your man, Tom, Tom Whipple, he told me to tell you that he loved you. Miss Emily, you were in his last thoughts. I know how that must grieve you, and I know I did wrong."

Anger flashed across her face and her finger went back on the trigger. "You people are all alike."

His face went white and he backed up a step.

"You're sorry." A sneer creased her lips. "You all say you're sorry, but the facts are, you're not sorry when you do these things, you're just sorry when you're caught."

"Please, Miss Emily, don't kill me! I told you the truth. You can believe it or not, but that's the gospel truth, it is."

"No, I won't kill you, Toby Summers. I'd like to, but I won't, not unless you force me to."

"Oh no, ma'am, I won't do that."

"All right then. We're both going downstairs to the storage closet. I'm gonna lock you in there till this thing's over, and then you can face whatever happens along with the rest of us."

CHAPTER 30

✦ ✦ ✦ ✦ ✦ ✦ ✦

THE CROWD WAS BEING ENTERTAINED by a juggler, while the men who were posting bets were busy scratching down the names of those who had now taken a good look at Zac's well-muscled body and glanced over the enormous size of Marshal Breaker Morgan. Morgan still had his shirt on. He had pulled it out of his trousers, and it hung like a gigantic tent over his massive chest.

Even the casual observer could see the fire in the marshal's eyes. He stood at one corner of the makeshift ring and glared at Zac. The wounds on Zac's body were clearly visible. At least one of them dated from the War Between the States, and the rest of them came from scrapes earned in the service of Wells Fargo. Zac wasn't a gunslinger. Many men he'd faced had successfully gotten off a first shot, but never the last.

Doc Lewis had elbowed his way through the crowd and stood at Zac's side. "What the blazes are you doing here? You can't fight that man, not in your condition. I'm going to call this thing off."

"Doc, you can't do that. The die's been cast. I couldn't back out of this thing if I wanted to." He pointed his chin at the crowd. "Those folks out there would get out of control. With all the money they've got down on this thing, they'd more than likely leave me gurgling underneath a four-hand knot."

"Well, that's a maybe," Lewis said, "but what's for darn sure is, if you fight Morgan over there, he's gonna kill you."

Zac looked Lewis in the eye. "I've hooked horns with bigger

257

men than that." He looked over at Morgan. "He's just got size, that's all, soft size. Probably's only bashed the heads of a few drunks these last few years and survives on his reputation."

He smiled. "One of my best friends is a fella that's taught me a bunch about fightin'. He's the sheriff in San Luis Obispo, and he's every bit as big as Morgan over there. He's not as big around, but he's taller and in a whole lot better shape."

"I don't think you understand, Cobb. That wound of yours just ain't healed yet. You could seize up anytime you move around, and when that man gets you in his grip, I don't think even I could help you."

Zac blinked at the man and looked him in the eyes. "Thanks, Doc, for all the help you've been already, and for the warning, but this has got to happen."

"All right, all right. Can't say as it'll do much good, but if things get too much outta hand, I'll try to stop the thing. Nobody'll listen, but I'll try."

"Thanks, Doc."

Every head went up when a shot was fired from the balcony of the judge's office. He held the small revolver in his hand and continued to chomp on his cigar. "All right, all bets are down. We're gonna commence this fight."

A cheer went up from the crowd and numerous hats flew into the air. The small brass band that Volcano boasted burst into a rendition of "Yankee Doodle Dandy," and more cheers rose from the crowd. The judge fired a second shot, and then a third.

"Enough!" he yelled. "That's enough. Now we're going to start. This will be a fight to the finish." Numerous "ohs" came from members of the crowd. "The rounds will last ten minutes each. I'll end each round with a shot. Now, I only got three more shots. 'Course, I don't expect this to go that long."

There was laughter in the crowd and Morgan beamed. "But if it should go longer," Harkness went on, "then I'll reload, don't worry about that. Okay, you men, mix it up. Give these miners out here a real good fight."

Emily had made her way out of the hotel and stood at the

back of the crowd under the judge's balcony. She watched as the two men approached each other and began to circle.

Morgan lunged for Zac, who quickly stepped aside and left the big man grabbing at midair and stumbling forward. Sniggers rippled through the crowd. The marshal quickly swiveled around and started back toward Cobb.

"Where you going? You gonna run from me?" He grabbed out for Zac, who once again stepped aside, this time landing a punch on the big man's jaw. It rocked the marshal's head, snapping it sideways."

Breaker stood still and blinked. Several men near the ring pointed at him and one laughed. He grimaced. Holding out his hands, he stretched out his long arms and moved slowly toward Zac. He wasn't trying to move fast anymore, just with deliberation. He had a bigger reach than Zac, and he was determined to use every advantage that he could.

He lashed out with a left and caught Zac on the jaw, then followed through with a right to Zac's ribs. Zac felt his air give way slightly; dizzy, he stumbled backward.

Morgan paused for a moment and looked at the men in the front row, who had appeared to be taunting him. He was a man of great pride, and to be laughed at was something that galled him. "You're next," he said, pointing at one of the men. Morgan didn't see him coming, but Zac sent a hard right hand into the marshal's midsection. Stepping in between the big man's arms, he pounded away at Morgan's belly.

It was soft and ample, just like he'd suspected. Zac surmised it was why the man had neglected to take off his shirt. He didn't want to show how out of shape he really was. Morgan had won every fight he'd been in since he'd come to manhood, but now Zac was determined to take advantage of his own superior speed and condition and make sure the big man wouldn't walk away from this one.

Morgan's belly gave way to the punches that Zac was sending below his ribs, and Zac could see the look of surprise in the big man's eyes as he stepped closer and intensified the blows. Perhaps deep down Morgan knew that his time was up.

Squeezing in between the men who were standing in front of her, Emily pressed herself closer to the ring. She'd never seen the look in her brother's eyes that she was seeing now. He was in pain, and she thought she saw a look that spelled fear as well. Across the ring, Jenny's eyes showed her anguish. She knew how Jenny was feeling, but now Emily was feeling something else, something she'd never felt before—pity, pity for a brother she had hated.

Zac threw a roundhouse punch that landed on Morgan's jaw, snapping his head around and making him stagger on his feet. The punches to the gut had started to take their toll. Morgan knew he had to do something and do it fast; otherwise, he might not make it to the first gunshot.

He knew that Summers would kill Zac if anything went wrong, but he also knew that some of the respect and fear that he'd cultivated in the town would disappear, never to return. He was being embarrassed and he knew it. It was something he hadn't known since he was a boy.

He reached out and lurched forward, grabbing Zac around the waist. He began to squeeze. Locking his hands behind Zac's waist, he pulled with a jerk and tightened his grip. "Now," he said, "now it's time for my kinda fightin'." He jerked Zac and, lifting him off the ground, slammed him back into the dirt with a thud.

Zac rolled over and arched his back. The pain from his wound was knifing into him now, doubling him up. He closed his eyes as his head began to spin.

Morgan reached down and grabbed him, lifting him up. Belly to belly, he held him and began a slow squeeze. Zac's face was against Morgan's now, and he heard the big man grunt loudly as he pressed. "I'm gonna kill you now—kill you, or turn you into a cripple." He squeezed harder. Zac felt the bones in his rib cage give and his spine start to torque. The pain was fierce.

He moved his arm under the marshal's chin and began to work at prying the big man's head back. He knew this was it. If he couldn't free himself from Breaker's grasp and do it right now, the best he could hope for would be crutches.

Neither man was hearing the crowd. They were both totally focused on one thing, the deathlike grip that Morgan was maintaining and Zac's own attempt to push the marshal's head back to loosen that hold.

Zac pushed Morgan's chin back with his left hand. The strain on his back was intense. The pain had returned now, and he was feeling faint. He blinked back the tears in his eyes and with all his might sent a blow with his right fist into Morgan's neck. The first punch startled him, but didn't loosen his grip. Zac sent several more chops into the marshal's Adam's apple and finally felt the death embrace loosen.

He hit Morgan again, and then again. Finally, the big man dropped Zac to the ground and held his throat. Zac rolled over and began panting for breath on the ground. He could barely move, and the pain was racing through the length of his body like a freight train on a downhill run.

Morgan had shaken off the effects of the punches to his throat and now stepped forward and cranked back, unleashing a kick that made Zac's side cave in with agony.

The crowd gasped at the sound the kick made and, turning their heads to one another, stared first at each other and then back at the men in the ring. They were silent, but each suspected that the fight was almost over.

Morgan kicked him again, harder this time, and Zac let out a cry of pain. He clutched his sides. Sending his leg back, Morgan prepared for yet another devastating blow. Zac found the strength, however, to turn over as the big man brought his boot forward, and the blow glanced off his side.

Running forward, Morgan left his feet and headed shoulder first for Zac's prone body. Again Zac rolled, sending his attacker to the turf with a crash that brought the crowd to its feet. Some laughed, and Zac got to his feet as a number of the men slapped their knees and howled with approval.

Morgan had thrown himself to the ground for nothing. What moments before had appeared to be the final blow had proved to provoke a growing number of the crowd with amusement. He got to his hands and knees and watched the crowd laugh. Hearing the laughter made him wonder. Why was he doing this? Why was he being Harkness's clown, being laughed at to make another man rich?

Zac was still dazed and Morgan stumbled to his feet. He reeled and got off several swift blows to Zac's head, rapping his head backward and creating a trickle of blood at the corner of Zac's mouth. Stepping into him, Morgan landed repeated unre-turned punches to Zac's midsection, and Zac found himself draped over the marshal's shoulders as the man continued to hit him in the stomach.

The pain now knifed into Zac's back. He'd been waiting for it. He was surprised it hadn't happened before now, but it froze him, helpless and limp. Zac grabbed onto the marshal's shirt to hold himself up, but slipped to the ground, tearing the home-spun cloth off of the big lawman's back.

The crowd gasped. Across Morgan's back were the track marks of a well-placed bullwhip. They crisscrossed his backside at every angle and were angry and red. Anyone who had ever seen a whipping knew that these were the marks of a man who had lost a lot of blood during many a severe beating.

Emily stepped forward, closer to the ring, and looked at the scars on her brother's back. She could tell from the marks that Breaker had suffered through numerous whippings as a boy. She hadn't seen his back since they were children, and now the sting on her own back made her feel closer to the man she had hated, closer to him and sorry for him.

She watched the people point and stare. It was as if the Hunchback of Notre Dame had been unmasked in front of the whole town and they didn't know what to do. The man who frightened them the most was obviously someone who had been bested before—bested many times, in fact. And now, he was be-ing challenged again. Standing there, exposed, they could all see the life go out of him—his pride, the only thing he had.

Breaker stood there before the crowd feeling naked and ashamed. It was as if he were ten years old again, ten years old and just whipped by his father. He looked up at the judge on the balcony and felt anger surge through him when he realized the man was eyeing him with disgust.

Zac took advantage of the marshal's embarrassment and, stepping into him, delivered an upper cut to the chin that rocked the big man. Zac could see Morgan's knees wobble. He had to get him now, had to bring this thing to a finish.

Zac began a series of punches back to Morgan's middle that drove him backward, step by step, toward the ropes. Each blow jerked Morgan's body, and although he stayed on his feet, he stumbled backward. Deep down inside, the marshal knew he had little left to give. He was out of steam and he knew it. Zac came on, moving forward, swinging hard now from behind his waist and up into the lawman's belly.

Zac was calm now. He could see the look of surrender written all over the marshal. He was a beaten man, looking for somewhere to drop. Standing still, Zac took aim and sent a right hand solidly into the side of Morgan's skull. The blow staggered the big man and he sank to his knees beside the ropes.

The shot roared out from atop the balcony. "That's time, that's ten minutes. Stop your fighting."

Emily ducked down beneath the ropes and was beside her brother. She put her arms around him and lightly fingered the scars on his back. "I'm sorry," she said. "I didn't know Papa had been that hard on you, too."

Morgan simply stared at her through the blood running out a cut that had opened up on one of his eyes. It trickled down his cheek and into the corner of his mouth, where he could taste its salt.

She lifted a cup of water to his lips and he drank. "Look at these people," she said. "They don't care about you. You don't have any friends in this town. You're just a bet to them. You're being used."

She looked up at the judge sitting on his balcony and Breaker's eyes followed hers. "He's the one that's using you the most, killing innocent people and using you to do the dirty work while he gets the money. He's just like Papa."

When Emily said that, Breaker's eyes flashed with fire. The

judge was looking down on him and smoking his cigar. He recognized the look. He was being used, and Harkness was Papa all over again. He looked at Emily. "I swore that would never happen to me again."

"But it is happening again," Emily said. "And that man up there is doing it."

Morgan staggered to his feet and saw the crowd staring at him. They had begun to talk back and forth to each other, and he could see the anger in their faces. They were no longer afraid of him. In fact, he felt a certain amount of fear toward them.

He raised his head and saw Zac; Jenny was wiping the blood from around his mouth. Looking up once again, he noticed Judge Harkness lighting another cigar and looking toward the corner window of the St. George.

He stumbled over toward Zac. His ribs were on fire now and all the wind was gone out of him. He blinked back the blood from his eyes. He knew that if he had to fight another round, he wouldn't last. His voice was low and subdued. "I ain't gonna fight you no more. You done whipped me fair and square."

He looked back toward the judge on the balcony. "You watch that man, Cobb. He's got a shooter in the St. George. Toby Summers. If you beat me, Toby's suppose to kill you."

He turned his head and looked back up at the judge. The gray-haired man was staring at his watch now and cocking his revolver to announce the new round. Harkness looked down at Zac and the marshal. "Gentlemen, are you ready to fight? So far you haven't shown me much. There is lots of money riding on this thing, and I for one hope you'll both put on a better show for these good folks."

Jenny and Zac stood stunned as Morgan walked toward his sister in the ring. He stood there for a moment and looked at her. "I'm sorry about Whipple," he said. "I didn't have anything to do with it. I want you to know that."

"I know," she said.

"I hope you won't go on hating me forever," he said.

"No, I won't. Whatever else you've done, you're still my brother."

As he turned on his heels and walked toward the Jug and Rose, the crowd was so shocked they barely noticed the stage-coach as it rolled down the hill and onto the street. It pulled up at the edge of the crowd and behind it were Marshal Frazier and the tiny posse that had ridden out with him, along with the gang of men who had robbed the coach earlier in the day.

Zac kept his eye trained on the windows of the St. George and, taking Jenny's arm, moved her toward the overhang on the far sidewalk.

"What's wrong?" she asked.

"This crowd don't look too friendly, and if there's a shooter up there and there's gonna be some gunplay," he said, "I don't want you nowheres near me."

Frazier guided his horse toward the edge of the crowd, with one of the bandits tied up and in tow.

"All right, listen up, you men. I'm here to place"—he looked up at the balcony where Harkness was now leaning forward on his rocking chair—"Judge Ruben Harkness and Marshals Brea-ker Morgan and Toby Summers under arrest. The charge is con-spiracy to murder and rob the stage lines. These men here, who you all know, will testify to that fact."

The crowd at first seemed confused, but then turned angry. They mixed around the marshal and began to try to pull the hold-up man who was seated alongside him down from his sad-dle.

"Here now," Frazier said, "back off, that's enough." Frazier lifted his boot from the stirrup and kicked one of the crowd onto the ground.

"What makes you believe these hooligans?" Harkness stood at the balcony with his revolver. "You caught them red-handed and they just made up this cockamamie story to get off. You can't believe riffraff like that."

The crowd was beginning to form around the bottom of the judge's balcony and hurl insults at him, along with taunts. "We believe 'em, Ruben, your honor, high-and-mighty." Another miner shouted from the back of the crowd. "You done got the claims of friends of mine you hung, and now we're gonna hang you."

From below the balcony, the ringing sound of Hattie Woodruff's voice sounded out. She shook her finger at him. "You done made a deal with the devil, you twisted Yankee wolf. Now you're a gwine to see him."

The crowd stood back and watched. From behind the judge, Breaker Morgan walked out onto the balcony. Just the look in the man's eye made Harkness retreat and put his back to the balcony rail.

"Them boys is right," Breaker shouted. He kept his eyes riveted on the judge while he yelled down at the crowd. "We done it all right, we done everything. Harkness paid us, but we done it—Roman Evers, Toby Summers, and me."

Harkness pointed the gun at Morgan's midsection and pulled the trigger. The smoke clouded the balcony and the marshal staggered slightly.

"Get him, Breaker," the mob shouted. "Get him and throw him down."

With that, Morgan took Harkness's arm and shook the gun free. Then he picked up the struggling man and, walking to the edge of the balcony, held the writhing man over his head.

The entire crowd could see the wound made by the judge's shot. They saw the stream of crimson running down Morgan's belly and marveled at how anyone could bear up under the strain.

He held the slight, gray-haired man over his head and called out. "Where's Summers; where's Toby Summers?"

Emily still stood in the ring. She was twisting her handkerchief. "He's in the hotel. I left him locked up in the storage closet, Breaker."

A number of men from the crowd yelled out, "We'll get him, we'll get him and bring him out."

"Throw him down, Marshal, throw him down," the people began to chant and rave below. There was a bloodlust that rang out in their voices. The sight of the powerful judge still suspended above Morgan's head had whipped them into a frenzy.

"Throw him down and let us hang him like he done to us."

Frazier fired several shots into the air. "Here now," he called out. "I'm placing him and these other men under arrest. They're under the protective custody of the United States Marshal's office." He motioned to his small posse to come forward and help to calm the crowd, but they shook their heads in refusal.

The mob surged forward, yelling for Breaker to toss the man down. They refused to pay attention to Frazier on the edge of the crowd or to the posse of men from among them who were sheepishly retreating back toward the parked stagecoach.

Zac tried to move through the crowd, but now their bodies were so packed together that no one could squeeze through. He couldn't reach the front of the group, and no matter how loud he tried to yell, the noise of the chants and shouts from the mob made everything he did useless.

"You want this man, boys?" Breaker yelled out at the crowd.

They responded first with independent calls and then in unison began to chant, "Down, down, down, down. Throw him down, down, down."

Breaker leaned forward and sailed the struggling man into the midst of the crowd. Numerous men broke Harkness's fall and, hoisting him over their shoulders, they began to move toward the livery stable with its overhanging beams.

The men who had gone into the St. George to find Summers had now produced him, struggling in their arms on the porch. They marched him ahead of the mob toward the livery stable and behind them, the remnants of the band began to form and strike up "Yankee Doodle" once again.

Zac turned around and took Jenny's arm. "Find Doc Lewis and get him to Breaker. I'm going to the livery—we got to stop this thing!"

Zac raced ahead of the mob and circled through the back street on a run. Galloping up behind him was Sam Frazier. He brought his horse to a stop and pulled the Winchester from its scabbard. "Here, Cobb, take this. I need you." Tossing the rifle to Zac, he bolted on ahead.

When Zac entered the backdoor of the livery, he saw part of

the mob that had crowded into the stable. They had thrown ropes over the rafters of the barn and were leading two horses from their stalls. Frazier had drawn his revolver and was facing them down.

"That's far enough," he said. "Stand right where you are."

Two miners who were leading the mob stepped forward. "These people been killin' us and stealin' our claims. How you 'spect us to turn 'em over to the law? They are the law."

Zac fired the rifle into the roof. The explosion turned every eye toward him. "Nobody has more right to see these men hung than me," he said. "You saw me come into town. You know I won't abide the guilty going free."

A number of men in the mob nodded their heads, and others began to mumble. One of the men from the group spoke up, "We want to see these men hang. They've had their way enough round here."

Marshal Frazier backed away. He was the legal authority now in town and he knew it, but after what Zac had gone through, he knew Cobb was the best man to speak to the crowd. Zac looked to him for direction, and he simply nodded back.

"No one wants them to hang more than I do," Zac said, "and you can be on the jury that sends 'em to the gallows, but if you try to hang them here and now, then you're goin' to have to kill me to do it." They could see the steely look in his eyes. "The issue is the rule of law here. I don't want to die for trash like this, and I don't want to have to kill any of you in the process, but I will." He put the rifle to his shoulder. "You can be sure I will."

CHA31PTER

+ + + + + + +

IT HAD BEEN OVER A WEEK since the fight. A quiet normalcy had gripped the town, and the newness of life with law had taken hold. Zac stood at the stagecoach with the new agent in charge, a bespeckled young man with wavy blond hair.

"It's almost time to pull out, Mr. Cobb."

Emily had said her goodbyes and walked off, back toward her job at the hotel. Now it was up to Zac and Hattie to wish Jenny a safe trip.

"Listen here, lamb," Hattie said. "I brung you somethin'." She handed a basket through the open door of the coach. "It's some ham and a little bit a cheese. I don't make cheese my own self, mind you, but I traded for it. Anyhow, it's a fine one and it'll last you to the coast."

"Thank you, Hattie," Jenny said. "I'll never forget you."

"Chile, you ain't gonna have to try to remember me, you're a gonna be seein' me regular like." She shot Zac a look. "And I'd rightly appreciate it if'n you called me Aunt Hattie. It'd do me right smart to hear it from you."

"All right, Aunt Hattie, I'd be proud to call you that."

"Shoot fire, girl, in the South a body calls anybody that's older than them by aunt and uncle." She smiled. "'Course I ain't quite that old, leastways not just yet, but you go ahead and call me aunt anyways, ya hear? I got myself other reasons what might make thet proper."

She cast a glance at Zac and stuck out her lower lip. "Here." She handed Jenny the burlap bag she'd been carrying. "Take Ev-

269

elina's violin back with you. He ain't gonna treat it too kindly on horseback when he starts home, and I'm a lookin' to you to protect it."

Jenny held the bag and, pulling it open slightly, felt the smooth lacquered cherrywood. "I'll guard it and keep it safe," she said. Jenny looked at Zac. She knew what his mother meant to him and right now understood a little more of what he had meant to his mother. She patted it. "I'll keep it safe for you."

"Miss Jenny, comin' from you, that's safer'n a bank." Hat looked at Zac and the new agent. "And a whole lot safer than this here outfit."

She turned to the men. "Blondie, you shoo yourself outta here and see to your business."

The new agent looked flustered. "Yes, ma'am, I got things to do." And he scurried off.

Hattie took out another small bag from her pocket. "Here's somethin' else, deary. It's a solid gold nugget. I wants you to have it. When it comes time to melt it down and use it to put a ring round yer finger, then I want it to be my gold that's in it, ya hear?"

Jenny smiled. "I don't know . . ."

Hattie put her hand up to Jenny's mouth and cut her off. "Now that's enough. I ain't a gonna have that kinda talk." She looked back at Zac. "What do these fool men know about sech things anyway."

She dabbed a handkerchief to her eyes. "Look at me, I'm a mess. I'm powerful sorry to be at your 'get gone' like this. Since I went to church, I been turnin' into a blubberin' fool." She dabbed the cloth at her eyes once again. "Only thing worse than a fool is an old fool."

"Look, Zac," Hattie said. "This ain't becomin' to me atall. I'll let you say your goodbyes to the little gal here. I'll be over at the Jug and Rose, gettin' me some washin's fer my innards. When yer done, jes' come and fetch me out."

They both watched the old woman walk off toward the saloon. They watched her and smiled. "I'm proud to know your Aunt Hattie," Jenny said.

Zac moved closer to the open coach door. "I ought to be another two weeks hereabouts, before I get back to Cambria. I got the trial in Jackson to go to, and I need to see that everybody who's been involved with these robberies is turned over to the law. Without Harkness and his men to frighten them, people around here are all too willing to talk."

"This may sound strange," Jenny confessed, "but I hope Breaker gets by that trial without going to the gallows." She reached out her hand and took his. "Hurry home," she said.

"Will I really be coming home?" he asked. He looked directly into her eyes.

She paused. "I don't know. This thing inside me for you isn't going away, I know that much. I just don't think I could ever take this life of yours home with me."

He looked up at her with his brown eyes. "I understand," he said.

"Of course," Jenny said, "I'm not sure anywhere I'd be is a place I could call home without you."